FOR WHOM THE FURY ROLLS

LUNA JOYA

MYSTIC OWL

FOR WHOM THE FURY ROLLS
San City Shifters, Book 2

MYSTIC OWL
A City Owl Press Imprint
www.cityowlpress.com

Cover Design by MiblArt. All stock photos licensed appropriately.

Edited by Lisa Green.

For information on subsidiary rights, please contact the publisher at info@cityowlpress.com.

Print Edition ISBN: 978-1-64898-355-9

Digital Edition ISBN: 978-1-64898-356-6

Printed in the United States of America

LUNA JOYA

FOR WHOM THE
FURY
ROLLS

SYN CITY SHIFTERS
🐾 BOOK TWO 🐾

MYSTIC OWL

AN IMPRINT OF CITY OWL PRESS

ALSO BY LUNA JOYA

PRAISE FOR THE WORKS OF LUNA JOYA

"A witch and an FBI agent find love while solving a years-old murder in the wickedly delightful second paranormal romance in Joya's *Legacy* series. The anticipation is delicious, and the eventual romance is well worth the wait. This sexy love story will entice longtime paranormal fans and draw in new readers." — *Publishers Weekly*

"Passionate and heartfelt, *Wicked Crown* delivers! Step into the goblin realm where court intrigue mixes with page-turning plot, Joya's electric foray into fantasy romance." — *J.E. McDonald, author of the Wickwood Chronicles*

"A magical debut full of unique, complex characters, fabulous sisterhood and an adorable dog. Who could ask for anything more?" — *Felicia Grossman, Historical Romance Author*

"With fast paced, heart pounding, thrilling suspense and fantastic displays of supernatural powers, *Magic Touch* is a paranormal delight! The romance isn't anything to sneeze at either! There is romance echoing through time and scorching the present. Readers will feel the heat of instant attraction and the sorcery of levitating passions." – *InD'tale*

"*Tides of Time* was one of those reads that kept my hands locked around my e-reader and my butt firmly planted in my chair. This book promises witchy mystery and romance, and it doesn't disappoint." — *Evie Drae, author of Queer Romance*

"A HOT romance with excellent chemistry between the characters, and a paranormal aspect that was both intriguing and contained a unique spin on magical powers." — *Amber K. Bryant, Award-Winning Author*

"Highly enjoyable. I was engaged from beginning to end. I was delighted in the different ways the author chose to incorporate magic into the book. These characters were well written. I hope to read more about these witchy sisters! I loved the chemistry between Cami and Sam. A wonderful debut for Luna Joya." — *The Literary Vixen*

"*Killing Song* is the high-octane third paranormal romance in Joya's *Legacy* series. Joya holds the reader in her grip with action-packed intrigue and an expertly paced will-they-or-won't-they. The satisfying ending still leaves plenty of room for the series to continue; readers will be eager to see that it does." — *Publisher's Weekly*

"*Heart and Seek* is a powerhouse of political intrigue, magical secrets, and sexy characters... For readers who love witches flexing their magical muscle, who drool over an intricate plot, and who believe that a love match should always prevail over a power match – this is it! This is a fabulous read. What will the delightfully devious Luna Joya bring us next?" — *InD'tale*

"Joya sends out her *Legacy* series with an enticing fifth paranormal romance, *Flash Point,* that finds the five Donovan sisters working to defeat the demon Nymvyra once and for all. The emotional friends-to-lovers romance plays out as a tantalizing tug-of-war between Mina and Josh, while the multilayered suspense plot provides satisfying answers to series-long questions. Readers are sure to be pleased." — *Publisher's Weekly*

For all the soap opera/telenovela fans like me who are suckers for a romance that absolutely nothing—not even amnesia—can stop

PROLOGUE

STONE

Seven proposals, six rejections, and one *THANK THE GODS SHE finally said yes* later, I can't deny my fated mate anything, even something so dangerous as leading this rescue mission for a runaway cub.

The winter wind stings my eyes and burns my nose. If I'm chilled, my human wife must be freezing. Dead branches snap under our feet, followed by the rustling of nearby wildlife curious about the predators in their midst. Beneath the creak of swaying, barren trees, the swift footfalls of other searchers scatter as they move in opposite directions.

My wife put a search team together in mere minutes. While I'm my alpha's lieutenant, I lead with thought and careful planning. Kiva's the spontaneous motivator. I'm damn proud of her ability to inspire, but wariness gnaws at me like a vicious inner monster. A smoky earthiness fills my senses, the only scent other than my mate's sexy sweetness.

Her flashlight blinks out again. Electricity has been spotty all week, and the damn thing's batteries probably only had a half charge to begin with. I can handle the transition, but she must be totally blind. The moon's a sliver in the sky. Its faint light reflected in the snow seems more shadow than brightness.

"Want me to take point?" I ask her yet again.

"No, I've got this," she says. "There's probably an emergency glow stick in the pack. I could check if my big strong bear hadn't insisted on carrying everything."

"It's our first wedding anniversary. The least I could do was offer to lug around the medic kit." That I hope we won't need.

"I know you didn't want me coming along." She speaks the truth. "But the kid's gotta be terrified."

"Or Rylie's a rebellious teenager who has outsmarted us. She probably shifted hours ago and snuggled up with wild bears in a warm cave somewhere."

"She's fifteen and crying over her crush being an idiot to her. Stupid bear shifter male."

I don't respond because arguing that point with my mate would make me one of said stupid bear shifter males. At least the rest of the search team is far enough back that we don't have an open debate of the issue. Making light of our runaway's situation doesn't help release the pressure valve on my worry about her, about Kiva, about all of us right now.

"We'll find her," my wife says. "Rylie's close. I can feel it."

My senses don't pick up any trail, not the slightest scent or sound to confirm my mate's instinct, but if she says the kid's near, I trust her to know the truth. My Kiva doesn't talk about being witch-born, mage-born, or whatever those who came into this world with magic in their blood call themselves these days. Her human half makes her an outcast to their kind, but she has an instinct that's infallible if she doesn't let doubts get in the way. "The lake's less than a quarter mile ahead. We can regroup there."

"Hate the water." Her muttered gruffness doesn't hide her fear, not from me.

Reaching for her gloved hand, I squeeze when she links her

fingers through mine. "Me too." I don't have Kiva's brutal past that she doesn't talk about, but nightmares of drowning have haunted me from childhood.

"We'll find Rylie," she says, "and we'll all go home to a nice fire."

"We will." Silence surrounds us like a thick wool blanket, but I don't miss the chattering of Kiva's teeth. Despite supply issues, she wears the best in winter gear that we can find over her skintight jeans and a She-Devils jersey for her hockey league. But she's shivering. I should've insisted she stay behind or wear another layer or...

"Stop worrying," she says. "I can practically hear you making a list of worst-case scenarios and fixes for them."

"It's my job as your mate to protect you, provide for you even though—"

"I can do it myself."

I grin at the truth. A trained fighter with a sharp wit and sharper tongue, no one is tougher than my wife. "True, but I like taking care of you. It's why I have dinner waiting at home for our anniversary celebration."

"You only remember because I wrote it on the cabinet door, right over your favorite honey taffy."

"No, I remembered first. You slapped the note up after asking me why you shouldn't schedule a hockey practice for tonight, and you put the date there because you'd see it when going for your stash of crab chips." Yuck. Why my woman loves to ruin good potato chips with crab cake seasoning, I'll never understand. Must be a Jersey thing. "I'd already wrapped your gift before your note went up."

"You got me a present? What is it?" Her enthusiasm and refusal to focus on anything I might've said other than gift makes me laugh.

"You'll have to wait and see."

"New skates?" Happiness threads through our mating bond, as radiant and warm as Kiva herself. "They are, aren't they?"

Her single-minded devotion to her sport despite spending half of every game in the penalty box might be one of the many reasons I fell hard for her. "You think I'd give you skates for our anniversary? To celebrate finally getting you to marry me after I proposed seven times?"

"I'm picky. Even my team says that about me."

Her teammates call her prickly, but I'm not going to argue semantics. "You can be picky as long as you're mine." I kiss her cheek.

Twisting so that our lips meet, she licks at me with the tip of her tongue. "Let's find Rylie and get home so I can get my present. I'll protect you out here in the woods, my big were-bear."

"I'll let the *were-bear* insult slide this time if you let me lead until we get to the lake." Where the light might be better.

"Fine." She hands me the dead flashlight. "I should get my pick of your latest creations for my anniversary."

I'm ridiculously happy that she wants something from my forge. My blades bring in top dollar, a benefit to our entire den since who knows when the next battle between supernaturals and humans will leave us scrambling for yet another new normal.

Had the modern world seen a fighter like Kiva before magic was outed? One who relied on steel and iron and silver rather than guns? Maybe. Maybe not. We shifters rely on fangs and teeth, and the uppity magic-slingers who fought the Witching Wars a half century ago retreated to their sanctuary cities, leaving the rest of us to struggle for survival in the combat still happening around the globe. To fight things that can't be killed by technology or weapons from the past few centuries. To be what Kiva was raised to become, a hunter of the gods-spawned. She doesn't do that anymore. Not since she said yes to *us*.

"The pretty hatchet you finished last week will be mine," she says.

"We'll see." I force as much doubt as I can into my voice. The hatchet's wrapped and hidden at home. My woman loves her weapons. I got her to finally agree to my proposal with a dagger that has our intertwined initials hidden in the intricate engraving, the one strapped to her thigh now. "Almost to the lake. You want me to radio the rest of the crew?" Here's hoping the batteries in the comms held more of a charge than the defunct flashlight.

"Not yet." She edges close to the lake that's now a frozen sheet of ice. The moon's rays fall brighter here, making the ice shine like broken glass. "Do you hear something?"

"You don't have to tell me my stomach's growling. Every shifter in a mile radius knows it." The steak dinner I'd planned sounds really good right now.

She smacks my gut as if that'll make the hunger stop. "I could've sworn someone called my name."

A trickle of fear snakes its way up my spine to the base of my skull where a pounding ache kicks in. "No. I would've heard that." My senses go on full alert. "Grab the shotgun strapped to the pack."

She curves her mouth into a wicked grin. "Mmm, dirty talk from my grizzly. Someone's getting lucky tonight."

"Promise?" I ask, pretending I'm not panicking about the voice she thinks she heard. Every one of those times I proposed? Worth it for all the nights coming for the rest of our lives. "I know all kinds of ways to warm you up."

"Yeah you do." She steps away from me, studying the ground. "Hey, fresh tracks leading toward the lake." She puts her boot next to the smaller print in the snow. "Rylie went this way."

I take a deep breath. "I can't smell her, and the tracks don't look like her sneakers. You sure those are hers?"

Kiva bristles worse than any housecat, and the scent of annoyance rolls off her. "They're fresh. I've got snowflakes stuck in my lashes, and we've had at least another inch tonight. Who else would've come this way?" She yells the girl's name.

Dread has my bear rising within me, ready to shift and defend our mate, and I want to snatch back Kiva's voice from booming over the frozen expanse. "We need to get back to the den. Now."

"But Rylie—"

"Whoever's been hunting shifters these past few years? They're still out there." The few detailed reports we've gotten say the killer rips dead shifters apart in a way no human could manage. But who knows the reality? News usually favors whatever group reports it. The witch sanctuary hours south of here doesn't care about us, and to many humans, the only good shifter is a dead shifter. "Rylie's smart. She's probably already back at the den."

"Their last murder happened months ago all the way across country. Whoever's killing East Coast shifters wouldn't risk the Sierra Nevada mountains in the winter. Besides, the marshal's office said—"

"I'm not trusting any damn wolves with my mate's safety."

She opens her mouth to argue but closes it just as quickly and cocks her head toward the lake. "You had to hear her calling that time."

"That voice?" The one sending giant warnings screaming along my spine? It's wrong, magical and singsong. "That doesn't sound like Rylie."

"She's out there across the lake. I'm going after her."

"No way you're walking on that ice. We'll go around." Or I'll toss her over my shoulder and run as far as I can get her from that voice.

"This high up? It'll hold." She hurries onto the ice. I grab for her, and she dodges my grip.

"Come back, sweetheart." While I love my mate's boldness and courage, in this moment, I need her to be impulsive somewhere far away from whatever's out there. "The ice can't be more than an inch or two thick this early in the season. It's not solid enough for Rylie to cross. Or you."

Keeping my big bear body on land and not chancing the ice giving beneath my heavy weight, I reach for her, and she dashes past my fingertips, farther onto the ice. "No ocean water," she whispers. "Can't be sea witches here." Her mumbling makes no sense.

The creepy call dances across the lake again. Saltwater scents wash over me as if we've traveled to a distant ocean and not a still, freshwater lake.

"Wait." I go after her, and the ice cracks under my weight with a loud pop. "Shit."

"I'm coming, Rylie." My mate glances over her shoulder at me. "I'll be right back to you. Promise."

"Kiva, love, that's not Rylie." I don't know what the hell the voice could be, but I don't want it anywhere near my wife. Unfastening the pack, I heft it off my shoulders and to the ground.

"No. Rylie! Oh gods." Kiva takes off at a sprint.

Something whizzes across the lake, a zipping noise that echoes with a zing. Kiva stops with a jerk and spins to face me.

Fear and pain punch through our mating bond. My pulse thunders in my ears, my lungs stop working, and my vision narrows in a dizzying darkness to getting to my wife.

"Kiva?" I don't have the oxygen for a yell, don't have the grace not to scramble and slip as I rush to her. A silver-tipped arrow coated in blood gleams on the ice, the spray of vivid red leading to my wife. Her legs buckle, and she crumbles, her head thudding against the frozen hardness.

My link with Kiva—the vibrant warmth I've known since the first time I saw her—it's fading beat by slowing heartbeat. I can't breathe, can't think.

"Hold on, love." I rush to her until a loud crack beneath me sounds like a gunshot. I'm too heavy. I'll bring us both down.

Dropping to my hands and knees, I crawl inch by agonizing blood-smeared inch to her.

She doesn't answer, doesn't whimper, doesn't tell me to stop being such a scaredy were-bear like she has a million times since we first kissed. I'm losing her in a fight I can't win, one I didn't even see coming. The ice groans loud and long, a fracture ready to tear us apart forever.

Farther out, a butchered and broken body sprawls as though dropped there like a gruesome gift. A bright red sneaker lies closer to us. *Rylie.* It has to be Rylie. Dear gods. I can't hear the heavy thud of her bear shifter heart or feel the hum of pack connection. Pushing down panic, I strategize. I'll save my wounded mate first and then crawl back out for Rylie.

Going down to my belly, I pull myself to Kiva. Blood rushes out of her so fast, a river I can't hold back. "Hang on, love." There's no healer or apprentice for miles. I drag her oh-so-slowly off the ice, never stopping my pleading.

Her heart goes silent.

"Don't leave me." The instant we hit solid ground again, I drop to my knees with her in my arms, the need to do anything but hold her leaving me in a rush. "Just stay with me."

I could call to the others, but they wouldn't get here in time. Not for anything but to watch the end of us.

"Please, please, please," I beg her, beg the gods, beg anyone who might listen, but the only answer comes from deep within.

Kiva's death hits like a boulder being dropped on me, the mating bond going still and silent, a void where there'd been so much life before. "No." My roar shakes the ground, thunders through the trees, and sends birds flapping away. The flapping comes so loud I can hear it over the deafening boom of blood in my ears.

I glance up at the dark night that stretches endlessly with only the ice's glare cutting into the abyss. A cloaked figure wreathed in black blinks to existence in front of us. "Are you

Death? Have you come for her?" My words come out thick around the sob stuck in my throat. "Take me instead. Or let me come with her? Please?"

"You called me here with a *please*, so I've come." A woman's voice—one full of venom and fury—comes from inside the black hood. "She's a fighter?"

"Yes."

"She was your mate? The one you swore to protect with your life?"

The truth in her judgment lashes through me. "Yes." I failed to save my Kiva.

"What price are you willing to pay?" The coldness in her tone matches the shivers racking my body. Her scent isn't human, isn't shifter, isn't anything I've smelled before. "To give her another chance at life, what would you give?"

"Anything." I flinch when Kiva's head lolls to the side. "Everything." My voice cracks around the word.

"Then it's done," the woman says.

Kiva vanishes from my arms.

I scramble to grab at empty air. "Where'd she go? What've you done to her?"

"She's alive and well and far from here with no memory of this life."

My heart hooks on her last words, floundering like a fish speared. "Will she remember me? She's my mate. We're fated to be together."

"Perhaps your mating bond stopped with her death. She's beginning a new life, one where she'll have the chance to choose again if she wants a mate—whether that's you or someone else."

"I'll find her." I will. No matter how long it takes me.

"You cannot interfere with her new life."

"She needs me like I need her."

"What *you* need is not my concern. She had a brutal start to this life, and I won't burden her with such horrific memories to weigh down her next." She pauses as if thinking through possibilities. "*If* you find her, you're forbidden to speak to her of this life until you've convinced her to fall in love with you again."

"I can't tell her anything?" It took me forever to convince my mate of our destined bond the first time. Those six proposals and rejections play in a repeat loop in my mind. Sure, she'd said yes in the end, but each *no* had been devastating in its own way.

"Nothing of this life. Nor can you have someone else tell her. Until—what's it your sanitized fairy tales speak of?" She sneers. "True love's kiss? Unless or until she falls in love with you again, she must remember on her own or not at all. It's the price for her second chance. You did say you'd pay anything."

But to give up love? Her memories of the life we'd made together? "She prefers to be called Kiva. Will you at least let her keep her name?"

"Perhaps." Her tone screams no, and I scramble for any hope to clutch in the wake of this horror.

The calls of the other rescuers who must've heard my pained roar come closer. My gut instinct screams I'm running out of precious time to find out anything about what has happened to my mate. "Can you tell me where to look for her? What kind of life you're giving her?" *Please, please be a good one.*

"I've no answers for you, only questions. Is pursuing her in her new life worth the risk of her rejecting you forever?" The woman disappears, not waiting for my answer.

Kiva's worth everything. I'll find her, and I'll win her back. I'll bring her home, and I'll never let her go again.

1

KIVA

FAMILY FESTIVAL NIGHT MAKES ME THE ABSOLUTE CRANKIEST, which says a lot considering I've spent the last few weeks tracking a serial killer. Weighed down by presents and wearing huge smiles, passengers hurry off the ferry below to find their deity daughters waiting on the dock. Their happy cheers, imagining what those squishy hugs might feel like, wishing someone would ask for me?

It sucks.

No one's coming to see me.

My brain knows the truth, but every single time, my heart hopes. Stupid heart.

Sitting on The Rink's roof, dangling my sneakers into the open air six stories up, I have the best view of Syn City. If we had a roller derby exhibition or a concert here tonight, the signs and strobes would be blinding, but now, only a smattering of twinkling lights shine for this quiet homecoming that most of the seven Houses celebrate twice a year.

The hotels and restaurants of the pleasure district glow in the distance. I let the night and my wings wrap around me, the inky black sky and bright pinprick of stars a giant mirror of my dark feathers with their silver blade edges.

Battling nightmares for months has left my eyes gritty and my nerves buzzing like a Mad Mae pinging on pills and a weeklong booze binge. The daughters of Bacchus know how to party, but I'm not asking a manic maenad for help with my sleep situation or to dull the ache of Family Fest.

A *whoosh* of wings sounding like the rustle of pages from some old, pre-Witching Wars book lets me know who lands beside me without looking.

"Thought I might find you here." Sadie's posh Southern accent stretches the words like taffy left outside in this muggy heat. "Anyone interesting turn up for the family freakshow?"

I snort, unable to stay mopey around her snark. "Who are you calling freaks? The mostly human families or us?" Everyone who belongs to a House in Syn City has been chosen to become the mortal kid of an immortal Greek god, which doesn't fit any definition of *typical*. Sadie and I had been chosen by the original Furies to dish out vengeance one ass-whooping at a time, which made us extra weird even among the other deity daughters.

"Them, *obviously*." Sadie sounds as though our wings and occasional murderous instincts should be the norm. She settles on the ledge next to me, careful not to break a nail or scuff her high heels. "See anyone you know?"

"Even if I did, I wouldn't recognize them. The problems of not remembering my human life before the turn." *Before* I'd been murdered and become a Fury. "At least no one can get pissed at the amnesiac for forgetting birthdays or anniversaries."

Sadie doesn't smile at my bad joke, but then she's probably thinking of the family she lost. Where my past stretches like an infinite blankness, hers weighs her down more than any boulder ever could.

Her black-paper wings with blood-red symbols represent the spell from her family's grimoire that she tried to invoke before her murderer caught her. Given our wings reflect our demise, perhaps I should be happy whatever vicious death that granted me blade-edged feathers has let me block the memory. Trauma-based amnesia seems safer than the other option—that I did something so horrible that someone cursed me.

I nudge her with my shoulder. "You shouldn't be up here watching this."

"Neither should you. Every family night, you come up here, knowing you don't remember. Kiva, it's been almost two years."

Twenty-one months and two weeks since I woke up to a second life in Syn City, but who's counting? While I don't want to confess the real reason I torture myself with watching these reunions, I can share a tiny sliver of truth. "I keep thinking someone might be out there looking for me, that maybe this time, my family will find me."

She shoots me a look completely at odds with her snobbish, smart-ass self. Her gaze goes intense but soft. "Our immortal mothers chose Dottie and me to be your triad sisters in a bond as strong as blood. *We're* your family."

Well, damn, I don't know how to answer that emotional sucker-punch. "I feel like we should hug it out or something."

She huffs a too-refined laugh. "We aren't *that* kind of family. Challenging each other to a duel would be more our style. We could ask our triad sister to summon her magical weapon to call."

Excitement buzzes through me. "Ooh, the fiery Grim Reaper sickles."

"Scythes," Sadie corrects. "Don't tell Dottie, but while my whip satisfies my inner badass, I'm sorta jealous that I didn't get something with flames. You?"

"Nope." I reach for the magic granted by the immortals who turned us, and my weapon to call materializes in my palm a second later. "I couldn't ask for anything better than my hatchet." Fancy etchings decorate the blade, and the handle has the initials

KT carved in the bottom. I tell myself *K* stands for Kiva, but maybe not. I've no idea what the *T* might mean.

"Come on." Sadie pushes to her feet. "I'm not staring at the swamp all night. Unless you're debating whether to dive in for a deadly swim? If so, I'll stay for the show."

"Ugh, I don't want to imagine the sea hags, gator shifters, harpies, and whatever other supernatural beasties live under the water out there." I stretch my wings, working out the tenseness the same as rolling my neck or cracking my knuckles. The rush of air lifts sweat-dampened curls from my neck. "Gods, I hate water. I've no idea what cosmic joke our immortal mothers intended when they landed me here for my second life."

"Good thing you're not a Nymph with Lover's Lagoon running through your bedroom." She lifts into the night sky. "Race you home?"

Home. If only I could remember where my last had been.

"Slacker," Sadie yells down at me.

With a tight hold on my hatchet and a grin chasing away the sadness, I leap off the roof and zoom toward the House of Furies.

2

STONE

SWEAT POURS OFF ME. I'VE STOKED THE FORGE'S FIRE HIGHER AND hotter than ever, as if I can burn away the memories of the night I lost my fated mate. If I'd known what would happen, I would've locked my mate in our house, no matter how many times she called me a possessive alphahole bear.

I clang the hammer again and again onto the glowing metal, using precision as much as force. The hatchet takes shape—the same as the one that I'd made to give my wife as an anniversary present. The exact copy of the dozens lining the far wall of my workshop beside her ice hockey trophies. By now, my movements for this design have become a steady dance, a routine without wasted efforts. I put the piece in the fire to heat again, yanking off the protective gear.

"Making a hundred hatchets won't help you find her," Beryl, my younger sister, says from where she props in the big open door to the shop.

"I know that." Or my head does. My heart's not so sure. "I still haven't found the one I'd planned to give her."

"We all went through so much that night with losing Kiva and Rylie." She pushes off the carved wood, putting away the chisels and steel punches I've left out. "How would you remember losing a single weapon among a thousand?"

"Because I hid her hatchet in our closet with her skates. The ice skates I found? I didn't lose her gift, didn't lose her."

My sister doesn't meet my gaze. "Rylie's death was horrific."

"True." How some psycho could brutally murder a teenager and leave her splayed across the ice, I would never understand. The poor kid must've gone through hell before her drained body was dumped like trash, and guilt plagues me that I couldn't even grieve properly for her while drowning in the overwhelming loss of my mate.

"Trauma can play tricks with the memory." Beryl sounds as if she has rehearsed whatever she's about to say, and I don't want to hear it.

"I didn't hallucinate a woman in a black cloak appearing out of nowhere, or how she brought my mate back to life, cast a curse on me, and stole Kiva's memories until I can give her true love's kiss."

"Except we haven't been able to find your wife." Beryl softens her voice, which does nothing to soften the blow. "It's been almost two years."

Twenty-one months and two weeks ago, I lost my mate. "My Kiva's alive."

"I'm not suggesting you stop looking. I'm saying stop living in the past." She gestures toward the hatchets, Kiva's hockey jersey with the nickname "Penalty Box," the notes in my mate's handwriting still tacked to the mini fridge, the wall, the toolbox, everywhere.

"She's out there."

"*Out there* is a very big place to search. She might not even be in this realm. You know as well as I do that some worlds—like the goblins'—are closed off to ours unless you happen to be friends with a mage capable of dimensional travel. You won't let me dig into whatever past Kiva hid."

"No, I have to respect her decision not to talk about her history."

"But if I could find just one thing from her past to use in tracking her—"

I interrupt. "There was nothing left except the bracelet she had on her when she vanished." I've spent hours wishing for one clue that might lead us to her. "Her mom spelled a poppet she called Peter that meant a lot to her, but it disappeared with her mother. She didn't own anything from her past."

My sister shakes her head. "Then we've no way to track her, and without her memory, she has no leads to find her way back to you."

The truth of the last hits me like a blow from my biggest hammer. I stare at these familiar tools and four walls that've been my refuge, my hiding place to pound away my rage if not my grief. Every corner, every inch holds a memory of her, of us.

Sometimes, when the breeze blows the right way, I can almost scent her here, can imagine that she's walking through the doorway that's always open for her return. Then I look up to find an empty room. Kiva's not a ghost, yet she haunts me.

"Come on now." Beryl yanks me into a side hug. "When we find your mate, how do you plan to introduce yourself? Offer her a hundred hatchets? It's not exactly a romantic bouquet." She teases while we skirt the straw dummies and speed drills that serve as the training grounds for our Warrior's Den Weaponry school. Beryl's the only teacher now with Kiva gone.

My sister keeps adding to her list of ways I could fail at wooing my mate, using the many times my wife turned me down as examples, until we're almost to the house that used to be a home when I shared it with Kiva. When I find her, I'll bring her back here, and I'll never let her go.

The smell of beer and the sound of a sports broadcast from inside tips me off that Beryl has been avoiding something, and

I'm not talking about the spotty electricity working well enough today to power the television. "Dad's inside, isn't he?" I ask.

"Yeah." She uses her *I know you're not happy but* voice.

"I hate surprises."

"As well as any and all change, yeah, I get it, but Mom's off on one of her geology digs, and he didn't want to be alone."

"You mean he didn't want to miss an opportunity to preach about how he could've been the next alpha *if only*. Talk like that will get him killed." I push through the back door into the house.

Kiva's boots sit under the bench where she left them. Her coat hangs on the peg. Moving through the kitchen, I glance to make sure her reminder note about our first anniversary still sticks to the cabinet. I don't have to look to know her favorite chips and soda stock the shelves one over. For our entire courtship, I teased her about how she ruined good potato chips with crab cake seasoning, and now, I'd do anything to have her be here, to wrinkle her nose, to call me her were-bear as only she could.

Pushing the thought aside until I'm alone, I attempt to be pleasant. "Hiya, Dad."

"Stone." He says my name as though the weight of the word should pull me down, down, down like irons strapped to my ankle. "Talk to the alpha today since you're his big bad lieutenant? Or did you walk away from your responsibilities to the den the same way you forgot about your family? Maybe your fearless leader knows a female shifter looking for a new mate."

I ignore the unfounded insult about me ignoring any duties since my role is between my alpha and me. "I don't need a new mate when mine waits out there for me to find her."

"But you don't know that, do you?" Dad makes his question sound like anything but asking. "You're still alive and healthy, which isn't normal for a man who has lost his true mate."

The earlier simmering rage builds into a full roar, an anger with the heat of my forge and the quick temper that has become my constant companion. "How would you know? You can't stand to be in the room with *your* mate. Why do you think Mom's gone ten months out of the year digging up rocks?"

"What I'm saying is maybe that girl wasn't your real mate."

"*That girl*? You mean my wife?" My bear rises within, ready to lash out with claws, no matter the family relationship. No one talks bad about my mate.

Beryl pushes between us. "The scent can't lie. Kiva was his mate...*is* his mate."

Dad finally glances at his daughter. "You had it right with the past tense." He snarls the last, sounding like the surly Kodiak he becomes. Then he's back to lecturing me. "We shifters mate for life. Your human didn't live through that night any more than that sweet cub, Rylie. It's sad, sure, but it's the truth. You need to concentrate on moving up in the power structure here, which requires a shifter mate."

The blaring television blasts across my senses, and I struggle to hold back my anger. "I'm the alpha's sworn second. There is no *up* for me. Stop thinking that garbage, let alone talking about it before you drag our family down with you."

He slams a fist into the arm of the chair, and a crack means he didn't restrain his shifter strength when abusing the furniture in his toddler tantrum. "I don't—"

"Stop," Beryl orders, startling us both into silence. "Pause whatever you're watching on the television."

Dad doesn't move. "Why?"

"Now," she insists.

"Do as she says for once," I argue. "What is it?" I ask my sister.

Dad doesn't give her a chance to answer me, but he pauses the show. "I'm watching highlights from a roller derby championship down in Syn City."

"Syn City?" I've heard of the place. *Everyone* has. Magic being outed woke some of the Greek gods who'd been relegated to mythology for millennia. Those gods created children—daughters—who run the city. Tourism brings in humans from far and wide, guaranteed safety while enjoying the entertainment provided at ridiculously expensive prices. "Is the championship one of their money grabs?"

"It's not just about the cash. Those players have got real grit, and they put on a good show, but the bootleg recording's over a year old. The deity daughters don't allow their bouts to be filmed. They get touchy, thinking they're so high and mighty as the children of immortals. They can still die as easily as any shifter. In my day—"

"Shh." Beryl steps close to the screen. "Go back a few seconds."

Dad shakes his head. "That part's not even the bout."

"The bout?" Beryl asks.

"The match. The game. In derby, it's called it a bout." My dad sounds annoyed. "Why would you want to watch a bunch of girls on time out?"

My anger flares again on its short choke chain. "Back up to the part she asked you to play."

He does in a slow, sulky way that sets my fangs on edge. "Happy now?"

Beryl waves a hand, the golden honeybee charm on her bracelet swinging as if it's drunk flying. "A little further back." The screen flickers in reverse. "Stop. Let it play again." She points at the group wearing black surrounding a silver-haired woman. "Slow it down."

"All right. Don't be so pushy." Dad sounds put out, but he leans forward, searching like me for whatever my sister spotted.

The scene bounces between the packed stands, a team of skaters in green, and the group in black around the silver-haired woman.

Dad's posture takes on a supernatural predator's stalk even in the recliner, and his gaze glows amber, keen interest in the old bear's eyes. And Beryl? My sister, who hates team sports and would rather say something about the objectification of those women in skimpy outfits and fishnet stockings? Her shoulders tense, her body practically shaking as nervous energy radiates off her.

She jabs her finger at the screen. "There." Hope lifts her voice at the end, a helium balloon rising to a happy exclamation point. The kind of exclamation point where Kiva would've drawn a heart on the bottom and then put crossbones through it with a mischievous grin.

I shake off the memory and stare, looking for what my sister has spotted. The picture's angle is off, and the image blurs. The close circle the players stand in hides their faces. They're dressed in black with matching tank tops that have silver wings and teeny-tiny shorts. The image fuzzes on the paused screen, and I can't figure out what captured Beryl's attention. "What are we looking for?" I ask. "Who are they?"

"The Furies," Dad says. "Spitfires, every one of them."

"Watch her." Beryl gestures toward a woman with her back to the camera.

There's an achingly familiar, confident pose from the woman's squared shoulders to the luscious curve of her hips. My breath slices out in ax-edged slashes, and my heart knocks in my chest like an old combustion engine with faulty spark plugs.

"It can't be," I whisper. If only I could see the woman's face.

As though she hears my thought in this old recording, the woman turns and glares at the camera. The same brown eyes I've dreamed of for two years, those eyes that can go from the cranky annoyance she's giving the camera lens to a devilish twinkle.

My vision narrows to those eyes, to that wicked mouth I've kissed a million times. The picture blurs, and the world around me seems to spin. I need to sit down, I need air in my lungs, I need to get to her—now. But I *don't need* more than the split-second image to recognize my mate.

"Kiva."

3

STONE

A MILLION QUESTIONS RACE THROUGH MY MIND. DID KIVA RECOVER completely? Is she happy in Syn City? How did she end up there? What in the world is she doing playing roller derby? Although that last makes sense with my woman's love of hockey.

"I need to see her, to bring her home." My words come out a whisper, but they're the most passionate and determined I've been able to string together since she died in my arms. "I have to go to her."

"To Syn City?" Dad asks. "No one messes with those Furies. I hear their house is a fortress built out of bones and magic in the middle of a swamp. Even if that alpha of yours will let you go, they'd never let you in to see her."

I ignore him. "I need a car that'll make the cross-country trip. The one time I wish airplanes still—"

"Whoa." Beryl grabs my arm, stopping me.

"What?" I'm ready to pick up my sister and move her out of my way if necessary, and Beryl's a warrior who can hold her own, so that won't be an easy fight. I bite back a snarl from my bear. "I've waited almost two years."

"She doesn't remember you." My sister's tone isn't cruel, but Kiva forgetting me? It's a brutal punishment.

I've never told anyone that I blamed myself for Kiva's death, for not keeping her from following whatever sorcery wove itself over the frozen lake. I couldn't stand to say the truth aloud, that I could've saved her if I had just held onto her. I tried to follow her that night, but the ice cracked beneath me with a loud pop like a gunshot. I'd cradled her while our link—the vibrant warmth I'd known since the first time I'd seen her—faded beat by slowing heartbeat. When I'd agreed to be cursed by the woman shrouded in black who'd appeared out of nothingness in exchange for her giving Kiva a chance at a second life, I would've promised to give anything, *anything* for her to live again.

"Kiva might remember me." A jumble of hope and worry tie my muscles into knots. "What if the curse didn't take?"

Beryl shakes her head. "Your mate would've found a way to contact you if she had remembered who you were, who you are to her. The deal you made with the woman in black—how exactly did she word it?"

"She said if I found Kiva, I'm forbidden to speak of her first life until I convince her to fall in love with me all over again." It'd taken me forever to convince my mate of our destined bond the first time. "I can't even have someone else tell her. Only true love's kiss will break the curse."

"Like some messed up fairy tale?"

"Yeah." My nerves rattle worse than a badly made sword in an oversized sheath. "Maybe seeing me will make her remember."

"And if it doesn't?" she asks. "You can't go charging in there all possessive stalker bear. Whatever brought her back to life—"

"A Fury," Dad interrupts. "That means she's a deity daughter now, one of the seven Houses of Syn City. The news said they're bringing in a big music star for a charity concert soon."

I stare at him. "How is it you know so much about a city you've never seen?"

Beryl huffs a hard laugh. "Because they sell the fantasy of hot women rolling around on skates wearing almost nothing."

"They're not all hot." Dad puffs up, more bullfrog than bear boar. "The Gorgons don't have a single looker among them."

"Really?" my sister asks. "You'd think being married to a world-renowned scientist for decades would prove to you that women are so much more than their looks, but no."

"Those derby women are tough." Dad clearly doesn't get her point, and I'm not correcting him because that would mean yet more time between now and me seeing my wife again. "The Houses don't just have the skating stuff," our father insists. "The Muses? Their shows sell out every time, and those tickets aren't cheap."

I move to go around Beryl, but she crosses her arms and blocks my path. Gods save me from a pissed off female bear. Yet, she doesn't yell at me. No, she asks Dad, "What else do you know about the Houses?"

"Lots." He sounds proud of himself.

"Take a seat," my sister tells me.

"Why?" My bear roars in frustration inside me, and my voice comes out rough with his need to be with our mate now. "I need to get to Kiva, not listen to whatever Dad has to say."

She doesn't back down at the viciousness in my tone, not the least little bit. "What you *need* is a crash course in the Houses. Do you understand the nuances of the power structure and social dynamics of Kiva's new city? Because she will."

Her heavy know-it-all emphasis on the last has me sitting. As much as my bear grumbles and my human side hates the delay, she's right. I know nothing of my mate's new life, a life without me. But we've found her. I can learn enough about her temporary situation to make her love me so I can bring her home.

I've won her once. I'll do it again. The challenge has me ready to go in prepared. "All right."

"Good," she says. "We'll need to know as much as we can before we head to Syn City."

"*We?*" I ask.

"You can't go by yourself. You'll screw it up."

"I won't." I'm pissed that my sister has so little faith in me.

"You already have. She turned you down six times." She holds up her fingers like I can't count that high.

Dad nods in solemn agreement. Great, the one time they can agree, it has to be against me.

"Fine," I say, the grumpy bear that Kiva loves to tease. *Or my Kiva did.* A sliver of doubt slides through me. What will she say about me now? *No, don't think like that.* We're fated to be together forever. "I'm listening."

"Good," Beryl says. "If she doesn't remember who you are, we're going to need a cover story to stay in the city for a while. Lucky for us, we have a business that deity daughters love since their mythological mommies and daddies don't condone guns. The marketing potential already had Syn City on my shortlist to scout for business expansion."

"I can get them to buy. I don't need help." What I *really* don't need is a babysitter—especially not my sister, who thinks I'm an idiot when it comes to my mate.

"I wouldn't trust you with advertising the Warrior's Den to such an important clientele even without your dead-and-comeback mate being there."

Ouch. Beryl has never been so cutthroat about my position in the family business. "I make the weapons we sell."

"And you run off potential clients. Plus, you almost decapitated a student a year ago."

"Almost, but I didn't."

"Yeah, that's why you're not going to Syn City alone." She sits beside me, crowding me. "Okay, Dad, tell us everything you know about the women who run the place."

Dad lists off seven Houses of deity daughters who claim

parents from Greek mythology. I forget half of the House names before he's finished with his spiel. He's more animated than I've seen him in years. Maybe he can make flash cards or cheat sheets because there's no way I'm remembering all this.

Two days later, I'm no closer to finding answers about Kiva's new life except for a photo of her skating and flashing a playful smirk that looks as though she'll annihilate the competition. The Furies call her *Killa* and don't use her real name. Syn City must spend a fortune to buy such widespread publicity, but they leave plenty of mystery when it comes to the actual Houses and the players. I've looked for Kiva by her actual name all this time, and no one had leaked it.

An illustration of a wicked-looking dagger shows up on Killa's fan site—a blade that looks just like the one I gave her for our engagement, the one I've carried every day since. The sight of it twists something low in my gut. I have to win her again.

On the drive in our borrowed truck, my nerves jangle with anxiety over getting to my mate now that we've found her. I manage to route us through safe harbor stops without crossing into human-only territories. The never-ending clashes between species has pockmarked the countryside with ghost towns. When a new skirmish arises, things get lean—*really* lean—which makes normally nice people go nasty no matter the species. I map around each obstacle with the same meticulous detail I bring to mobilize shifter soldiers in battle.

Propped in the passenger seat, Beryl memorizes a Syn City visitor's guide she managed to score at a diner. In the last stretch of the journey, when I'm too tired and wired to think, she announces, "We have to park the truck and take the ferry over."

"A boat?" Just what my heave-or-hurl stomach doesn't need right now.

"It's a hover ferry, partially powered by magic. They closed the one bridge into the swamp. No vehicles allowed in Syn City."

"Any other way in other than by boat?"

"Nope. No flights allowed even if we could trade a kidney or two for the fuel costs and find someone willing to pilot." She cuts a teasing *oh you're in for it* look my way that only a sister can give. "Want me to protect you from the gator shifters and harpies? Or maybe your Fury can."

If Kiva remembers me. I stop the pity party. *When* she remembers me.

Beryl takes care of the ferry tickets, herding me along with our massive trunks of weapons and tools. "Try not to vomit on the boat," she says. "You don't look so good."

My fear of water began years ago, but the phobia has soared since Kiva's death. I prefer to keep my feet, paws, whatever on solid ground.

Knowing the boat hovers just above the dirty water and its magical beasts doesn't help. I breathe in great gulps of air, pushing down my panic whenever a choppy wave reaches high enough to bump the craft and send us reeling on a roller coaster with no safety straps. Worse, I'm trapped with my sister, who thinks it's pop quiz time. Kiva hated when Beryl played this game, and I'm beginning to see why.

"Name the Houses in Syn City," she says.

"Uh, they have seven. They're all women." I take my time with each word, buying a few seconds. "The Furies." Kiva's group, named after the original Furies who went around handing out vengeance to murderers and rapists, focusing mostly on those who hurt women and children. Their justice sounds shifter-style.

Beryl pinches my arm the way she did when she was a cub, and she's still got the pincer grip of a crab.

I pull away and glare.

She doesn't look at all sorry. "You're not even trying. You got one of the seven Houses—*one*—and the easy one at that."

"I can name the rest," I lie.

"Prove it."

Other than Dad's horrible descriptions, my mind goes blank.

Don't say the ugly ones, the undead ones, or for gods' sakes, the sexy ones. "Um, the talented group that sings and dances and wears too much pink."

"The Muses." She gives me a *try again buddy* look. "You have five more Houses to go."

"The drunk ones that drive you insane."

"The Mad Maes—Syn City's version of Maenads. So far, *I'm* doing great on this test. You? Not so much."

I'm over this. "Kiva's my mate. That's all I need to know."

"Then I'll talk business, and you can stay quiet, broody bear."

We hit a puke-inducing pitch of waves coming at the boat. A giant tentacle shoots up from the water, curling toward us. What monsters lurk down there? For a moment, Beryl's face flickers the shade of green I'm sure I've been wearing since we boarded. She pushes to her feet, wobbling. "I'll talk with the crew, see what I can find out before we arrive."

I don't take my gaze off that greyish green tentacle, but I catch Beryl playing with her bracelet as she walks past, my little sister's tell that she's nervous. About the massive squid, the upcoming trip, or me fumbling my chance at convincing my mate to come home? I'm not sure, and she's not the only one worried.

A slim man in the ferry company's uniform of black slacks and a blue vest stops walking and stands close, but not too close. A quick inhale tells me he's a shifter—a turtle shifter, if I'm reading his scent right.

"Coming to Syn City for the concert this weekend?" he asks, his cadence syrupy slow.

"The Muses having a concert?" See, I'd listened to my sister's quiz. I could name Houses like any other tourist not here to find their dead-and-come-back mate.

"No." He slides a sluggish glance toward the shore, the movement heavy as if he's too tired to do more. "A country music star." Each word plods along like its own sentence. "Trick Peterson. The city'll be packed." The shifter shuffles toward a door marked

EMPLOYEES ONLY, his trudge steady and unhurried. "We'll be so busy with female fans. Smart of you to come early." The door finally closes behind him.

Hordes of fans along with everything else keeping me apart from my mate? How will I ever get to her?

"We are *in*." Excitement fills Beryl's voice as she comes through the same staff-only door. I don't want to know how she bossed her way back there. "I got us vendor access to The Rink tonight." The Rink has been spelled in capital letters in her tour guide like The Center of the Universe or The Shrine to All That's Holy. These people are serious about their roller derby. Beryl stabs at me with her pointy nail, her human ones almost as sharp as her bear claws. "Are you listening?"

"I am. You got us to in to see the building. How will this help me win back Kiva? I thought you said they're not playing a bout tonight."

"Yes, but the Furies practice tonight. Your mate will be there."

My world circles around the possibility. After two long years of nothing but hard and horrible, could finding Kiva be this easy? "We won't have to search the entire city? We simply walk into this one place and she'll be there? I don't... I can't..." My tongue tangles and trips over anything I try to say.

Beryl squeezes my arm, the same as she used to do when our parents fought. "You don't have to say anything. I know."

She's the comfort I didn't realize I'd needed until now. I've blustered through confidence and conviction in a world I know nothing about for the past two years. The hope that all my questions could end in the next hour is both thrilling and terrifying.

The ferry blasts closer to the shore where a gigantic coliseum looms on the horizon at least six stories tall. It takes over most of the skyline. "No wonder they capitalize The Rink."

"The pleasure district is farther inland. Our hotel's there, along with restaurants, shops, and a casino. Other than housing for staff, the rest is woodland and swamp. The Syndicate controls even the ferry schedule. No private access privileges in or out of the city. Except for Trick Peterson." She says the name on a sigh.

"The music guy?"

"The country music star." Beryl bites off each word. "I know you live in your forge, but you should occasionally catch up with this decade's pop culture."

"So he's a big deal?"

"He's the biggest name in showbiz right now. To think, he's coming to Syn City while we're here. It's so exciting. I booked our rooms through a shifter-only source, or we wouldn't have been able to stay. Maybe his concert tickets haven't completely sold out."

Beryl keeps talking, but I tune her out. I'm going to be near Kiva again—finally. I can't believe it. Walking off the boat and onto the shore? It's like moving through a dream. Instead of scanning the water and every face for danger, I'm living in a fog despite the clear night.

The pleasure district glows in the distance like a small town, and most of the lights are switched off on the coliseum. A jumbo screen stands two stories high on one curve of the round building. Based on the images in Beryl's guide, if we'd been coming in for a bout, we could've seen the sign a mile away. Electricity apparently doesn't blink, flicker, or shut off for weeks at a time in Syn City like it does at home. I wonder how much of that is hard-won peace, functioning tech, or magic.

"Can you imagine our Warrior's Den logo flashing on that screen?" she asks, then pushes me to grab our trunks.

An hour later, we've checked into the hotel, dumped our baggage in our rooms, and caught a courtesy hover shuttle to The Rink. Or rather, I've followed my sister like a robot with half of his sensors turned off. All I can think about is finding Kiva.

"It's a pain they put us in separate wings with the trunks and our weapons," Beryl says. "If Trick hadn't been coming, I'm sure our rooms would've been closer together, but I insisted on king beds. I need my space when I sleep." Which is my sister's polite way of commenting that her shifter self might send a smaller bed crashing to the floor.

I grunt a version of "I don't care," which seems to pacify her.

We step into the coliseum, air conditioning blasting away the sticky swamp heat. Yep, no electricity issues here.

I've been in a sports stadium that could've compared to a tiny version of this, but there'd been shops and concessions in a main corridor outside the seating. Not here. No, here, the oval flat track that is the skating rink at the bottom stands as the clear star of the building, visible from every entrance. Thousands of stadium seats climb upward from the rink both below and above the central door we'd stepped through.

Bars, food stands, merchandise dealers, and autograph tables line this level. Enormous banners from each of the seven Houses hang from the rafters. The sheer size of the place overwhelms, but they've maximized the space. Screens bigger than a house drop above the main rink. I bet they're double-sided. If so, even ticket holders in the highest seats would be able to see the game. Unfortunately, they aren't switched on now, so I can't make out the faces of the women in black circling the track.

But I don't need to see their faces. The mating bond calls to me just as it did the first time I met her. I hadn't needed a visual that night either. She's *here*. I can sense her. The same as if I could catch her scent over the smells of sweat, stale popcorn, and spilled beer. I hurry to get closer.

The shrill bleat of a whistle has me wincing. Judging by the faces of a few people around us, some of these workers must be shifters with equally sensitive hearing. Looks like the rumors that the Syndicate prefers to hire supernaturals might be true.

"Foul," a woman yells from the middle of the rink. "Penalty box."

"Are you kidding me?" a heartbreakingly familiar voice yells. "*She* skated into *me*."

"Did not." A ponytailed woman circles my mate. "If you wanted to cop a feel of my butt, you should've waited 'til we're off the track."

"As if you have enough to grope," Kiva fires back.

"We can't all be heifers like you."

My mate smacks her own gorgeous ass. "You're so jealous."

"Still a penalty," the woman with the whistle hollers. "Take a seat."

Kiva spins and looks at me. I swear I can feel her gaze on me. I haven't asked the gods for anything since the woman in black brought her back. But tonight, I do.

Please let my mate remember me, remember us.

Please.

4

KIVA

I'M TOO MUCH OF A BADASS FURY TO POUT, BUT I DROP WITH A bang onto the penalty bench, kicking out my skates and wiping the copper tang of blood from my mouth. Crashing into a team-mate's bony elbow had been the least of my mistakes tonight.

Thank the gods this is only a practice session, but we're so close to real bouts that matter, and I'm *waaay* off my game. The past week since Family Fest, I've had a weird feeling that some-thing or someone's coming for me. Above the clack of skates and music blaring through the speakers, I can almost imagine they're here in the stands...watching.

The prickle across my neck, the shivers sending goose bumps across my skin, the *pull*.

The bone-deep feeling that's making me breathless? It's not fear.

No, it's so much *more*.

It's also the first hint of anything outside of roller derby that's sparked my interest in two years. Of course, who knows what I liked before then because I'm the only freak in my House who doesn't remember her pre-Fury life. No, I just woke up in Syn

City with nothing but the bloody clothes on my back and an engraved bracelet that I run my fingers over now.

"Kiva, what were you doing out there on the rink?" Maizie, our new coach for the House of Furies, jabs a thumb toward the track. With brown skin and muscles that inspire envy, she's the ideal boss badass even though grief and fatigue drag down the few lines in her face. "You skate mean, but you don't skate illegal. That's what makes you so damn effective."

"It—" Glancing up in the stands, I spot members of the House of Huntresses and bite off any explanation. Why those smug know-it-all's are shadowing our practice session, I have no idea, but I don't like it, and I'm not telling my new coach any of my *woe is me* problems in front of them. I lift my chin in their direction. "Huntresses." I don't bother hiding my snarl.

Maizie follows my gaze. "Damnit." She has been in charge of the Furies for only a few weeks. "They're doing their best to hit us while we're weak, with our coach being gone—"

"*You're* our coach now." I keep my voice low, not wanting to undermine her authority but not letting her forget that she's in power. She's the one we believe in while we all mourn the death of our last leader. "Show them how we'll beat them this year in the championships." Because they are going down, way down.

She sets her jaw, staring at the Huntresses as though she's about to pop a top on a ferocious can of Fury kickass. "I'm still not letting you off the bench. You're out for the rest of practice."

"Come on," I whisper. Playing might be the only time I'm not tormenting myself about the nightmares that have me roaming the halls every night. "Let me skate. You know they hate me. Maybe it'll make them run back to their crappy archery ranges." If the Huntresses had proper weapons to call like we Furies do, they wouldn't need to practice so much.

"Nope, my penalty call was legit. You play that sloppy in a real bout, and I'll throw you out of The Rink myself. In fact..." Maizie whips her head around, her dreadlocks flying out of their messy bun. "I've got the perfect punishment."

She motions toward a brown-haired girl who's lugging water and towels and gods-know-what-else across the track. The teenaged, two-legged equivalent of a golden retriever breaks into a run. Normally, there'd be no humans at The Rink unless they're married to a House member or they're the uber-rich tourists packing the stands who pay good money for the privilege of putting their butts in seats. But this perky superfan is our exception.

I wave to her, and Connie drops half of what she's holding when she tries to wave back. Oops. "What kind of punishment?" I ask Maizie. "Having to actually talk to the Huntress hags?"

"No, this will be so much better." Our new coach looks positively gleeful with a smile that promises retribution. "Connie belongs to one of your triad sisters. You would do anything for the two of them, right? I mean the three of you just took down a serial killer. Handling one annoying teenager shouldn't be a problem for you."

"Connie's not annoying, and I didn't take anyone down." Not false modesty on my part. My triad sister Dottie sliced and diced the guy with two scary sickles that would make her a grim reaper if you stuck a handle on the damn things.

"Maybe the kid's not a complete pest, but she's studying for a test on city infrastructure—"

"Which I know nothing about."

"But you'd make the perfect tutor." Maizie sounds so smarty pants she might as well be a Huntress, although I'd never wish that on anyone.

Connie barrels into the pit, looking like an overgrown puppy ready for a training class full of treats, petting, and *atta-girls*. "Can I get you anything?" A pair of skates falls from her arms with a clatter. "Sorry about that."

Before I can open my mouth to ask what she's doing, Maizie butts in. "Kiva volunteered to help you study for your test."

"You did?" Connie turns those big brown eyes on me, so wide her gaze could belong on a cartoon character. Disappointing her now would be as cruel as kicking a kitten. I can't do it.

"Sure." I shoot Maizie a you're-killing-me look as she rolls backward onto the rink, but I can respect when I've been well and truly played. Connie might be the distraction I need to take my mind off the nightmares. At least until the doc picks them apart at our session tomorrow. Plus, I love the teen. She reminds me of someone—except I have no memory, so maybe I dreamed up a teenaged girl to look after. "How about a rundown of everything Syn City-related you should know in ten minutes or less?" Since that's what's left of practice tonight.

Connie heaves a huge, dramatic sigh that should be a show-stopper on the soap opera the Nymphs and Muses binge watch. "Maizie forced you to tutor me, didn't she?"

"Busted." I pat my palm against the wooden bench with its dents and bumps of derby destruction. "Join me in the penalty box, and I promise I'll give you the skivvy on anything Fury-related you want."

"Anything?" She sits beside me, shooting me an excited grin.

"Return the favor by letting me know how things are going with your cousin and her were-kitty?" My triad sister and her mountain lion shifter had finally made good on their mating bond.

"Only if you can help me convince Dottie to let me stay in the city. My cousin's *sooo* overprotective with, you know..."

"The serial killer who murdered her, caused her to go Fury, kidnapped you, and killed Coach so that Maizie had to take over?" I summed up the last few weeks in one line. "You should cut your cousin some slack for a while."

"But my sixteenth birthday's soon, and Dottie still treats me like a kid. I'm not that much younger than you, right?"

"I don't know how old I am." I tap my temple. "Amnesiac."

"Sorrry." She drawls out the word like a toddler caught with her fists jammed in a cookie jar. "I'm the worst."

"Nah, I figure I'm mid-twenties." But who the hell knew for sure? Not me, no matter how many leads I'd tracked. It was as if *before* me hadn't existed. Spinning the big bracelet on my wrist, I rub my thumb over the engraving of my first name from my human life. Or at least it's mine now. No one knows where I came from or if this was where I'd wanted to end up. "You sure Syn City's what you want?"

"Definitely. I've followed the seven Houses since before I could read the captions beneath the pictures." Starry-eyed and as dreamy-toned as the House of Mad Maes strung out on the good stuff, there will be no talking Connie out of staying.

"Okay, superfan, you shouldn't be worried about passing any test. You already know everything."

"Except who's on the Syndicate, what they do, what's behind the mysteries of the Houses—"

"Whoa, whoa. No one knows those things." Syn City's run by a secret Syndicate that makes the rules, runs the Houses, and keeps The Rink bringing in enough cash to support us. "Only the Syndicate knows its members or what they do other than bossing the coaches."

"Maybe the coaches *are* the Syndicate members." Her words tumble faster, amped on some weird teen adrenaline high. "Or maybe only immortals make up the Syndicate."

"You talk conspiracy crap like that around Maizie, and you'll make her mad. Not that I care about her feelings right now."

"Especially after she called you out for a foul when you *barely* bumped into someone and then she stuck you with me." She makes the offense sound worse than a being crammed in an elevator full of smelly Gorgons.

"You're all right, Connie."

She beams as if I've given her the keys to a bang bike. Not that

I've been on one, but they look like the loudest fun possible. I can't let her think I've gone soft. "For a human," I add.

"Yeah, yeah." She glances toward the stands. "What's with the Huntresses being here?"

"I don't know, but they're here without their coach." Thank the gods for small favors since Devlyn would've taken over The Rink the minute she walked in as if she owned it.

Connie frowns. "I didn't know practice was open to other Houses to scope out the competition?"

"I don't think they're here to study our plays." Since they barely glance at the track.

"Why else would they be here if not to steal ideas from other teams? Is that how they win the championships every year?"

I wince. Damn, I didn't need yet another reminder that we lose. Every. Single. Year. But not this one. "No, Huntresses wouldn't stoop to cheating. They're above breaking rules. Just ask the self-righteous bitches."

She snickers. "If that's what you call them, what're the Muses?"

"Rich bitches."

"And the Styx?"

"Undead bitches. No one's sure whether they're vampires or wraiths hiding behind those faceless masks."

"And everyone knows Furies get whacked and come back."

I almost choke. "Look at you, rhyming. That's not half bad. You been raiding my archived mob movies?" The ones made back before humans realized magic is real or that the dust bunnies under the bed might eat you and everyone else in the house. "The Furies have a known past because we have people from our *before* lives—like you with your cousin."

"Except you?" She sounds worried.

"Clearly, I was in the witness protection program." One of the many lies I've spun to ease other people's discomfort more than my own. In the almost two years since I turned, *no one* has shown up to claim me. Not family or friends or a crazy ex-boyfriend whose life I destroyed when I disappeared. What if they hadn't come because there'd been no one to miss me?

"You okay?" she asks.

"Yeah." Except for crazy nightmares where I'm covered in blood. Normal Furies—or however normal we get—don't remember details of their dreams. What if I was a psycho murderer in my first life? Here's hoping that being a vengeance killer ordained by the goddesses in my second life would cause less insomnia. "I've got a lot on my mind."

Connie digs at a crack in the floor with the side of her sneaker. "Do you know Dr. Bomani, the House shrink? I have to talk with her if I want to be allowed to stay."

"Of course I know Dr. Bo. Every Fury has to see her after the turn." I'm in her office every week now that the dream has gotten worse. But that's not what Connie's asking. "And?" I nudge her shoe with my toe stop.

"What if the doc finds something really wrong with me? What if she won't let me stay?"

"Dr. Bo is not going to make you go home to whatever back-woods town you and Dottie came from."

"But will she make me talk about the kidnapping? I mean, I'm good, totally over it."

Sure she is, with the way her voice sped up and she digs harder at the concrete floor as if she hopes the crack might widen enough she could fall into it. "Are you? I mean, I'm no therapist, but that's got to mess with your head."

"Going home won't make things any better. I'd rather stay here with my cousin and you Furies."

"Then tell Dr. Bo that. She'll let you talk about your problems, maybe ask you some questions or give you some help figuring things out or seeing a new perspective."

"But what if she thinks I'm, you know, too broken to keep in the city?"

"Hello? Have you met the Furies? We're all broken here, just in different ways. I can't think of a single member of any House who had a great *before* life or whatever the Styx might've had. We're deity daughters, chosen by the immortals for a reason. Not a sunshine-and-sparkly-baby-unicorns kind of reason. Syn City is the chance to get things a little bit better this time around." Which might be why I have no real desire to know the truth about my first life. If I can avoid knowing more, I can keep everything exactly the way it is now. Derby, triad sisters...not a bad life.

"So you're all here to prove something?"

"Deity daughters are created to fulfill a mission given to them by their immortal for as long as our mortal bodies allow us. Furies seek vengeance. Muses talent. We all have a legit purpose except the House of Mad Maes."

"Are they really as crazy as they seem? Or is it an act with the harlequin masks?"

"Stay away from the Maes. They're not just broken. They're out to break everyone else, then throw a hell of a party while watching the place burn around us. The only reason they don't win on the track is because they don't care about derby except for the mayhem."

"Good to know. Glad I won't be on the rink with them. Any other advice?"

"No hooking up with the shifter staff. Not unless you want your cousin to unleash holy hell on them."

"Pfft. That's not happening. It would take a supersized dose of stupid for someone to date Fury family."

"Shifter hormones can mean legendary levels of thinking they're invincible." Now what made me say that? I don't know many shifters, and I certainly don't talk to them about sexy times. Those supernaturals have fated mates—insta-love with lifelong complications and endless devotion. Something beyond me or I'd have found mine by now, right?

"Who's that? He's huge...shifter huge." Connie's eyes go wide, and her posture tenses. "And he's heading this way." Her voice climbs higher and squeakier. Had trauma from the kidnapping kicked in?

I snap my head in the direction she stares. Holy Hades and Persephone doing it doggy-style. The guy coming toward us is massive...massively hot. He looks like he stepped out of my favorite video game after raiding while wielding a jumbo version of my hatchet and riding a rhino.

"Kiva?" Connie whispers in a voice that's not at all soft. The girl has got to work on stealth.

"Yeah?" The man's biceps must be thicker than my thighs.

"He's looking at you."

"Huh?" Maybe two years of focusing on Furies, derby, and avoiding the past mean it's been too long since I've gotten laid. I don't have a former life to compare the present to. Maybe past-me kissed every guy she met and screwed twenty on Sunday. Or maybe she'd been a virgin. Jumping Jupiter, am I a virgin? No, I would know, right? Except I wouldn't. "No," I drawled in a grumpy version of the sweet Southern accent my triad sisters have.

"Yes, he is. Oh gods, oh my gods—" Connie jumps to her feet and erupts into some teenager tantrum seizure. I'm so glad I don't remember my teen years because no way could I have survived being as awkward as her right now. Okay, okay, so the guy looks like a hot Viking plunderer from one of the Nymphs' romance novels I swiped. But my staring and drooling at him routine has to be *way* less creepy than whatever the hell Connie's doing.

The pull I felt earlier? The one that stole my breath, made my heart pound, and had a magnetic tug? The come-closer urge that made me wonder if I wouldn't mind drowning in its whirlpool? It's back.

Sticky wetness drips from my nose to my lip, and I swipe the back of my hand over my face because I'm already struggling not to stand and move. Toward the pull? Away from it? I'm not sure.

But the crimson streaks across my wrist make me go still. My nightmares rush to fill my vision as much as if I'm living them.

The blood.

So much blood.

I'm drowning in it.

I can't breathe.

Panic shoots through me, squeezing my chest ten sizes too tight. Nightmares in waking hours? Or are these memories? *What did I do in my last life?* I don't want to know.

A piercing screech from where the Huntresses huddle makes me scan for the threat. My Fury senses haven't ignited with revenge-hack-kill fervor. I catch the big guy wincing as if an operatic kid in the crystal shop has had a glass-shattering meltdown. He's probably a shifter. They're not the only supernaturals with sensitive hearing, but they're the most common. What kind of animal shifts to something so big that *this* is his human, smaller side? And what the frick is this pull coming from his direction?

"Thank you," a deep voice croons. "I appreciate the welcome." Trick Peterson, the country music star, steps out of a doorway below the shifter stranger and onto the now silent track where practice has stopped. "I came to let you know I'm throwing a party in two nights exclusively for House members and their guests."

A cheer goes up from the Huntresses. Trick's not-so-subtle surprise appearance explains why they're here. But could he be the reason I'd felt the pull, and if so, what kind of magic does he sling? A power that could make me believe I'd seen my bloody nightmares while awake? A knot of sickness and dread spins in my stomach.

Or was that last part all me? Are my twisted memories haunting me?

I don't want to know. It's time to see Dr. Bo for another session.

5

STONE

My heart bangs worse than a faulty hammer on a warped sword, and time slows as though I'm swimming through the swamp that surrounds this damn city. I can't see Kiva in the swarm of women crowding around Trick What's-His-Face, and I storm down the few remaining stairs toward the track.

Beryl's big bear feet *clomp, clomp* closer behind me. "Hold up." My sister grabs my shoulder, and I barely resist the urge to growl and toss her off. "What's your plan?"

"To get to Kiva."

"You step on that skating rink, and you can kiss any chance of talking to her good-bye. Trick keeps magic-slingers in his entourage, and the Furies can be as predatory and deadly as any pissed off momma bear."

"How do you know that?" My mate might have a temper, but she wouldn't hurt me.

"While you've been sulking, I've talked with shifters on the ferry, at the hotel, working here in the concessions and maintenance." Beryl gestures toward my mate. "*She* is not the same Kiva as you remember."

"I need to see her." To touch her. To hold her. To make sure she's okay. "To talk to her."

"And say what? Me big bear. You mate. Run away with me, a complete stranger, to get lucky and hibernate?"

I stop. "She has to remember me."

"She doesn't." My sister's intense whisper carries Kodiak female ferocity. "Did you see her sprinting into the stands to hug you and start another happily ever after? She doesn't know you, just like the curse said. You're going to have to do this super slowly, or she'll tell you no, and you won't get to propose another six times—or even once."

Kiva walks out of the crowd, and her gaze flicks to mine. Hope rockets through me.

I yell to be heard above the cheers about the upcoming party —a carnival. "Kiva, I—" My voice cuts out, the words sticking in my throat. I can't physically tell her. When the cloaked immortal had said I couldn't talk to my mate about our past, she must've invoked magic to make sure her curse held. *Damn it.*

Kiva looks at me, through me, past me. Her gaze slides away, and she pushes through a door marked HOUSES ONLY. My gut twists and burns as if someone has stabbed me with one of my blades. My mate didn't recognize me, and I can't tell her who I really am, what we meant to each other.

Beryl tugs on me, and I can't move. My feet stick as though I'm rooted to this spot, the last place I could see her. "You know it's her," my sister says. "That she's alive and she's here. That's what really matters. Come back to the hotel, and we can plan over a meal. They have honey beer and a baklava cookie bar on the menu."

Food. The answer to all problems according to Beryl. But she's right. Rushing after a woman who doesn't know me would scare Kiva, and I don't want to see fear in my mate's eyes. If she didn't feel the same mating bond, the same tug that links us, I don't know if I can handle losing her all over again.

Hours later, with a full belly and empty heart, I stare at the walls of my hotel room, the space seeming to shrink by the second. I still haven't figured out how to approach Kiva. The business plan Beryl outlined over dinner makes sense, but there's no passion in approaching my mate's House as a weapons artisan.

Sure, Kiva likes blades, but she prefers quiet and steadfast devotion. She wants a mate who knows her favorites—which song she loves to sing badly and loudly, what ratty old sweatshirt of mine she wants to curl up in when she's cold, which scents make her wrinkle her nose or sigh with sweet memories, what salty snacks she craves when she's stressed.

Snacks. Food. *The answer to all problems.* Gods bless Beryl.

I jump to my feet and toss open the trunks full of weapons and tools. Packed among the hatchets and hammers in protective wrap is a box with a half-gallon of Kiva's favorite soda and a bag of crab chips. I could drop it off on her doorstep like I used to when we dated, before she said yes. Perhaps it would remind her of those times, of how I loved being the guy she let take care of little things.

Tucking the box in the crook of my arm, I hurry from my room and step out of the hotel. The pleasure district doesn't pack the partying-vibe punch of its name tonight. Other than a diner and a bar, everything looks closed. Perhaps everyone's resting up for the pretty music boy's promised carnival or his concert.

All right, so I'd been jealous of the way he'd stolen Kiva's attention when he'd announced his presence like he was one of their gods come down from Olympus. But he also saved me the embarrassment of charging onto the track and rushing up to my mate without being able to say a word about our past.

Leaving her a present? That couldn't be banned by whatever curse Kiva's Fury creator cooked up as my punishment. Outside, I take a deep, centering breath. If the mating bond truly began its dance again tonight, I should be able to sense her. While I won't be able to experience her joy, feel her pain, and be as connected as we'd been before, I could track her if needed.

I exhale in a hurried rush.

Nothing happens.

On the second breath, I pause after the inhale, savoring the movement and memories. *There.* A flutter of *something.*

With the next, I connect to the hope, leaning into the supernatural sense that lets shifter males put on courtship displays to rival our animal counterparts. An echo of our faint mating link ricochets inside me, sparking brighter. Kiva's answering my call whether she knows it or not. I follow the thrumming of the bond between us. Deeper and deeper into the woods I plunge, closer to the swamp surrounding the city. The buzz of bugs and bigger threats doesn't stop me, although the sweltering heat and giant mosquitos make me wish for home—my home with Kiva and all its comforts.

Here, far from the pleasure district, an enormous tree stands that's way too big to be found in this part of the world. The thick trunk, the towering mass—it must be thousands of years old, which seems impossible. The most logical explanation? Divine powers. If immortals staked this city as the home of deity daughters, how much of a stretch would it be for them to alter the natural landscape?

Every tiny thread of the tentative mating link leads me here. I glance up, looking for the place where prey or a stealthy predator like a Fury might hide. There's nothing to see, but my other senses tell me that's a lie, a facade of something concealed in plain sight. Several heartbeats reach my ears, not frantic beats of small animals but the steady pulse of humans or those who could pass for human. I breathe in the scents of spices, metal, and perfume.

The pull of Kiva? It comes from above. The Fury home must be a winding tree house hidden by the leaves, the moss, and magic.

I heft the box from beneath the crook of my arm, testing its weight. I would've brought a bag if I'd known I'd be climbing tonight. No time for regrets. I check for nearby branches and footholds, preparing to ascend one-handed. There'd better be a damn doorstep up there to leave this on.

A thud of boots and a soft *whoosh* have me spinning, preparing for whatever magical creature comes out of the trees.

Only the mating link throbs, raw and exposed.

Kiva.

"It's a little late to be strolling through the woods to grandma's house." Her voice carries the same one-two punch of sarcasm and sweetness that it always did. Her Jersey accent's slight, but it still remains. Hearing her speak after only dreaming of her voice for two long years hits me hard, and I have to concentrate on her words. A joke. A twist on a human fairy tale from before the Witching Wars. How very Kiva.

"I'm no wolf, and I wasn't looking for grandma." I can barely force the words past the thickness of emotions clogging my throat.

"Oh really?" She huffs a little laugh of menace. "You could meet worse than wolves in these woods. Why don't you run home?"

"Because I was looking for you."

Her eyes widen, surprise filling her gaze. "I'm *way* worse than any wolf."

Yeah, she's more dangerous for me than anyone else, but not for any reason she seems to know.

She studies me like she's trying to figure out a stranger, assess his strengths and weaknesses, his intent and threat level. I've seen her do this to hockey opponents. The distance in her gaze guts me, but she hasn't left me standing here, and I'll take whatever crumbs of attention she's handing out. "What's with the box?" she asks.

"I brought you a gift."

She tips her head, narrowing her eyes. "What kind of gift?" Suspicion rides the nosiness in her tone.

"A late-night snack."

"Why?"

"I saw you at practice earlier, working hard. Figured you might be hungry." She was always hungry after hockey.

"You wandered out in the woods in the middle of the night to bring me a present?" She makes it clear she's not buying it. "Put the box on the ground and back away."

Two years ago, she would've snatched the box unopened from my hands. Even before we were a couple, she would've taken it with a grin. Now, she sounds so distrustful. My Kiva wouldn't have—I stop myself. She's the same, she's still *my* Kiva. I slowly lower the box and put distance between us, stretching out my hands. "Nothing but food and drink," I tell her.

"Why were you at our practice?"

I open my mouth to tell her that I love her, that we're mates fated by destiny, that I want nothing more than to take her home and give her everything she wants, to make up for the night I failed her. But no words come out.

The curse. It has to be.

She quirks her lips. "While you're deciding what lie you want to pile on to your earlier assumption that I'd be hungry after practice, let me tell you again not to go nosing around places where you haven't been invited. It'll get what's left of you dumped in the swamp for the gators and sea hags to chomp on."

"I thought Syn City guarantees safety to its tourists." Another fact Beryl had read aloud from the visitor brochure.

"The Syndicate protects human tourists, but that doesn't apply to you, does it shifter?"

Had she remembered me? A hopeful *maybe* bubbled in my gut. "You know I'm a shifter?"

She steps closer, and the urge to touch her overcomes me so badly that I have to curl my hands into fists to keep from reaching for her. "The only question I have is what kind of shifter are you?" she asks. "We have werewolves." I almost wrinkle my nose at the suggestion. What an insult. "But you're bigger, broader, and you said no to that. One of my triad dates a were-kitty—a mountain lion," she adds. "You don't have his cat qualities. My money's on some mutant variation of a prehistoric Mongolian mammal." Her speech speeds up, excitement running through her voice as lively as an electric current. "Am I right?"

"A what?" I have no idea what she's talking about, but she's staring at me expectantly. "I'm a Kodiak shifter—a bear."

"Oh." She sounds disappointed. Somehow, I'm failing her test.

A *whoosh* the same as the one that came before Kiva appeared comes from behind me. *Not this time.* No one will hurt my mate. I step between her and whatever just landed, ready to serve as a shield.

Except my woman peers around me and smacks my arm. "Hey, Sadie," she says. "Meet our visitor. He's a were-bear."

Were-bear. It's the horrible nickname that would've made me want to tear someone's limbs off...except this came from Kiva. *My* Kiva. Said with the same snarky sass she used to give me.

The blonde who must be Sadie shoots me a look from head to toe before dismissing me as if I present no threat. "When did we start inviting random shifters?" she asks in a posh Southern drawl that sounds far richer than redneck, tossing her sleek blonde ponytail over her shoulder while saying the word *shifters* like smelly garbage. But what has me staring isn't her uppity nose in the air. Nor her perma-scowl. No, she has wings—giant black wings with blood red drawings that scribble and fade as if someone's writing an archaic language across a living book. "We let one mountain lion in here to date our triad sister, and suddenly we're running a shifter sanctuary?"

"He's not coming to the House," Kiva answers. "He worried that I had post-practice munchies and brought me snacks."

"Did you order something?" Sadie asks her, completely ignoring me.

"No," my mate says softly. "It's a gift."

"Ooh, a superfan." The other Fury doesn't sound impressed. "We need to work on our defenses so random shifters like... what's your name?"

"Stone," I say, and both of them stare at me.

"Your *real* name?" The rich accent doesn't cover Sadie's witchy snideness. "Not your performance name."

"That is my real name."

"Shut up," Kiva exclaims. "You wouldn't even have to fake a derby name. Like mine's Killa, but my real name is Kiva. And Slaya here is really Sadie."

"Don't tell him anything, motormouth," Sadie says, folding her wings behind her. They vanish—just *poof*, those enormous feathers that rustle like pages disappear. "He could be a psycho serial killer."

Why is their first thought *serial killer*? What has Kiva been through since I lost her? I don't get a chance to ask because she's already talking.

"Nah," she says. "We've already had one of those living in Syn City, and we just got rid of him. Snacks won't kill me."

Sadie steps forward, opening the box. "Unless they're poisoned." She yanks out the chips.

Kiva snatches them away. "They're not poisoned. The bag's not even open." She rips into the top. "See? Just plain old chips."

"Crab chips," I say for no smart reason whatsoever. My IQ obviously got zapped along with my ability to talk about my mate's life before she was a Fury.

Sadie takes a whiff of the bag and wrinkles her nose. "Ew. Disgusting."

A sudden thought occurs to me. What if Furies don't eat normal food? Sure, The Rink had every fat-laden, salt-soaked snack anyone could want on the menus, but those are meant for human tourists. Shifters hunt, but what do Furies eat? *They feast on the souls of evil*, a sly voice that sounds too much like the mystery woman in black whispers in my head. I'd clearly spent way too many nights watching horror movie marathons sacked out on the couch these last few months.

My worries churn in my gut as Kiva pulls a crab chip from the bag, sticks it under her nose, and sniffs.

"Seems fine to me," she announces and bites into an oversized chip. "Mmm, spicy," she mumbles around the mouthful.

Her friend, coworker, teammate, whatever Furies call each other, stares at her in revulsion. "Didn't anyone teach you the concept of stranger danger?'

"Maybe." Kiva gives a half shrug and taps her head. "Amnesiac."

My brain skids to a full halt. The immortal had said she wouldn't remember me, but she doesn't remember *anything*? "What kind of amnesia?" I ask and then wonder if different kinds exist or if I came off as an idiot—again.

"What are you?" Sadie asks. "A shifter doctor? Does that mean you're a veterinarian or an actual people doctor?" She glares at me.

"No, but..." How the hell do I explain my interest without sounding like the crazy man who brings snacks to the middle of nowhere well past midnight? "I see a lot of concussions. My sister and I run a school for medieval weaponry." Yeah, I haven't been allowed to teach a class in well over a year, but I'm not mentioning that. "Jousting and sword fighting—even with practice weapons—can mean a lot of blows to the head if there's too much aggression flowing." Which is most of the time with shifters.

"You teach sword fighting?" Kiva asks, finally looking at me with some interest other than as a trespasser she might want to hack into bits. "What do you know about hatchets?"

The simple question about the gift I'd never been able to give her twists me into knots. So much that I don't have an answer.

"No," Sadie says. "We're not whipping out our weapons to call so you can ask a random shifter for tips. Just because he teaches humans how to smack at each other with sticks doesn't mean he knows anything about real weapons."

"I own a forge." My words creak much like the noise my ancient vise in my workshop lets out no matter how much upkeep I do. "I make weapons."

"That's why he's here." Sadie drawls each word like an indictment for treason. "He wants to sell us blades so he brought bad food to bribe us for a meeting. Not such a smart tactic, shifter."

"I dunno." Kiva crunches another chip. "I think it's a solid plan. Got any of the weapons you made on you?"

My chest squeezes, my throat tightens, and my bear claws at me from inside. *I have the dagger I made for you, the one you took when you finally said yes, the one I've kept on me every day since you've been gone.* "Yeah." I fumble to unsnap the sheath hooked to my waist and hold out her dagger. I don't want to give up the tiny piece of her that I've been holding on to, but it's hers, and maybe she'll remember something if she sees it again.

Her eyes light up as if I've handed her the holy friggin' grail. "This is gorgeous," she murmurs, tracing her thumb over the engravings. "You made this?"

"I did." I want to say I made it for her, but the words get stuck in my throat so I change tactics. "It's yours." Holy mother of shifter saints, I managed to say something right and not be cut off by the curse.

"Yeah?" she asks even as she tightens her hold on the hilt.

Her tone says she thinks I mean *yours* as in a gift. That's fair. "Yeah." My world centers on her, on the happiness shining from her face, on a memory of the first time she took this dagger and agreed to be mates forever.

"Cool." She clutches the dagger to her the same way she did then—as if history repeats itself.

"Come on," Sadie says. I'd forgotten she's still here. "Let's say good-bye to the shifter. He impressed you with his sales pitch. Job well done." She says the last as though she means the opposite. The woman hates me personally or all shifters. I'm betting on the latter.

Kiva looks up at me. "Can you fix roller skates?"

No, but if it means time with her, I'll learn how. "Sure."

"My left rear wheel's been a little wobbly, and our last props guy... Well, he was a serial killer so..." She trails off, staring at me and holding the gifts I've brought her.

"I'd be happy to look at it."

"Thanks." She follows Sadie a couple of steps into the darkness of dense trees but stops to glance over her shoulder. "Hey were-bear, see you at Trick's party?"

"Wouldn't miss it." Not if it means spending another moment with her.

"Awesome." She walks away. I listen to her steps, the crunch of dead leaves and twigs under her feet, and the *whoosh* like earlier. Then there's nothing.

My heart lifts. I'm here less than twelve hours and already Kiva has taken a gift from me and eaten the food I offered her. The mating dance has formally initiated. A few more days, and I'll have her back. A few weeks, and we can go home together.

6

KIVA

"KIVA, YOU SCHEDULED THIS EMERGENCY SESSION. YOU DON'T HAVE to talk about your reasons, but it might help." Dr. Bo's soothing spa voice makes the suggestion sound so appealing like *yes, please, I'll talk about my trauma with a second helping of pie.* Or maybe some of those damn addictive crab chips that the werebear brought me.

The good doctor gives me a patient gaze as I pace back and forth across the thick carpeting in her office. "Why don't you begin with helping me understand what's making you feel agitated?"

"I'm not agitated." My tone chops at the denial as much as shouting *yes, yes, I'm ready to shriek like a banshee.*

Dr. Bo aims a pointed look at the throw pillow I'm holding. I've slowly plucked at the tassels as though it's some poor chicken about to meet its end in a pot.

I stop manhandling the pillow. Agreeing with Dr. Bo should be so easy. Same with telling her the real, unfiltered truth about my life, because she's the one person I trust with my crap. But...I can't. Sure, I told Connie the teenaged Fury mascot that Dr. Bo's on our side, that she gets how all of us are broken in our own way here in Syn City, but I don't want to admit that I might be as messed up as a Mad Mae.

"The nightmare comes all the time now," I say. The one that plays on repeat because my brain doesn't create another when this one is so much gory fun. I don't call it *my* nightmare because that's too close to an admission that it might be *my* memories.

"Every night?" Her expression doesn't change. She keeps that steady *not judging* solemness without being super serious.

"Yes and..." I take a deep breath and force out the words. If I admit the delusion out loud, maybe I can be done with the heaviness of it haunting me. "At the track last night during practice, I spaced for a few seconds and thought I was literally in my nightmare."

"That must've been a lot to handle." She doesn't say *a lot* of what—worry, anger, fear, fucked-up frustration. "How did that make you feel?"

Oh, so I have to fill in the blank that came after her mysterious "a lot" statement?

No surprise there.

Welcome to how Dr. Bo works. She asks questions, gets me talking, has me spinning out details that I've sometimes overlooked or dodged on purpose. The woman can out-stare, out-think, and outmaneuver the toughest of us. In her fifties, with warm brown skin and as much grey in her hair as black, she exudes authentic classy—the kind that makes you stop snarking at her and get real for a minute. *How do I feel about the nightmare popping up in the middle of practice?*

"I honestly don't know." I drop my butt on the couch with a *pfft* of plush cushions deflating. "The dream's bad enough when I'm asleep. I don't need it creeping into my waking hours."

"Talk me through what happened right before you saw the dream at the track."

"There was so much going on. Trick Peterson showed up, which made people lose their minds." I check my neuro-judging

tone, but seriously, some of the Huntresses had made my delu-
sional state seem damn near normal next to their orgasmic
screams at a celebrity showing up. Especially when half the
House of Muses are worshipped as celebrities in the rest of the
world. "He's throwing a party tonight."

"Are you going?" She lets me switch the subjects so easily that
I wonder what the catch will be.

"Yeah. I guess. I mean, everyone's going, and there's this guy.
When the nightmare wouldn't stop, I went for a short flight a
couple of nights ago in the woods—"

"Going outside by yourself was risky, especially in light of
recent events." Dr. Bo sounds so calm discussing the serial killer
who showed up at our house to kill my triad sister Dottie.

"I stayed alert, and I have my weapon to call. No one wants to
come up against me and my hatchet, especially when I'm magi-
cally guaranteed not to miss."

"Still, did you leave the well-guarded Fury house for a
reason?"

She sets up the equation like I'm an adrenaline junkie who
might've been on the prowl for more danger. *Okay*, so I am, but
that wasn't why I went outside. Although maybe it's as reasonable
as confessing I followed the weird pull in my gut that started
around the time Mr. Country Music Star showed up at The Rink.
That pull roared through me at the track and has been a low hum
through my head and heart ever since. "I heard noises outside
and went to check it out."

"By yourself?"

"Yeah. Weapon to call. Literal blades built into my wings." I
spin my bracelet, needing the solid reassurance of the cool metal.
"Anyway, there was a guy, a shifter... We talked and he said he
would be at Trick's party."

"So you have a date?"

"What? No." Nerves bubble up and over my tongue like soda
that's way too carbonated, almost choking me.

"You work hard, you've been through a lot, and you've overcome extreme struggles. You deserve to date if you choose to."

"Why does everyone assume I'm into this were-bear? I mean he's hot and all, but I didn't know taking food from the man apparently equals some kind of mating ritual initiation. Who could ever think that? Not me." Until Sadie and I had gone yesterday afternoon to visit our third triad sister and her mountain lion shifter. Dottie's man had mouthed off the "food means forever together" nonsense.

"Then what has you making that correlation if you don't believe it to be true?"

"Sadie brought up meeting Stone in front of Dottie's shifter. Who names their kid Stone anyway? That's like a setup for being awesome with a cape and a funny hat. Maybe her man was just pulling my leg or wing or whatever about the snacks leading to *let's have sex and mate for the rest of our lives.*" I shut my mouth, cutting off the babble before I convince myself I'm a were-bear's bride.

Dr. Bo watches me like I'm her favorite freak at the sideshow, and I wish she'd relax her rule about not allowing punching bags in the therapy office. "I'm not sure what Dottie's cat shifter told you, but food and courtship have gone together throughout time in several cultures. What makes you so uncomfortable about dating?"

"I have derby and stuff." And if my nightmare comes from memories, I might've been a killer in my past life. "It's not like someone is here yelling 'fated mates' or 'forever kind of love' for me like Dottie has with her were-kitty."

"How do you feel about your triad sister finding a romantic partner?"

"They're engaged." I don't want to explain my tone because hell, I don't even understand it myself. "They're so disgustingly cute that I wonder when they plan to pop out a litter of were-kittens. Probably before the championship playoffs, which will be terrible because Dottie's the fastest Fury we have on the track."

"You know there's life beyond roller derby, yes?"

"But I'm damned good at derby." And not at much else except wielding my hatchet, but since it's what I was given by the immortals as my weapon to call, I can't take credit for any skill there. No Fury misses when she aims her weapon to call at a target—unless she wants to.

"Your Fury status doesn't mean you can't have meaningful relationships. Do you have anyone you trust enough to open up to so they might help you with the nightmare? Your triad sisters, perhaps?"

"Sadie already has enough bad stuff to deal with that she won't talk about. While she may come across as a beauty queen with bookish wings, I know she struggles with her history. And Dottie—well, she only died and came back a few weeks ago, and now she's got a teenager to look after. Connie's great, but she's still a responsibility. I'm not unloading my violent dreams on my triad sisters." Or how I might've been as bad as their murderers in my last life.

"Is this really about what you think they can handle, or is it more about your worry that they might judge you?"

Well, whack the truth nail on the head a little harder and maybe it'll knock me out next time, Doc. I hate when she cuts past my partial bullshit and goes straight to ripping into my real issues. Naturally, I sidestep her pointed question and answer with minimal sarcasm. "Judge *me*?" I manage a snort of a laugh that comes out more like a weak sob.

Dr. Bo gives me a stare so piercing I swear she looks through me. "You can't avoid your past forever. You'll have to deal with it whether by coming to terms with your amnesia or working through your fears surrounding this nightmare." She slices away layers of my mental armor, leaving me hurting and quicker to lash out than Sadie would be with her whip.

I don't keep the hatchet-sharp bitterness out of my tone. "My amnesia exists whether I want it to or not. I've done every scan, every test, every friggin' needle poke. There's no medical explanation, so that means my psyche must have a damn good reason for me not to remember." Like me hacking people with a knife that made the blood in my nightmare or the fact my Fury wings came edged in silver blades. Yeah, I don't want to dig into that abyss of issues.

"I'm not telling you to go seeking answers all at once, but perhaps you could slowly piece together your past through new experiences. Going to the party with this shifter could be a first step to testing your boundaries beyond derby or vengeance. Whether it's a date or not."

She wraps up the session, and I leave with my invisible wounds open, stinging in the wake of how easily I'd jumped to shove blame and hurt anywhere but on my empty past. My forgotten memories throb a constant ache, a raw and hollow gape for my conscience to poke at like a tongue searching for a missing tooth. I don't want to know if I committed horrible atrocities, except what if not knowing means I repeat those crimes in this life?

Releasing my wings, I take comfort in the familiar *whoosh* and weight and rightness of them. My past life might've been shit, and I could've been evil incarnate, but my flying makes me smile every time they unfurl.

The party. I just need to go to the party, have a good time, and forget about the nightmare. Flirting with a bear shifter who brought me food and an awesome dagger would be entirely optional—if Stone even shows. Maybe he'd made his sales pitch for his weapons business and would be moving on to another potential customer. A pinch of hurt slams into me as I take to the air, and I push it aside. Winning the roller derby championship— that's all I need to concentrate on. Hours later, I show up at the party ready to dance, drink, and not think about my nightmare.

Trick isn't a star. He's a *mega*star. I knew that, but still, taking in the full extravagance of the event he'd put together for a single night astounds. A gigantic circus tent of red and white takes up most of the grounds outside The Rink with bright lights, dazzling displays, and bold colors. Wandering between the performers and exhibitions, I ease by grunting Gorgons clustered around a strong-woman competition. Several Nymphs *ooh* over a muscled man juggling fire and knives. The crackle of flame and zing of the blades almost keep time to the drumbeats coming from another part of the tent.

A stranger dressed in a lavish gown of the darkest blue shimmering like ocean waves in the moonlight reaches for my upper arm. "Kiva?"

I jerk away from her touch, checking myself before Fury magic brings my hatchet into my hand. Something isn't right about this woman. She's elegant with streaks of lavender through her white hair and a shark-like coldness in her eyes. *Run*, a feminine voice I don't recognize urges in my head.

"Don't be afraid." The woman's voice soothes with its hush, a whisper that tugs at my lost memories the same as pulling on a loose thread that threatens to unravel my entire existence.

Suspicion has me ready to call supreme bullshit, but a comforting warmth settles around me as if the stranger wraps me in a snuggly blanket. "Who are you?" I demand.

"Marina."

"Have we met before?" In the life I don't remember?

"No, but I'd like to be your friend." Her kindness draws me in, making me want to nod at her suggestion. "I've come to Syn City to help you remember your past and find your future."

Meeting new people to help unlock my past? Thanks, Dr. Bo for being as right as always.

Showing up to this party? Best idea ever.

7

STONE

"CRASHING A HOUSE-MEMBERS-ONLY PARTY MIGHT BE YOUR WORST idea ever," Beryl says, walking beside me toward the ridiculously large circus tent outside The Rink. "Oh wait, no, your *worst* idea would be showing up to surprise your mate in the middle of the night like a creepy stalker. What the hell did they put in that honey beer to make you pull that stunt? I've been talking to the locals, and Furies have notorious reputations in this city for violence, especially when it comes to defending their turf. You're lucky she didn't gut you."

"It's not stalking. I took her food because she's my mate, and it's my privilege to care for her."

"You took food because you wanted to initiate the mating ritual, and please tell me that you did not take her those gross chips. Didn't they expire? Gods, I knew I should've thrown them out the last time I was over at your house."

"She didn't complain, and she liked the dagger."

Beryl blinks at me. "You gave her the dagger you've had on you since..." Since Kiva died. She doesn't need to say that part for me to know the exact day and hour I started carrying that knife. My sister touches my arm. "Are you okay?"

"It's *her* dagger. She deserves to have it returned. Maybe it'll trigger a memory."

"So what's your grand plan to get access to your Fury?"

"She asked if I could fix her skates and if she would see me at this party."

"Which we're *not* invited to. It's House members and guests only. Not even the resident staff. What makes you think they'll let us in?"

I haven't thought that part through. I've been so caught up in what to say to Kiva, how to convince her that we belong together, that I haven't worked out the details. "I, uh—"

"Stone? Here to peddle weapons?" The Fury who'd been with Kiva last night walks toward me, along with several other women, only she doesn't have those wings of black with blood red writing that she had hours ago.

I search my memory for her name although I hadn't been paying much attention to anyone or anything but my mate. For so long, I'd dreamed of Kiva, and she'd been close enough to touch, to scent. The name clicks when I remember my warrior saying it in that rich voice of hers that I missed for so long. "Sadie?"

My sister pushes past me. "Hi, I'm his sister, Beryl."

"Beryl the Bear?" Sadie asks.

"Yeah." My sister waves away the insult. "I got the short end of the name stick, or rock in this case. Mom's a geologist. I'm the brains behind Warrior's Den Weaponry. Stone's the blacksmith."

Sadie glances to a dark-skinned woman with dreadlocks flanked by two tanned blondes who look enough alike to be sisters. "He made the dagger that Kiva was playing with this morning."

My heart beats faster at knowing Kiva has something of her old life, something of me with her again.

The woman with dreads looks to Beryl, ignoring me altogether. "Nice craftsmanship. I'm Maizie. Come with us. Let's talk business while we drink Trick's booze."

I follow the Furies, the pull of the mating ritual calling to me. Kiva's here. I can feel her.

The tangy scent of rum and spices fill the air along with the beats of drums and melodies of a strumming guitar, less country twang and more beach-soaked rockabilly. Trick Peterson may not play my kind of music, but the man knows how to throw a party. Dancers twist into contortions no human could manage, and a shifter hybrid male smelling of goat entertains by juggling fire. Laughter and roaring shouts compete with the music, a rowdy promise of fun and mischief. Feminine voices come from every direction, but I'm here for one woman. I drop my shields, tuning out the sensory overload for the lure I can't resist.

Kiva.

I spot her talking with a woman who wears a gown of the glittering seas come to life but pales in comparison to my mate. How could I have forgotten the smallest details of how Kiva moves, the way her eyes twinkle devilishly when she's amused, or the tiny lines at the edges of her mouth when she's fighting a smile? Photos captured her image, reminded me of her angles and curves, but not of the nuances—the fast clip of her speech, the sweetness of her scent.

I breathe deeply, and panic hits me. The woman standing with Kiva smells of wrongness, ocean water, and witchcraft.

Something magical murdered Kiva's father and sister when she was a kid, her mother when she was older. She refused to tell me details, and I wish more than ever that I'd pushed her to talk. Memories of Kiva saying *there can't be sea witches here* beside the frozen lake right before she died pound into me worse than a jackhammer to my heart. An arrow killed her, not magic, but something's wrong, and I don't know what.

I can't see my mate's face. Her back is to me, but her posture, the way she carries herself, she seems so relaxed—too relaxed. Kiva's a warrior. In public, she stays ready for a fight. I can hear their voices, muddled by the crowd at first, yet coming in clearer as I speed toward them.

"What do you want to know of your past? Of your future?" the woman asks Kiva. "Maybe you'd like to meet your fated mate?"

My gut twists into a knot upon hearing the words. How could this stranger know that Kiva and I are destined mates? Had she glimpsed our past somehow? Or maybe my wife had remembered a crucial piece of her history? I hurry closer, eager to be done with the curse's heavy secret that's beginning to feel like I'm lying by omission.

"I don't have a mate." Kiva sounds so sure, so unshakable that I want to plead with her to take a chance on me. But the words catch in my throat. I can't even gesture *me, me, look at me, I'm the man desperately in love with you*. The curse weighs down my arms as though I've fought a dozen long battles and drag invisible anchors behind me.

"Of course you have a mate fated for you." The woman, this stranger's voice, spins a sticky web thick with magic. What kind of creature is she?

"I do?" Kiva sounds dumbstruck, spellbound.

Hope rockets through me. I have to tell her, but I can't, and the world slows around us as if I'm watching bullet trains rocketing toward each other at dizzying speeds. They're destined for collision, but I can't stop the catastrophe or look away. Instead, I'm pulled along in their chaotic wake.

"He's here," the woman says. "Waiting for you. He's been searching for you."

"He has?" Kiva's voice breaks, that of someone lost in a storm who has spotted a safe harbor.

I open my mouth, but no sound comes.

The woman smiles, a sweet and tender grin that almost hides the sinister beneath. "Trick is your mate."

No.

"No," Kiva voices my thought as if she can hear the screaming in my head, only her voice shakes where my heartache is as solid and certain as if my chest cracks in two.

"It's true." Trick Peterson, the man whose face has been plastered around The Rink's jumbo screens, steps forward. With white-blond hair and bright blue eyes, he looks as though he's about to go to his knees in front of Kiva. He's declaring himself to *my* mate. "I've traveled the world looking for you."

The fuck he has. I want to rip the guy apart.

Except the boiling anger that shoots my blood pressure into the stratosphere takes a serious backseat to the crush of confusion radiating off Kiva.

"I, I..." Stammering as though whatever she'd wanted to say has become caught in a snare, she backs into me.

The urge to hold her and not let her go fills me. I've never wanted anything so much as to take my mate into my arms, to tell her how much I've missed her. My hands shake with need. But she glances up at me in hurt bafflement as if she has no idea how I ended up in her path or even how *she* got here. Delicate layers of sadness, fear, and dread weave through her scent, more powerful than my drowning need to touch her. Alpha females are the most dangerous killers in the world, especially when trapped as my sweet Kiva is now.

I stand as a shield for her if she needs it, but I'm no longer her sword, and the truth of that reality rips me into ribbons. In my single-minded focus on making her love me again, I overlooked the reason we're here. Because I failed her. I didn't save her. I lost her but never let her go. Yet, forcing a trapped Kiva into my arms? Caging her would be more devastating than watching her walk away.

Because now, I have a chance.

She's alive.

She's here.

I need to remember these critical pieces of the puzzle that had been a destroyed wreck of nothingness only days ago.

Holding out my hands, I keep my palms exposed and fingers spread to look as harmless as a bear shifter can. She's so beautiful with a spinning world of emotion in her brown eyes, her dark hair pulled up and away from her long neck. The black outfit she wears could've been a normal date night out for us before... before the one night I failed her.

Kiva presses her hand to my chest, pushing as though she's unsure I'm real. The dazed look clears from her gaze, and she stares at me for a moment—for one blissful moment—like she knows that we were an *us*, like she remembers. In a blink, the recognition disappears, and I'm a stranger again. Worse, the flush on her cheeks, the narrowing of her eyes, the mash of her lips—they're all big blinking signs that she's a powder keg of temper about to spark.

"No." She sounds as if she's convincing herself to either hold back or unleash holy hell. "I'm no one's fated mate, and I don't appreciate you playing head games with me," she says to the woman in the fancy dress. She looks to Trick. "Or being used in anyone's schemes to get ahead."

"But—" The country music star croons the word, and she cuts him off as if he's called her an ugly name.

"Don't use me as a lovesick publicity stunt to sell concert tickets." She hurls that verbal missile with astonishing precision given the hurt in his ice-blue eyes. Rounding on me, she says, "Don't bring me food like some screwed-up mating ritual induction so you can sell weapons. I don't care how awesome your daggers are."

I'm not sure whether to take her accusation as a supreme insult or flattery, and she doesn't give me or anyone else time to speak.

"My blank slate of a past isn't some billboard for sale," she says. "*I'm* not for sale. No fated mates. Not for me. No way, no how."

Trick ducks his head with an *aw shucks, I only want to make you happy* grin that's patronizing as fuck. "I feel as if I've known you my whole life."

"Yeah?" she asks. "Then where have you been the last couple of years?"

I could warn him that he's asking for her to punch him in the face because I've seen Kiva do it before, but I don't. Better that *she* knock some sense into him than me. She draws back her hand, only she doesn't ball it into a fist as my Kiva would. No, she flexes her fingers like she's reaching for something.

Maizie, the Fury with dreads, rushes forward. "Kiva, don't." She pushes the order through the air like a sword to cut through the thick tension in the tent right now. "No magic. He's not a target."

My mate glares at Maizie for a long moment, the shaking in her outstretched arm going from a tremble to an outright jerk. Finally, she nods and crosses her arms, turning her back on the celebrity with one last glance at me.

"Sadie," Maizie says, "get your sister out of here before she destroys our headliner's pretty face."

"Yes, Coach." Sadie moves to Kiva's side, the blonde's anger radiating off her as she and my mate leave.

I don't understand. Kiva lost her only sibling decades ago. How does she have a sister now?

Maizie sends a look at the spell-slinging woman that makes tingles of dread crawl along my skin. "Mr. Peterson, I need a word with you and your entourage later about fortune telling with my Furies. We don't welcome strange magic here." She aims that commanding stare at me. "I don't know what you did or didn't do to Kiva in the past to piss her off, but you didn't provoke her now, and for that I'm grateful. We'll talk business later."

They leave, and I'm still watching the spot where Kiva disappeared into the crowd—the now gossiping crowd. Their accusations swirl around me, and I don't need shifter senses to sort through the hateful whispers.

Gods, Kiva's so weird, even for a Fury.

Can you believe she turned down Trick? What an idiot.

Did she almost go after him with her weapon to call? She should be exiled.

The immortal mothers never should've turned her.

What a disaster of a deity daughter.

She's a psycho.

Weirdo.

Freak.

My bear wants to roar, and our heart lurches after our mate. What's this horrible new world she has fallen into, and how the hell do I haul her out of it and get her home?

8

KIVA

"Harder, Connie," I yell from across the Fury house's training room to be heard above the pounding rock music, squeaking sneakers, and *thwomp* of a stick hitting padding. The teen's taking whatever hormonal angst she's got out on a padded figure with a Huntress face painted on. I added that little House-hating anger incentive. "You got this. Teach that dummy who's boss."

"I am." She slams the wood again and again with focused, heavy breathing.

Her cousin stands next to me at the workstation with finishing sanders, whetstones, and ammunition littering the high bench the same as vegetables, spoons, and pots might a kitchen countertop. These oil-soaked and metallic scents comfort me as if I grew up in an armory instead of an actual home.

Dottie cleans weapons and disassembles parts like the novice she is, hesitating between each step of habit so routine to me that I can do them without looking. Thank goodness my triad sister has a magical weapon to call, which doesn't require any maintenance or special skills. She holds a mace like the thing's a ticking bomb. "You didn't holler such nice things at me when I was new to fight training," she says.

"Your human cousin doesn't have to earn her wings and her weapon to call. You did." I shove a heavy-duty cleaning cloth at her, listening for the telltale slowing of the *thwacks* from across the room. Switching the music to a chill playlist, I call out to Connie, "Transition into your staff kata drills. Great job."

The teen beams and glides into an impressive lunge-and-thrust routine with perfect form. Stepping from the shining hardwood floor to the cushioned dark mats, her footfalls become silent, her actions as brutal as if she had an opponent in front of her. Light pours from the open doors onto her black training uniform, cutting slices of bright and dark against her skin and developing muscles with each steady movement as part of a seamless flow.

"Thank you," Dottie says.

"For what?" I check my need to yank the mace away from her before she coddles it some more.

She stares at the teenager like the kid might disappear if she looks away. The two cousins have the same brown hair, the same brown eyes, the same stubborn chin. "Connie's had the most awful time since she arrived with the kidnapping and Coach's murder right in front of her, and I just don't want to screw up her life any more than I already have."

"You didn't ask some crazy killer to come after you, Connie, or Coach."

"My cousin came here looking for me, so it's—"

"Not. Your. Fault." I bite off each word and punctuate it with a wag of the pointy end of the dagger I'm holding. "Don't make me hurt you in front of your mini-me. She might come after me in some sad, little payback scheme."

"Please." Dottie stretches the word into its own paragraph. Her twang would put a sugar-shine on anything. "Connie adores you."

"The adoration's mutual." I glance at the smooth, precise moves of the teen's choreographed moves. Her swinging ponytail, her need to prove herself, her desire to be strong against the monsters of the world, her wishing to belong with the Furies like we're the grown-up version of a cool girls' clique... Everything about her buzzes around in my brain as an almost flashback, hazy and not nearly as clear or as graphic as my nightmares, but still—the familiarity is there. "She reminds me of someone."

"Oh my gawds," Dottie whispers. "Have you gotten some of your memory back?"

"No. Or at least I don't think so." I'm so tired that stopping the sigh that escapes me would take too much damn energy. "I don't know."

"Sadie mentioned you aren't sleeping, said you've been wandering around the halls and outside. Want to talk about what's keeping you awake at night?"

"Well, it's not Trick or the bear shifter." I grab a whetstone and sharpen, staring too hard at my hands, the knife, anywhere but toward Dottie. The woman's like a walking mood ring who deals in emotions as easily as I wield weapons. "This blade's dull. Might as well stab someone with a spoon."

"Stop changing the subject unless you need to take the edge off more than that blade. Maybe one of those men could be your answer. Or both of them."

"Geez, Dottie."

"What? You can't keep going without sleep."

I move the blade faster. "I'm not buying into the *fated mate* crap with either of them. No offense to you and your were-kitty."

"None taken. Did you talk to the shifter? I mean the way Sadie told how it all went down, with the fortune teller predicting you and Trick would be mates, but no one mentioned the bear saying anything."

"He kept quiet." Which hadn't kept me from biting his were-bear head off for simply standing there and being a big, muscle-bound safety net to keep me from tumbling over. Plus, he'd grounded me somehow, helped me shake off whatever daze had come over me. I would be sure in the future to stay away from whatever Mad Mae levels of high that Trick Peterson might be piping through his parties. "He's been nothing but nice."

"So why did you accuse him of using you to sell weapons— very expensive and fancy weapons, but still?"

Guilt eats at me, gnawing at my stomach as if I've swallowed the worst sour candy coated in chili pepper, but I refuse to give in. "He shows up in town to score a vendor contract and that same night he's bringing me a random gift?" Yummy chips, which is beside the point.

"This isn't like you. When I became a Fury, you welcomed me with the subtlety of a war hammer. You've been nothing but friendly to my human cousin and my mountain lion fiancé, so I know it's not a bias against shifters for you like it is for Sadie. What has this bear done to make you so suspicious of him?"

I can't tell her that I'm suspicious of myself these days with the nightmares which cause me to lose sleep and go crazy paranoid, even if that includes unleashing some maybe undeserved distrust of Stone. Instead, I stick with a safer subject, shift the blame and deflect. "What difference does it make to you how I treat a guy you've never met?"

"Because you don't act to hurt someone's feelings for no other reason than they've been genuinely *nice* to you—except the Huntresses."

"Hey, those bitches are never actually nice, and they don't fake it like the Muses." Yet she has a point, and judging by the stare she's giving me, she doesn't plan to let this go. Had I hurt Stone's feelings? I don't need to ask because I saw the answer in his eyes for myself. He'd controlled it well, remained the stoic badass bear, but I hadn't imagined the flash of pain that I'd caused. Knowing I hurt him without any real reason? It left a knot of suckiness in my throat. "I shouldn't have said those things to him. I got so mad, and he made for a big, easy target."

"Who didn't confront you at all in a public setting for coming at him?"

A sinking feeling pulled at me, making me feel oh-so-heavy. I quit grinding the poor blade into oblivion. "Does that mean something in fangs-and-claw land?" Because Dottie made it sound as though it did.

"Girl, bear shifters have seriously sensitive egos. He didn't say anything?"

I thought through what had gone down as best I could remember it with the weird, magical fog. "He might've kept Trick from pushing the whole fated-mates thing. While he didn't *say* anything, he stared at the celebrity like he was stanky poop he'd stepped in."

"Which he would've done if he wanted to date you like a normal person, not as a beat-you-over-the-head cave-bear who forces you into a fated-mate deal, not that he could do that anyway."

"What do you mean?" I figure fated mates means...well... fated. As in, once the connection is made, there aren't any loop-holes or wiggle room.

Dottie frowns, getting an I'm-thinking-hard-not-mad, little crease in her forehead. "I'm still fuzzy on the details because I haven't met another mated pair, but I know that while one partner begins the mating dance, the other must willingly accept the bond. I first felt my link with Chase through a kiss, but he was already half a dozen steps ahead of me. I had to *choose* to finish the connection. Your bear shifter might've asked to dance, but you would have to commit to any forever-together stuff. As a shifter, he would know that. He can't trick you into being with him."

"Shit, then I shouldn't have gone quite so aggro on him. I've been a tiny bit touchy lately."

"You? *Nooo*." She dodges my half-hearted shove with a giggle. "If you don't get some sleep, you may mow us all down with your hatchet."

Damnit, that momentary impulse I'd had to draw my weapon to call against Trick and his fortune teller—it'd been inexcusable, and I'd been damn lucky Maizie had put a stop to my crazy impulse. "You heard about that, huh?"

"Everyone did. You're lucky that Maizie didn't ground you."

Grounded. Such a gentle euphemism for stuck in my rooms, banned from The Rink, kicked off the derby team for an indefinite suspension, and reported to the Syndicate, my immortal creator, or who knows who?

"Yeah. I don't know what came over me. It felt like I'd been there, done that before, except I've never met them."

She stares at me, silence between us but for Connie's occasional whooshed exhale on a hard strike. "Or maybe you had," Dottie says.

"Listen, I love you and all, but I had enough cryptic bullshit with the lady last night—Marina—so even with your countrified cuteness, I'm gonna hard pass on the psychic stuff."

"I don't know any woo woo, remember? I'm the one who didn't fully believe in Furies having wings and being magical until I became one. But muscle memory, the ability we have to remember things beyond the conscious because we've done them or seen them so often that they're engrained deep within us— that's science. Kind of like how I could gear up in a hazmat suit as a human while half asleep because I'd put the darn thing on so many times that I didn't need to think."

"I'm not a fan of the analogy to my life being hazardous waste, but I'm listening."

"Then compare muscle memory to the reason you have Connie doing those drills so that the moves become as natural to her as flying is to you."

I glance toward the teen's progress, the slow, strong dance of a girl and her staff. "Fair enough. So talk and, dear gods, stop fondling that mace. It's clean enough."

Dottie drops the weapon to the table with a thud as if she's been waiting to get rid of it the entire time. "Could you fly when you first got your wings?"

"I wouldn't call what I did flying so much as avoiding crash landings." I hadn't thought about those early days after waking up here in Syn City as a Fury in a while. "Why?"

"What about wielding a blade? Not your weapon to call, but the others—swords, daggers, regular axes."

"I could use them instantly. The training room's always been my playground. Why?"

"And skating?"

"Came naturally except the adjustments we make for the weight and drag of our wings the few times we're allowed to use them on the track. Your point?" Because I'm losing focus with the zen music floating through the room, and the last thing I need to do is give over to sleep and nightmares in front of anyone else.

"My point is that you already had the weapons training and skating experience from your first life. You simply brought them with you into this life as a Fury. We aren't human anymore, but we used to be."

I hate her analysis. *Hate* it with a capital H. No way does this sister deserve me taking my temper out on her. Sadie might, but not Dottie when she's been nothing but nice to me. *Much like Stone*, my annoying conscience reminds me. "Maybe I skated in the first life, I'll give you that, but why would I have ever needed to learn sword fighting or hand-to-hand combat as a human?"

She glances toward Connie, who rolls through the strike and dodge combos like she's been doing these steps for years instead of weeks. Since the teenager witnessed the horrific murder of our House's last leader, I've put her through training with staffs, daggers, and a sword. I did worse to Dottie right after her transition to Fury, training her endlessly on every weapon we could find, other than guns since those aren't allowed in fights between the children of immortals. Plus, some supernaturals just won't die unless decapitated. Which I knew when I woke as a Fury.

The realization slams into me.

Shit, I'd known how to kill magical creatures as a human and had brought that knowledge to this life. Visions of my violent nightmare fill my head, from the screams to the blood to the familiar weight of weapons in my hands and in holsters hanging at my sides.

What the hell kind of human life had I lived? One of murder and destruction?

Had the immortal mothers simply looked down and thought *this one's already good at killing, so let's just give her another go at it?*

"Kiva, you okay?" Dottie looks concerned. I must've spaced out.

"Yeah." No, no I am definitely not okay. "What if—" My throat closes around the question, but I have to ask so I pull up my big Fury panties and force out the words. "What if my past is a dark one? What if it's not worth remembering?"

"Whatever it is, it's yours, so the decision would be yours too. Maybe talk to Dr. Bomani about it?"

"I have." Dear gods, I've discussed every possibility of getting my memories back and figuring out if anyone's out there who might've missed me when I left my first life. "She says there may be no getting it back." Last night's weird conversation with Marina plays in my head again. "But what if there was a way? A magical way?"

Dottie shakes her head. "I don't know much about magic, but aren't the med mages gone? Didn't all the magic-born healers retreat to the Sanctuaries after the Witching Wars? I mean, maybe some are still out there, but you'd think the immortals would've already brought them here. Otherwise, they'd be at risk of humans discovering their powers, and while Syn City's cool with supernaturals, I can tell you firsthand that a lot of the world isn't. My hometown would've chased any med mages away—or worse."

The quiet way she says the awful last reminds me that I haven't known a world where magic isn't accepted. Or if I have, I don't remember it. Furies, immortals, wings, and weapons to call...those have been my life. This life anyway. "But if someone *could* magic my past back to me, would you say go for it?"

"I don't know." Dottie watches Connie like the teen's kata movements might hold the answers to my question. "Part of me wants to say no, but I'd written off Chase as someone from my past who I would never see again. Now, he's the love of my life."

"Seems he would've been then, too, whether you knew it or not." Since those two had been fated mates, they had ended up together no matter their tangled past. "So maybe you didn't need to remember him from before. You still were destined to be together."

"I know that having a *kismet* soul mate sounds wonderful, but I've also seen that supernatural stuff can twist the truth. Like it did with the guy who murdered me and Coach, who would've murdered Connie." Her voice goes rough with the last. "What if magic gave you a messed-up past that comes back to haunt you?"

Except I'm pretty sure my past already haunts me every night. The nightmare lurks at the edge of my thoughts, playing out the same way with me running after someone, away from someone, or maybe both. The bitter cold stings my face, burns my lungs. The acrid taste of smoke rolls over my tongue. I want to scream and cry, the anger and frustration for whatever lies just out of my reach making me shake and shiver and weep. Then the blood— so much blood.

"Kiva," Connie yells, rushing toward us. "I finished. How'd I do?"

"Awesome." I'm on autopilot. It's not Connie's fault. Fatigue drags at me, and this heavy conversation pulls at me like I'm sinking in the muck of the swamp outside the city with the sea hags tugging me down, down, down.

"Really?" she asks, her higher pitch giving away how she's still a kid underneath all her wishing to be an adult.

I shake off the foreboding as best I can. Worrying won't solve anything. "You bet," I tell her. "You can even play with the mace Dottie didn't want to clean."

"Hey," Dottie protests, but I don't hear whatever she might've muttered next with Connie throwing her arms around me.

She hugs me so tightly that I can barely catch a breath, and in between the thudding heartbeats that fill my ears, I imagine another girl, another time. *Rylie*, a voice inside my head whispers as the nightmare plays out in my mind as real as Connie's soft training uniform, the excited tension in her muscles, the fiercely whispered *thank you, thank you, thank you* in my ear.

In the nightmare, the cold rips through my clothes to bite at my skin. Darkness surrounds me, the faint moonlight glowing white and silver off ice that slides beneath my feet. Faster and faster I run, trying to find Rylie, whoever she might be. I'm terrified but determined because she's out here somewhere beyond my reach, and it feels like I'm chasing a ghost who's constantly one step ahead of me—until she isn't.

Rylie's broken body, mangled and bloody, sprawls across the ice in front of me, and the blood—oh, the sticky, hot blood—it's everywhere. It's all I see, and I can't catch a breath. *How did I get it so wrong? What have I done?* A buzzing fills my ears, and sickness twists my stomach. Rage blasts through me, erasing everything in its wake. Rylie, oh gods, she's dead. This isn't a dream. It's so much more...dreadful, terrible, true.

I can't handle this.

Hugging Connie, I squeeze her solid, warm body to reassure me of the here and now. She's safe. She's alive.

Unlike the other girl, the one I may have killed in my last life, because how else could she be haunting my waking hours? That consuming anger clings to me like a sticky web.

The slick slip of ice that feels like skating? The knowledge of weapons and how to wound, maim, or murder whether the prey's human or supernatural? Muscle memory indeed.

I need to unravel my memories *now*—before the worst of my past repeats itself in my current life.

9

STONE

I DIDN'T EXPECT THE INVASION OF SYN CITY TODAY—THE HIGH-pitched shrieks, the clatter and clang of dishes and silverware in the hotel's café, the chatter of crowds in the lobby, and the rush of words. So many words. Their talking churns endlessly. Trick this, Trick that. His face stares out from shirts and signs and anywhere else they could plaster it. I'm sick of Trick Peterson, and I've known about the man for only days.

Bam. I slam a hammer hard against the metal on the anvil, harder than I needed to but not hard enough to destroy the shape. I yanked my ear protection off a few seconds ago, wanting the sound to chase away my thoughts. Dumb but effective, and Beryl's not here to insist otherwise.

The ringing echoes off the cement floor and sheet metal walls of my borrowed workshop, an empty storefront next to a bar where tourists can pretend to be ax-tossing barbarians for an hour while supervised by Gorgons. How the city keeps a perfect safety record for humans, I have no idea.

Maizie, the leader of the Furies, loves the weapons we brought. She bargained with Beryl to make sure I can deliver on the custom orders. Within an hour, she had me set up here with my tools, borrowed supplies, and an anvil that a Gorgon dragged over from the bar. I didn't ask why they keep an anvil in a bar, but the thing works for what I need it to do, and that's all I care about. Plus, Syn City has actual functioning electricity for air conditioning, saws, and lights so I won't have to rely on generators and a spotty power grid.

The shop has a huge glass window along the main walkway of the pleasure district, and I feel like a reenactment exhibit for the tourists who stop and gawk. Though it's not my first time doing live demonstrations, it *is* the first I've been asked to work over a forge shirtless. I declined, given the safety hazards, but Beryl had promised future exhibitions without flame and power tools and wearing less clothing, which makes me wonder exactly what we're selling. Doesn't matter as long as the work gets me closer to Kiva.

As if thinking about her conjures her, I feel the pull of the mating bond deep in my gut as though she's calling me. She's close.

The door opens, the bells above it letting out a sweet tinkling sound that has left my heart aching each time I heard it...until now. Kiva walks through, glancing at the bells. "Huh." She closes the door, then opens it again, setting off the chimes. "Such a pretty noise."

Her simple words punch me in the gut. The bells drove me crazy earlier because their chime reminds me of the ones she hung outside our home to scare off evil spirits. I figured she'd learned the trick during her horrible childhood, but I hadn't asked because I didn't want to risk triggering those awful memories.

I wish I had peppered her with hundreds of questions and pressed for details like who the hell the witch she'd mentioned moments before dying might've been. Had this sea witch been the reason Kiva avoided water? I'd passed it off as her being kind so I wouldn't dwell on my nightmarish memories of almost drowning as a cub.

I should've asked. Now, she won't have the answers.

Pushing aside wishes that can't come true, I ease the hammer onto the anvil and tug off my heavy work gloves, keeping my hands visible and my actions deliberately slow. After her accusing me of trying to trigger the mating bond at the party last night, I don't risk sudden movements. Kiva was fast and strong as a human. Something tells me that becoming a Fury didn't slow her down, and I don't want to fight my mate. Not now, not ever. Which is why I keep my mouth shut. If she's upset, she'll talk when she's ready and not before.

She crosses the room to inspect the steel on the anvil. "What's this piece gonna be?" she asks.

I struggle past memories of *us* to manage the answer. "A hatchet."

Her gaze sparks with interest. "Really?"

"Yeah." I wish that I could tell her how she wanted the one I made for our anniversary, how I engraved her married initials *KT* into the bottom since she'd loved things marked as her own after a childhood of so much being taken away. Her father, her older sister, her mom. I clear my throat, forcing down the fist-sized lump of emotions. "I have some finished if you want to see what it'll look like." *Like yours looked before it disappeared.*

"Definitely." She dances her fingers over my tools, not touching any but tracing the outlines as though she's trying to memorize the shapes. Or remember them. She spent countless hours in the workshop back home. "I have a soft spot for hatchets."

I know. The words hang unspoken between us because whatever curse her immortal put on me locks those key pieces of *us* behind my lips. "Good, practical choice," I say instead and feel a tiny piece of me die with the not-a-lie but a sickly imitation of the truth.

"Oh wow." She pushes past me to the hatchets scattered across a table. Beryl had shoved them out of the way in favor of flashier choices to show Maizie. "You made these?" There's wonder in her voice.

"I did."

She gives me a hopeful look, one of almost wonder. "Maybe you made mine."

"What?" It's the only response I can muster, my voice sandpaper rough with hurt and regrets.

"My weapon to call."

"Is that a Fury—"

Whatever nonsense I'm about to spout is cut off when she reaches her hand back as she did last night at the party—the movement I'd thought might've been her balling a fist, the one that'd made Maizie yell at her. Only she flexes her fingers, and a weapon appears out of thin air. The handle hits her palm a moment before she closes her hand around the wood as though she anticipated its arrival to the nanosecond.

But what comes when she "calls" isn't just any weapon. No, it's a hatchet—*the* hatchet I made her two years ago. The gift-wrapped one that disappeared on the night of her death, rebirth, whatever.

Impossible, yet by the engravings, I know it's the same. The powers that brought her back, the same ancient magic that allows me to shift from human to bear has willed the hatchet to follow her into this life. I reach for the handle, ready to check the bottom for her carved initials.

"Nuh uh." She stops me. "No grabbing a girl's magical weapon. You're likely to lose a hand like that."

"Sorry," I mutter, still staring at the weapon. Gods, how did the immortal who turned Kiva know about the blade, let alone swipe it from our bedroom? Then again, for an immortal with the power to bring back the dead, I guess burglary and gift-swiping's no big deal. "Inspecting quality work's a job hazard." Sure, my excuse sounds lame, but the immortal's curse keeps me from saying what I want—*it's yours, it always belonged to you even before I finished the design.*

"Each Fury receives a weapon to call, one specifically chosen for her by the gods." She sounds reverent, not at all like my Kiva, who talked about the gods and their spawned children as the villains of most stories. "When I first called my hatchet, I felt like I'd always known its weight even in my last life."

I want to scream *you did*, but nope, silence...that's all I can manage. I fumble for a subject not related to our past, maybe the curse will let me talk about something rather than staring at Kiva's dark hair that I've tangled in my fingers so many times when I've held her, the slope of her cute nose that she has rubbed against my neck, the lush fullness of her lips that I've kissed countless times. "It sounds like the, uh, gods..." I manage not to say the thieving, awful gods because I should be grateful to have Kiva back no matter what. "Sounds like they supply the House of Furies pretty well with weapons, so I'm not sure why Maizie wanted a demo."

"Because a woman can never have too many high-quality blades." Kiva flashes a smile—a gorgeous, too-wide, too-toothy smile that has me needing to fall to my knees and do whatever dirty deeds she'll let me get away with until she takes me back. Perhaps I won't have to say anything. I can just silently worship her with my mouth and body. "Besides, looks like you make other stuff too," she says.

I pull my mind out of the lick/devour/possess cycle that might get necessary body parts chopped off while she's holding that hatchet. "I work iron and steel into whatever comes to me, mainly weapons, but sometimes I make gates, tools, or rough jewelry."

"Like this?" She waves her hand, and the hatchet vanishes in an instant. Shoving up her sleeve, she reveals the cuff bracelet that I've never seen her without. "I think it's from my first life."

My heart pounds so fast and loud that any shifter in the area could hear it, my mouth goes dry, and my sweating has nothing to do with the heat of the forge. The last time I saw that bracelet? She'd stroked my jaw and told me we would find Rylie. Before that? She'd worn the cuff and nothing else while I kissed my way over every inch of my mate's curves. I want to hold her, to ask her how she's been and what put those dark circles under her eyes, to take her home where we can be together as we always should've been, to promise her that I won't fail her this time.

She blinks guileless eyes up at me. "Something I said?" she asks, coming closer.

The woman has no clue she's wreaking havoc on my emotions. Her gaze flicks to my mouth for a moment that feels endless. Or maybe she thinks she knows exactly what game she's playing with the temptation of touching her, tasting her. But there's no way I'm making the first move after she accused me of using mating traditions to sell weapons. No matter how much I want her, miss her, need her, love her.

"Why are you here?" My whisper comes out too rough, too damn broken.

Gnawing at her bottom lip, she's silent—her tell when she's nervous or hiding something. She's still my mate. I can feel the link so clearly, so deeply, but until she answers the call and lets me be a part of her life now, I'm left with emotions coming through the bond without context, so I wait until she speaks. "It's my city." That's the most half-assed answer I've heard from her in a long time.

"But not your shop, so what are you doing here?" I point to the floor. It's not my shop either except for today, but that's beside the point.

"Maybe I came to ask you for another pretty bracelet." She shoves the jewelry in my face, stalling because I know that's not at all why she came here. *If* she even knows the real reason.

Seizing on the chance to touch my mate, I reach for her wrist but stop an inch away, "May I?" I have to play this perfectly or I risk making my sister's barely veiled worry come true when she gives me the sad looks that suggest I've already used all my chances with Kiva.

"Yeah." She sounds less certain than her quick answer.

I wrap my fingers around her wrist and rub my thumb over the bracelet. Her breath catches on a sharp intake of air, her pulse speeds, and I catch the faintest trace of a long-lost familiar scent, the sweetness of Kiva's arousal. No matter what she might've said last night, she's interested. I'll take whatever crumbs of attention she'll give me. Forcing my gaze off her dilating pupils and parted lips, I glance toward the bracelet. "Hand-forged iron, the stone's red jasper."

"Could you have made this one?" Her scent changes to something else. Hope, maybe? Has she been trying to rediscover her past all this time? The possibility claws at me. I can't stand seeing my wife suffer.

"No, I didn't create this."

Kiva scoots closer. That's right, pretty mate, kill me slowly with each move you make. "Any idea who forged it?" she asks.

Your mom had it made. I want to tell her so badly, but the words stop on my tongue. Damn this curse. I can't even say that her mother had cast the spells on the bracelet to keep Kiva safe from something my mate wouldn't discuss.

Her mom had been a witch, but her father human, which meant Kiva hadn't been born with powers. Still, she'd been dragged into her mother's hatred of the gods' spawned, fighting the children of immortals when she'd been a human, a kid. I never met Kiva's mom since she'd died before I met my mate, but I never much liked the woman. No reason could've been enough to put my mate through that kind of hell.

I can't give her the answers, but maybe focusing on things from the past will help her remember the truth, remember me. "What makes you think this came from your last life?" I ask.

Twisting the bracelet toward its opening so that I can see the edges of the inside, she presses close to me, so close I can feel her skin against mine and her hair teases my nose. "My name's inside. See? Or at least, I hope I haven't been borrowing someone else's name for the last two years." She sounds concerned.

"It's your name." Holy Hades, I managed to get the truth out —not the entirety, but a sliver. For the first time since I tried speaking to her at The Rink, my tongue doesn't stick like I have a mouthful of glue. What does that mean? What else can I tell her? I'm having a crisis and strategizing as though I'm about to wage the most epic battle of my life, which perhaps I am, and she sighs a dismissive little sound of *maybe*.

"Well, it's my name now anyway," she says.

What if that's the key? What if I have to say things that bridge her two lives? Tricky, but I'll figure something out. Until then, I'll keep offering her food and gifts and whatever else she'll take from me.

She lowers the bracelet but doesn't move away. "You asked why I'm here. I came about last night at the party..." She trails off, and I don't interrupt while she decides whatever she wants to say next. It might be a trivial nothing for her, but it's not for me. I'm in her sphere again, breathing in her scent and remembering the little details of our life together like the lines between her eyebrows that she deepens when she's thinking. "You have nice eyes—brown but there's gold inside. Is that a bear thing?"

"That's a me thing. The bear is almost all gold. You came here to stare at my eyes?"

"If I did?"

"I'm good with that." More than good with it.

"I shouldn't have said what I did last night, especially not after you've been so nice. I snapped, and I'm not apologizing for snapping, but my anger shouldn't have been at you."

"You'd been backed into a corner. No surprise you came out fighting." Now that I've seen her weapon to call, I know why Maizie leashed my mate. The damage she could've done as a human would've been staggering, and she's probably more devastating as a Fury. Her heartbeat sounds the tiniest bit different, her scent flavored a little darker, and the edge in the way she carries herself makes me wonder if I underestimated the changes in her between one life to the next. What if I'm fighting a lost cause? No, I can't go there.

She twists away, ducking her head with the movement. I fight the need to take her by the chin and tip her face back up so I can savor every flickered expression, her hurtling-fast wit present in each of those racing and abrupt switches in her mood.

Dragging the sheathed dagger from her waistband, she offers it to me. "I can't keep this," she says.

"You can." Resisting the urge to touch her becomes too much, and I stop her, wrapping her slender hand with my larger one. "It's a gift."

"Nothing comes without a price."

The certainty and bite in her voice wounds me, but she won't understand the why. I would give her anything and ask absolutely nothing in return, but that unconditional devotion comes with our mating, and she still views me as little more than a stranger. "If I insist you keep it?"

"After the way I treated you last night? That kind of public insult?" She tugs her hand and the blade out of my grip, letting it drop the few inches to the table with a soft clunk, muted by the leather sheath. "I don't have the cash to repay you for a hand-crafted dagger plus whatever penalty tax comes with telling you off unfairly in front of the Houses."

A mad idea seizes me. Maybe I can unseal the immortal's curse of silence with a bargain. "What about a trade?"

She angles her head to study me, a questioning glint in her gaze. "What could I possibly have that you would want in trade for that steel?"

"A kiss."

10

KIVA

A KISS? HE WANTS A KISS? FROM ME? AFTER I ACCUSED HIM OF kicking off the mating ritual—a super sacred shifter tradition—and trying to bribe me to sell the weapons that he clearly won't be able to keep in stock given the quality? He would give me that gorgeous dagger that might as well have been forged to fit my hand for one kiss?

His steady gaze doesn't leave mine as if he worries that I'll disappear if he blinks. The sweltering heat of the room despite the blasting A/C isn't the reason my body goes hot and tight. No, it's the promise there in his eyes.

Stone's golden skin's damp with sweat, and his brown hair looks like he's either been worried or well-bedded. Someone's been mussing the tangle, and I suddenly wish it'd been me. If I take him up on his proposed trade, I could sink my fingers into those curls and find out whether they're as soft as they look.

If, if, if.

No, a kiss between us isn't a matter of if. It's more of a when.

Not giving myself time for second thoughts, I cup my hand around the back of his neck and pull him closer. He's sexy and solid beneath my touch despite the trace of sadness that clings to him as much as that air of barely restrained power. I want to take those walls around him and smash them to pieces as violently as if I'd shattered the barriers between us with my hatchet.

With a kiss, maybe I can.

He inhales a sharp breath, the soft sound snapping what little control I have over my impulses. I need him now. Not a gentle, sweet kiss. No, I need to drink him down to see if he could fill up the emptiness that I've carried for too long. I kiss him like I have something to prove and maybe I do. The clash of lips, the taste of him, the way he opens to me and takes over—there's a rawness and dark hunger laced with need—until he gentles the kiss in tempting sweeps of his mouth and swirls of his tongue.

Kissing Stone feels like coming home, sinking into a familiar floating sensation that wraps around me and carries me away to a place that's happy, safe, and everything else I've been missing since I woke in Syn City. I want to snuggle into his warmth and melt in his tenderness until we spiral into sinful possessive sexiness. But suddenly, we're not alone.

The jarring clang of the bell and raised voices have me pulling away, and I don't miss how Stone follows me as if he'd be content to ignore whoever has interrupted us and keep on kissing me.

In the next instant, he stiffens and sweeps me behind him almost as he did that first night we met below the Fury house when he acted like he would protect me from anyone. I want to protest, to tell him *I don't need a bodyguard, thank you very much,* yet the smell of saltwater and spices rolls over me.

Marina's here.

But I can't see her. I move to go around Stone, and he moves with me. Step, block, step, block. The man reacts as if we've done this dance before, but we haven't. He glances down at me, and I glare at him, but he stands there, filling up the space with his big bear self. I poke him in the side, pretending I can't still taste him on my lips and wouldn't rather have my hands on him in an equally demanding, possibly just as bossy, so much sexier and less irritating way.

"We're closed," a woman who sounds as aggravated as I feel says. I peek around Stone to see a tall and stacked brunette pushing past Marina to block her as much as he's currently blocking me. "If you're interested in purchasing ironwork, we can schedule a time when we're open."

"The place doesn't look closed," Marina says. "Kiva's here."

The dark-haired woman turns in our direction. Her facial features from her brown eyes and long lashes to her pouty mouth are a much softer but obviously related version of Stone's. She stares at me as if she knows way more about me than she should. Or as though she suspects I've been making out with Stone. I push at him and give her a little wave.

"My sister," he tells me. "Beryl."

She looks from her brother to me and back again, opening her mouth and closing it.

The bells above the door chime. Dottie peeks inside, her ponytail bouncing the same as her cousin's does when she's training. "Kiva? You in here?"

I glance at Stone and say low enough that only his supernatural hearing should catch my every word, "*My* sister this time. At least Sadie didn't show if your sister's a shifter like you."

Raising my voice, I call, "Back here."

"Oh good. Found her," Dottie yells over her shoulder. Seconds later, her mountain lion shifter and Sadie follow her inside. This small shop's getting real crowded real quick. "Hope we're not interrupting. It's crazy out there with screaming fans, and Maizie said we could find y'all here."

The door slams open, the bells banging so hard they damn near fly off the hook. In a room full of apex predators, everyone spins toward the intrusion, ready to handle whatever threat might be there. Everyone except Marina. Having ditched her ballgown in favor of a blue suit that looks custom-tailored to her slender body and platinum jewelry that plays up the lavender in her hair, the fortune teller looks bored and more than a touch annoyed. What magic does she have that makes her so sure of her safety? Or maybe she's simply used to the crowds that descend wherever Trick Peterson goes.

Because Trick's the problem right now. In his faded jeans with lipstick smeared across his face and shirt, the country heartthrob pushes into the shop and shuts the door. Two large bodyguards block the entrance from outside to the disappointment of his adoring fans. "Looks like I found the party," he says with his trademark, aw-shucks charm. "Guess my invite got lost."

"You won't get one." Stone's voice goes a little growly. It's hot. I step closer to see if I can feel the rumble.

His sister gives him a be-nice-or-be-quiet look. I've gotten that same look from both Dottie and once from Sadie when I was really mouthy. *So worth it.* Beryl stares at Trick with little hearts in her eyes, and she's fanning herself. "We're not yet open for business," she says, "but if you'll let us know what you're looking for, perhaps we can help." She seems to be struggling between fangirl overload and maintaining professional we're-closed-but-don't-hate-customers politeness.

"We're here for Kiva," Dottie says. "We're her triad sisters."

Oh great, now it's *my* turn to be on the receiving end of Stone's sister's WTF glare. Maybe her brain skipped over the *sisters* part and went straight to throuple. "Not a threesome menage-style," I clarify. "Triad sisters. Furies stuff."

Dottie's mountain lion snorts a small laugh, clearly the only person here with a sense of humor, although Stone cracks a smile.

"You're Furies?" Trick asks. "All of you?" He sweeps a gesture toward everyone in the room, including Marina and the men. Maybe the brain in his pretty head doesn't handle details like the fact that Furies are women, or how Dottie, Sadie, and I wear our

House's standard black while Marina's in blue and Beryl's rocking a bold red.

I want to point out what he missed with snarky subtext, but looking at his wide eyes and let's-be-friends charm, making fun of him would be like kicking a puppy. Guess I'll do the introductions so everyone knows who else is in the room.

"I'm a Fury. My sisters are too." When I gesture toward Dottie, she wiggles her fingers in a country, cutie-pie wave. Sadie gives him the chin tip, which is more than I'd expected. "Chase is Dottie's honey. Marina, you know." But none of the rest of us do. Not really. "Beryl and Stone are brother and sister visiting Syn City." I realize I have no idea where they're from. "Stone's a blacksmith and my were-bear."

A hot flush flashes up my neck to my hairline, and my hands sweat for reasons having nothing to do with the heat. *My were-bear?* Where the fresh Hephaestus did that come from? Chase had said it'd be an insult to the man to call him anything other than a bear shifter. Hell, it might be oversharing to say that much. I'd been told more than once that calling a shifter a were-bear was—in big capital letters—NOT okay.

Maybe no one noticed. Except now everyone is staring at me with mixed reactions of shock or horror. Not Stone. He's got this sweet grin curling one corner of his mouth that says he didn't mind my slip-up in the least and that he might throw down with anyone who has a problem with it.

Dottie's mouth rounds in a perfect *O* and she none-too-subtly elbows her were-kitty. Damn it, I'm gonna catch all kinds of shit for this.

Marina sniffs as if the air has taken on the stench of Gorgons. With gangrene. "I came to find you to see if you needed help untangling your past," she says. "While meditating earlier, I got flashes of distress that I thought might be coming from you."

Maybe when I'd been with Dottie and had seen myself finding Rylie's mauled, broken body. Somehow, my brain connected those horrible images of Rylie to another teen I care for—Connie. That'd been more than distress. It'd been straight-up terror.

No matter what scary psycho I might've been in my first life, I couldn't let this stronger, faster Fury body spin out of control. I would make my sisters promise to put me down if things went that horrifying direction. But if Marina could help me figure out whether the visions were real memories or monstrous creations of my imagination, should I refuse her offer when everything else I've tried has failed?

She stares in my direction as though she's reading the literal energies in the room. "Obviously I misread the signals as you seem to be fine."

"No, it was me." The truth slips from my mouth so fast that I can't reel it back. I slide closer to Stone, wishing I could borrow some of his easygoing solidness. With Fury strength, I'm scary, but he looks like the kind of guy who could weather chaos without flinching, much like his namesake. "I've had hints of memories returning—not all of them good."

"The nightmares," Sadie says, sharing my secrets that can't be anywhere near as secret as I'd hoped. "If they're memories, that explains why you haven't slept in weeks."

Maybe the cracks in the concrete floor will open and let me slip through. I don't want to be the center of attention for anything but roller derby. Certainly not for this.

Stone crowds me without making me claustrophobic. Instead, he creates a tiny—okay, not so tiny since he's a massive bear—bubble just for the two of us in this unwanted reveal party for my past. "What do you remember?" He sounds so hopeful, as if he thinks I have a past of rainbows and unicorns instead of murder and mayhem.

"It's bad." Not something that I want to share with a man whose honeyed taste lingers on my tongue. "Too awful to tell."

He opens his mouth as if he has the most important piece of

my past right there in the curves and lines of his lips, but not a sound escapes him. The determination on his face, the frustration that radiates off him—am I imagining those things? I mean, he came into town a couple of days ago. I barely know this man, and now, I'm reading snarled emotions coming off him.

Maybe my memories aren't memories at all.

Maybe I'm just slipping into psychotic delusions.

Moving to put space between us, I'm surprised when he steps closer, lowering his head so I could angle my face and kiss him again if there wasn't a murky swamp of tension between us. "The terrible things you think you remember?" he whispers, his warm breath a comfort against my cheek. "They're tearing you apart?"

I nod, unwilling to do more with the burning in my throat, the pressure behind my eyes of tears pricking that I can't let fall.

"Sharing's hard but bearing the heavy load by yourself might be worse." He sounds so reasonable, saying exactly what I need to hear. How does he do that? And why can't I hate him for being so damn sensible? "Maybe give me one possible memory to carry for you. I'm pretty strong."

With those massive shoulders, he could lift mountains, but will my past scare him away? Why does it matter to me if it does? It can't. Not with a guy I barely met. Not if I'm going to get my shit together and my head back in the roller derby championship.

One thing. I can share one thing. It doesn't have to be more. Just the name that invaded my thoughts earlier and haunted me ever since.

"Rylie."

11

STONE

"Rylie?" My whisper scrapes and scratches as if caught on my claws and fangs. The teen's name hits me low in the gut like a sucker punch. Oh gods, what could Kiva have seen the last few seconds of her first life? How much does she remember? The tortured look in her eyes suggests she recalls the worst. Not the teenager she adored and teased, but the girl's body after she'd been abandoned on the ice. "What do you remember of Rylie?"

Her gaze pins me to the spot. "You know who I'm talking about?" Her words tumble faster and faster. "Are you from my first life? Before I turned Fury?"

I don't answer. I can't. Explanations stick against the roof of my mouth, and I hate this damn curse. Why didn't the kiss break my silence? True love's kiss, the immortal had said. No one loves Kiva more than I have, than I did, than *I still do*. The last comes a second too late, a hesitation I can't afford to think about now.

She backs a step away as if seeing me as worse than a stranger —a liar who's keeping a secret she badly needs. "Who was Rylie?" Her voice comes out shaky but louder.

Beryl whips around, her gaze bouncing between me and Kiva.

"You remember Rylie?" Grief washes my sister's tone in the darkest shades of sadness.

Hurt flashes through Kiva's eyes, tugging down the corners of her mouth—the mouth I just tasted for the first time in so long. She touches her throat in a brush of fingertips in almost the same spot the arrowhead pierced her. "What did I do to her?"

"Nothing." The answer springs from me, and I choke with the need to tell her the rest of it, to hold her and say that everything's okay now, that we can go home to the life we had together. "You didn't—" My voice cuts out.

"Did I kill her?" The heartbreak in her question shatters something deep within me.

I shake my head, desperate to comfort her.

"No." Beryl reaches for Kiva, who backs away from us both— straight toward the woman who stinks of wrong magic, the one who claims Trick Peterson could possibly be meant for my mate.

Marina, Kiva had said. Sounds like an awfully clichéd name for a sea witch. Again, I think how I should've demanded more information from my wife about her childhood, but there'd been too much rage and sorrow over her mother's death. She'd gone quiet whenever I'd asked—she who'd so rarely been silent—so I hadn't pushed.

The fortune teller smiles like a lazy housecat with canary feathers stuck to her claws, a smug smirk showing no teeth. "Want me to read your past? You already know your future is with Trick."

For once, country music's golden boy quits grinning like a fool. He's staring at Kiva as if he knows her, as if he's her mate and he's worried about whatever his pet witch might tell her. I don't like the man for wanting to steal my wife, but I agree that getting her away from Marina's the smart play right now.

Except the crafty woman and her promises of the past sink their talons into Kiva. "Can you do that? Tell me about my life before I became a Fury? It's not *my* past so much as hers—the human I was."

The way she distinguishes the difference in her two lives has a sickly chill slithering along my spine. My mate doesn't recognize her past as her own?

"I can," Marina says. "Memories don't like being locked away. No mental door can hold them, no matter how powerful. Sometimes, they burst free all at once. Other times, they leak out around the cracks and openings. You're having nightmares? Sounds like your past already haunts you. A girl—you said her name was Rylie?"

Dottie, my mate's triad sister, pushes past her cat shifter. "Don't do it, Kiva. We talked about this. Things aren't always what they seem. Sadie and I'll go with you to Dr. Bomani to find out how we can help you deal with this in a legit way—not through some stranger's magic."

Kiva lifts the corner of her mouth. "We were strangers—the three of us—until some immortal we'd never met made a deal to make us Furies, to have us live a second go in the name of vengeance. What's the difference in that bargain and this?"

"A big damn difference," Sadie says. "We didn't have a choice then except to choose life or death. Now, you have options."

My mate shakes her head. "You have your pasts for better or worse. I need mine now before I repeat something horrible, before I hurt Connie."

"You would never," Dottie insists. "You're not sleeping, so there's no way you're thinking straight. Don't do this."

"What's your price?" Kiva asks Marina, but she glances at me when she speaks.

She might as well shove her dagger into my chest. *Nothing comes without a price.* Her words echo in my head. She'd traded a kiss for the blade, and here I'd been too stupid to see that the life-altering liplock that'd meant the world to me, to have my mate's taste on my tongue once again, it'd only been a business transaction for her. Everyone in the room keeps talking, the air conditioning keeps buzzing, the country music fans outside keep screaming—and no one notices I'm dying inside.

From the sickening satisfaction in the woman's gaze, Marina knows she has Kiva, no matter what price she might name. "For me to give you what you need to unlock your memories of Rylie, you only have to promise Trick a chance to prove his devotion to you as his fated mate, a single kiss. Hardly anything, right?" The horrible woman cuts a look to me as if she knows what she interrupted. I want to roar, to make her stop talking, to end this crazy bargain, but what if I'm no better than this witch?

For his part, Trick doesn't say anything. He's staring at Marina like he doesn't want her here, which makes me wonder why the hell she's part of his entourage. Is there something bigger going on between the two? Something more sinister?

Kiva's next question to Marina interrupts my spiraling thoughts. "If I ask you to help with other parts of my memory?" She raises her chin, sliding a wary gaze in my direction, and her lack of faith in me cuts the same as if she sliced me open with her hatchet.

Marina doesn't hesitate. "When my gifts help you with this piece of your past, we can negotiate terms before unlocking more. Let's start with one kiss." She reaches out toward my mate.

"Fine." Kiva takes the woman's hand then jumps like she has been electrocuted, squeezing her eyes shut with a low moan. "Nooo." She covers her face and sways as if the weight of whatever she sees has crashed down on her.

My gut bottoms out, my heart skips a beat, and I hurry toward my mate without thought, every protective instinct unleashing my claws and fangs. I can't lose her again, never again.

Despite my supernatural speed, I'm not the first to make it to Kiva. No, her Fury sisters zoom forward, both with black wings snapping out to block me. I snarl, ready to fight past them.

"Don't try it, bear." Sadie calls a whip into her hand the same way my mate conjured the hatchet I made her—through magic. "Kiva seems to like you sometimes. If we fight, our sister won't appreciate me hurting you."

Beryl gets in my face. "Think past the fear, past the instinct. She's your—" Her voice cuts out on a choked gasp. The damned curse might've robbed her of finishing her thought, but what's left unspoken shakes me into the here and now. *Mate.* "She's safe physically," my sister urges. "The Furies have her."

"The witch's still a danger." My words come out on a growl.

"She's leaving," a male voice drawls. The mountain lion shifter, mated to one of the Furies, stalks toward Marina. His fluid walk screams predator, and the witch doesn't argue.

Maybe Marina's smart enough to see she's done whatever damage she meant to do already. Or maybe she doesn't want to face off with me, two pissed-off Furies, and a cat shifter who moves like he likes to play with his prey. "Come on, Trick." She snaps her fingers at the singer, then walks out the door into the screaming mob of fans.

Trick stays put. "Is Kiva okay?" He sounds genuinely concerned.

"She will be," Sadie says. "It's best you go now, super star."

"All right." He meets my gaze, holding it. "Take care of her." With movements far jerkier than the cat shifter's, he follows Marina outside, closing the door behind him.

The room goes silent except for the rumble of Trick's roving fan club and the rustling of Sadie's massive black wings with throbbing blood-red symbols that block my view of her sisters.

"Let me out," Kiva says from within the winged wall. She's lost that curling-into-a-ball, eyes-squeezed-shut defensive stance from earlier. Now, she stares at me, and I can't read the look in her gaze or the emotions rolling off her. The mating link I'd relied on? It's gone silent, dormant.

"You okay?" Dottie's sugar-sweet worry pours like a healing

balm, but fear and confusion have my shields up, and the relief rolls off me instead of sinking deep.

Kiva gives her sister a quick nod that isn't reassuring while staring at me. "You were there that night at the lake." Her words come out halting, hesitating, but she's not inviting me to butt in. "Did you kill Rylie?" She touches her neck, her fingers brushing the place where her blood pumped out, where I held her so tightly as if I could wish the wound away. "Did you murder me?"

I can't breathe, my chest goes three sizes too small for my lungs, and some kind of Fury magic must be making the room spin as dizzy and sick as I suddenly feel. Staggering backward, I almost plow into the forge's fire, except Beryl grabs me, but my vision, my world narrows to Kiva.

My mate doesn't remember me, doesn't know me in the least if she could accuse me of this. Kiva's not at all the same. The truth has my stomach plummeting. What if she's not meant to be my mate this time around? What if I've lost her forever and the witch had it right? What if she belongs with someone else? *To* someone else?

"Did you?" she asks again, steel worthy of any immortal weapon in her voice. "Did you kill us?"

"No." I drag the word up my raw throat like a glass shard laced in acid.

"But you were there." Her blank expression, her flat tone? I'm not the only stranger in this relationship. She doesn't know me, but I don't recognize this version of her. "At the frozen lake when I died. You knew me in my first life."

I nod, waiting for the curse to kick in, for my body to seize with the movement.

"Tell me." Her order rips through me, tearing my heart to shreds more than any enemy claws could. "Who were you to me?"

Your mate, fated to be together forever. The answer freezes on my tongue as bitter and cold as the lake where I lost her. I want to tell her everything, but nothing comes out.

Her mouth twists in a snarl that would make any grizzly proud, that would be ugly on anyone but Kiva. "Say it." She practically spits the words.

"I can't." My body sags with the awful heaviness of the truth.

"Can't or won't?" Hate flashes through her gaze. "Was playing me a game for you? Some twisted joke? You come into town, seek me out, and then you let me believe we've never met while asking all about my amnesia and my first life." She huffs a hollow shell of her usual laugh. "You're worse than Marina with your tricks." She shakes her head and looks to her sisters. "I've learned more than I wanted to know. Let's go."

Sadie moves between us—judgment and contempt in her gaze—as if I might stop Kiva, as if I could hurt my mate any more than I just did through the fucking curse. I want to roar and tear the room apart, but what good would that do me? My mate hates me. I should've let her go. More than that, I should've saved her from dying. I should've taken the arrow, should've taken her place.

Dottie murmurs soothing reassurances, something about calling the doctor. Her mate brushes his hand along her arm, telling her he'll catch up.

I can hear their words, but none of it matters.

Nothing matters now.

"Oh g-gods," Beryl stammers. "She thinks...she...she..."

I wrap my shaking sister in a huge hug, letting her cry the tears for us, knowing I can't weld together the jagged pieces of what I've lost.

The other shifter watches us, catlike curiosity gleaming from his golden eyes. The nosiness pisses me off. What the hell could the mountain lion want? How does he think he could torture us further by sticking around?

"Yeah?" I don't bother hiding my gruffness.

He breathes in as though trying to scent the truth. "Why can't either of you tell Kiva about her life before she turned Fury?"

I'm ready to fight, and if he wants to be who I take my rage out on, then so be it. "I—"

"*Can't*." He emphasizes the word. "You said you can't. Why not?"

Shit, someone finally believes me—not the someone who mattered, but still. "A curse." The triumph of managing to say that aloud feels like a worthless win at this point.

He glances to Beryl, who's softly sobbing. "On both of you?"

"On anyone who tries to tell Kiva who I was to her, who we were to each other." I can't get any further explanation out, and I'm not sure if it's the curse, or if the emotion clogging my throat has me choking on the rest.

He stares at me, horror flickering across his face. "Fuck, she's your—" He coughs and rubs at his chest.

Mate. The word goes unspoken, but he knows. Why the hell the curse might affect him when Kiva's no longer here, I won't guess.

Instead, I nod. "She not only doesn't remember me, but she thinks I killed her." Grief rolls through me. "I've lost her all over again."

12

KIVA

I'VE REPLAYED THE SAME SCENE IN MY HEAD FOR DAYS LIKE A hologram loop on repeat—the moment I knew Stone had played me.

How had I misread the big were-bear so completely? We shared that kiss that shook me down to my core with the tendrils of hope for something more. I imagined him to be sweet, sensitive, a little sad, but oh-so-tempting when he'd been lying the whole time.

Tonight, Maizie pulled me from practice because I'd been operating on autopilot. Sure, I'd blocked and hit and held the line to keep anyone from getting by me, but I'd been skating through a mental fog. The clack and smack of skates against the track circle in my head, echoing up to the rafters where I'm lurking like a damn gargoyle.

Far above the best seats in the house, a steel catwalk maze winds beneath The Rink's ceiling. The cold of the metal bites into the back of my thighs as I dangle my feet off the side into the staggering empty space between me and the pits below. Up here, the scents of cleaning solution, beer, popcorn, and sweat circle in a calming sense of home. Or at least the only home I know other than my room in the Fury house. But now I know from the glimpse of the terrifying memory that I came from a vast, open place with ice, trees, mountains, snow, and Stone. His face, his quiet desperation, and the hidden secrets trapped behind his tormented gaze haunt me.

The heavy clunk of boots behind me almost has me wondering if my constant thinking about him has made him appear like Dottie's wishing for Chase pulls him to her through their "fated mates" connection, but no, while Stone is massive, he's also a shifter and more graceful than this *clomp-clomp-clomp.*

Trick Peterson stops a few feet away. "Would you like some company?"

Yes. No. I don't know. "Sure," I say before checking the impulse. It's not his fault I'd been half hoping to see someone I shouldn't want to ever talk to again.

Silence hangs between us as sure as the bulky cables that surround us, not the uneasy and awkward kind. No, it feels as if we've done this before even though he's not the guy I remember in my visions. Ugh, I have to stop thinking about Stone.

"Marina let you off your leash?" I regret the bitterness of my words the instant I snap out the question. This whole situation? Not his fault. He grins a cheeky, boyish curve of his mouth with no hint of anger. If only I could fantasize about his lips, his kiss instead of the one I shouldn't crave.

"Marina's never too far away," he says, and for the first time, I notice the gravity of his tone hidden beneath the *aw shucks* charm that's as real and staggering as the anxiety-inducing height between us and the floor. As far as I know, only one of us has wings. What the hell is he doing up here instead of lounging in some plush hotel suite surrounded by adoring fans and bodyguards?

"Why are you here?" Gods, the second I say the words I remember Stone asking me the same question about coming to see him. I need to clear the man from my thoughts.

Trick stares at me as if he can see past my expression to the hurt inside. "I hadn't seen you since Marina made her deal with you about the kiss."

Or maybe I'd been an idiot and every man visiting Syn City just wants to mess with my mind. "So you came up here to collect on her bargain? If I kiss you, will you go away?"

"I came up here..." He emphasizes the last bit as if parroting my words. "To check on you. Whatever you remembered, whatever happened between you and the shifter, it made you sad. I'd like to help."

"How?"

He frowns, drawing down his blond brows. "I don't know."

I expect him to say more, to explain the confusion clouding his gaze, but he doesn't. Instead, he watches me as if my face holds the answer. *Men.* For two years, I've had enough of a struggle trying to figure out who I was, and now they expect me to figure them out as well. No thanks. "I'm not up for another betrayal." Saying the truth of what Stone did twists the pain deeper the same as if he'd used one of his swords or a blade from my wings. "When Marina first talked about us being some sort of destined couple, you said you had traveled the world looking for me. If you knew me in my human life before I turned Fury, tell me now because I'd rather not have to find out for myself that someone else has been lying to me."

"We haven't met. I would've remembered you, but I feel like I've known you my whole life." He sounds honest if unsure. "Does that sound crazy?"

I swallow a laugh. "Don't use me as your sanity meter." No way am I talking about the lectures I got from Dr. Bomani about allowing Marina or anyone else not practiced in med-mage memory retrieval to tamper with my memories no matter how Stone may have confirmed the truth of them with his silence. "Amnesiac, remember? Only one of us should be able to claim that kind of crazy."

"Marina thinks we're mates. She's told me for almost two years of how I would meet my true love and know her instantly. Her talk of who I might find, the perfect woman out there meant for me, the one who inspires my songs? Well, you fit the description perfectly, and you're amazing. I don't know about the whole fated thing." He shakes his head. "But I like seeing you safe and smiling. Knowing you were sad? It made me want to fix everything for you to take that away."

His sweetness tugs at me. While I admit there's none of the heat and overwhelming intensity I feel around Stone, being with Trick is easy like knowing which weapon works against which supernatural, which side of the bed to sleep on so I can defend myself if necessary, what armor brings safety and comfort instead of slowing my movements. Maybe if I kiss Trick, I could find the same raw need, the same sense of coming home that I felt with Stone. Going on that impulse, I grab his collar and haul him down the few inches between us to press my lips to his.

His coldness startles me. Kissing Stone blazed like standing next to his makeshift forge, the heat spiraling over me, around me, through me. Trick's skin feels as though he's stepped in front of the rink's air conditioning with its vents switch to a deafening roar, startling me so that I pull away. I wait for the sweet sensations to sink in, to grow, to do anything, but instead, there's emptiness—a void of emotion other than embarrassment that maybe I read the situation wrong.

His stillness and wide-eyed stare doesn't help ease that fear. After a long, awkward pause, he says, "Thank you."

"Uh, you're welcome." I have no idea what else to say because he's making the whole thing weird, like he doesn't have thousands of fan girls throwing themselves at him for hugs, kisses, and way more. A tiny peck shouldn't have short-circuited his brain. Goose bumps prickle over my skin, and I wish I had a jacket to shove my hands into. Anything other than wondering if

I should use them to push over the side, fly away, and avoid the mortification.

"Why'd you do it?" he asks. "I don't want to think Marina's promise forced you into kissing me."

"A deal's a deal." I notice Trick isn't trying for another round, which screams the exact opposite message of kissing Stone when my were-bear would've been happy to keep going until we'd both drunk our fill of each other. Not *my* were-bear. He's not *my* anything. While my brain might've gotten the message loud and shattered-glass clear from his lies and refusal to tell me about my own past, apparently, other parts of me still haven't caught up.

Trick taps a rhythm against the steel with his thumb. "I don't want to make you uncomfortable." Well, he's too late to stop that ship from streaking along under hydro-speed sails with the clumsy kiss. "You talked about betrayal earlier. What'd you mean?"

Okay, so he simply wants me to relive the painful experience he already witnessed first-hand. That's not bizarre, really. Who could be uncomfortable? Except he doesn't sound like he's asking to punish me. No, he acts like he doesn't fully understand my emotions—or anyone's, which seems odd for a man who sings about heartbreak and hard partying.

"All right," I tell him. "You said you'd been looking for me? As your mate?"

He nods.

"Did it bother you not knowing whether you would find me or not?"

Confusion fills his face. "Marina said I would find you, and I didn't have a reason to think otherwise. I considered whether you would be okay until I found you, whether you would be safe, but beyond that, no."

"That doesn't sound like fated mates to me. What about passion or love?" The wildfire of chemical attraction that Dottie and her mountain lion shifter had.

Trick lifts a shoulder in a half-hearted, clunky shrug. "Caring for someone's safety can be love. For example, I wish you wouldn't sit way up here so far from the ground. You could slip, the railings could break, a thousand things could go wrong and you would fall."

"I come up here to think, and I have wings, so I won't go splat. What's your excuse?"

"I needed to make sure you were okay."

Wow, he's totally a daddy type and not in the kinky call-me-Daddy way. Not that I remember having a dad, but I could hope mine hadn't been an asshole, had been as devoted as Trick. Of course, Stone might know the answer to that question, but the bear bastard won't share. "Since I became a Fury, I've searched for any clues about my past. Stone keeping information from me would be bad enough, but he hid the fact he'd known me when I thought we were on our way to friendship." Or something more.

"Sometimes we keep secrets for good reasons." Trick glances down.

Marina walks up the stairs between the stadium seats, looking from one side of The Rink to the other. Her hair looks more lavender than white in this light, and her trademark blue shimmers a purple so dark she could almost be wearing Fury black.

Trick leans back, cloaking himself in the shadows.

I cut him a *caught you* look. "You sure coming up here was about me?"

"Yeah. Why?" He sounds so damn earnest that I almost feel bad teasing him, but come on, snark's so much fun.

I dip my head in Marina's direction. "You prowling the catwalks has nothing to do with hiding from her?"

"Nope," he says. "Well, maybe a little bit. You going to hold that against me?"

"Depends. You going to tell me what's going on with her?"

"I can't."

Rage simmers beneath my skin, making the place where my wings settle itch with the need to release. "I'm getting tired of people telling me that."

"I can't say what I don't know. Marina has been everywhere with me, handling the press and fans and whatever else so I can concentrate on music. I've known her since I was a kid, and we've had a good business partnership. Or at least we did until we got here and I saw how she acts with you." He hangs his head, the unruly platinum blond hair around his face falling forward. "Something's off. She says she wants to be a friend to you, but hurting you with your memories doesn't seem to bother her, and that's not right. I can't tell what's making her act this way, and she pretends I've made it all up when I mention it."

Sounds like gaslighting to me. "I don't trust her." I hope letting him know that truth doesn't bite me later.

Silence stretches, and this time it's not as comfortable ticking by. His expression closes off from his usual transparent sincerity. "I wouldn't either if I were you. I reckon I'd better see what she needs. The tech setup for our upcoming charity concert has been giving us problems, and I'd rather not disappoint the kids who'll be coming to town for it."

"Kids?" I ask, not bothering to hide my relief at the change in subjects because whatever agenda Marina's hiding might be more than I can handle right now.

"Yeah. Roller skates, glow sticks, and no booze to help anyone cope with the ear-piercing screeches, but it'll be worth it for those kids who won a ticket."

"You're a good guy, Trick."

His gaze drops to my mouth. "But not the guy you really wanted to kiss. Not the one you were thinking about when you kissed me."

He's got me there. I don't know what to say so I keep my mouth shut as he pulls to his feet, his boot heels clanking on the metal. He reaches a hand down to me, and I take it. I've already been rude to the man, and here he's being a gentleman.

"Do us both a favor," he says. "If you believe in fated mates, you believe destiny will work itself out. I don't think Stone meant to hurt you—he couldn't have faked his response to your pain—which means he has a reason for keeping secrets. Find him and figure out what's between the two of you, either in this life or your previous one."

He's asking me to consider his rival, to go to the one man who makes me hate and want and seethe and sob into my pillows.

I search for a hidden motive but find nothing in his voice or expression. "You're better than a good guy. Who'd have thought a celebrity might be the nicest man ever?"

"Yeah, yeah." He smiles a crooked half grin, his mouth hitching up on one side. "Don't make me regret it." With that parting shot, he's gone, and I'm alone again.

But for how long? I guess that's up to me. I prop on the railing, trying to convince myself that I shouldn't go see about a bear. And failing.

13

STONE

A LOW SNARL FROM THE MOUNTAIN LION SHIFTER IS THE ONLY warning I get before he's on me, hacking and slashing like a novice with a blade, but a supernaturally quick one who's a fast study. The ring of metal on metal and the crash of us knocking into furniture doesn't slow him. He's on me in two strikes, compensating for his shorter reach with catlike cunning and agility.

When he'd offered the distraction, I'd dragged my big bear paws just as I had since Kiva swept out of this room, leaving shattered pieces of me in her wake. Sure, I could stumble out of bed in the morning, make the same weapons I'd crafted for years, and fall back into bed at night, but I'd had no more spark of life than a machine since she'd stared at me with hurt, betrayal, and hatred in her beautiful brown eyes. Fighting gave me someone to take my guilt and regret out on, someone other than myself.

My muscles burn, my hands cramp, and my arms shake with the exertion of an hour of lessons before a solid hour of combat. I'm out of practice, and my body feels every slacker moment of the last two years right now.

The jingle of the bells over the door has me looking up,

hoping Kiva might walk in. Chase takes advantage of my preoccupation with feline grace. I block his sword, but he slams me in the gut with an elbow. Sneaky cat. I grunt and shove him away.

Beryl bustles into the shop. "Oh good, you two have finished swiping at each other. Thank the tech gods for Syn City's amazing resources." She looks to Chase. "Have you all always been so wired here?"

"We say y'all in this part of the country, and yes, Syn City didn't get hit by the Witching Wars and retaliation fallouts. If anything, the humans' propaganda attacks launched against us supes made this place even stronger."

She makes the *hmm* sound that means she's thinking. "The deity daughters fed the magic and the tech simultaneously. Makes sense." Looking to me, she says, "You'll never believe what I found on Trick Peterson. Or more importantly, what I didn't find."

"Oh?" I ask only because she'll keep staring until I express some sort of minute interest in what she obviously thinks I should care about. Although it's hard to see why anything the country star has or hasn't done matters now. Not when Kiva hates me.

Beryl splays her hands in *"Stop, listen to me"* fashion. "Trick has no verified history before he skyrocketed to fame almost two years ago. No school records, no work stuff, no photos. It's as if the man didn't exist."

"Okay, and?" I put away the swords. I'm tired, and she seems to have more to say—lots more. "Everyone knows public records have been shit these days."

"Not just public records," she insists. "No press, no social presence, no nothing."

"Look, I know you've got a crush on the guy—"

"Snap out of it." She clicks her fingers in my face. "Listen to what I'm telling you."

I don't even push her away. "Why does that matter?"

"He showed up on the music scene right after Kiva died."

When my mate had bled out in my arms, when her life had blinked out on the ice, when an immortal had given me the greatest gift and worst curse. "And? Other than Marina claiming they could be mates, there's no other connection."

Chase claps a hand on my shoulder. "He can't be her mate. Once destiny chooses us, we remain mated pairs."

"Through life." My gruff voice almost breaks on the last. "But she died."

He shakes his head. "It lasts through multiple lifetimes. Fated mates are literal soul mates, preordained to find each other again and again."

"Those are myths." I can barely manage the whisper.

He cuts me a look as if I'm an idiot, and I'm too gutted after what's happened since we came to Syn City to take offense. "I was meant for Dottie in her last life and in this one," he says. "Her death didn't keep us apart, although my stupidity and stubbornness almost did."

His words slam into me. If that's the truth, then maybe Kiva still might be meant for me. Except for the fact she's convinced I've lied to her, betrayed her, kept secrets from her without knowing why I had to do those things. But no, I've lost her. "The curse? It's supposed to break at true love's kiss. I kissed her, and nothing happened."

Beryl smacks my arm. "Of course that didn't work, you big dolt. It has to be true love from her, not you. You're not the star of this story, she is."

"What's that supposed to mean? Kiva's the center of my world."

"You *were* the center of hers, but not anymore." My sister sends me a pitying look. I freaking hate pity. "I love you, bro, but I get the feeling she's not coming home to be the little wife of the alpha's lieutenant."

Chase interrupts. "She can't. Furies don't leave Syn City.

They're bound here to the magic that's the source of their power. They leave the city to complete missions for the immortal three, but they live here."

"She can't leave?" I ask, the world falling out from beneath me. "She's trapped here forever? She would hate that."

Beryl sits heavily on a chair. "No more than she hated being stuck at the den with us."

My sister knows something that I've missed, something big, something that knocks me off-center when I was already unsteady. "Kiva didn't say anything about feeling trapped."

"She loved you too much. Not that she told me either, but sometimes she had this distant look like she was ready to bolt. I think she would've if she could have without making you give up your position as lieutenant. You were so happy with earning that title."

"The rank meant nothing to me once she was gone." Nothing had. "So what now?" I'm out of ideas.

"We have an amazing source of info about Furies and mates." Beryl glances at Chase, then to me. "But first, you need to decide. Kiva lived by your terms in her last life, but she's not the same and she won't go home with you. I don't think she would leave her triad sisters even if she could. So either you accept that you'll have to live in her world with her as a Fury, or you'll need to let her go. No matter how much the hotel owner loves you fixing her ironwork or how good business with the Syndicate has been, we can't stay here tormenting Kiva with possibilities and half-truths. You wouldn't want that anyway."

My heart slows in my chest, and my head pounds. "I want her any way I can get her. I always have, even if I screwed up the first time around not keeping her safe—"

Chase butts in again. "I'm going to stop you there. Furies take care of themselves, and she won't appreciate the whole knight-in-shining-armor thing, no matter how hot she might think your swords and hatchets may be." He waves a hand at all the shiny, pointy weapons I've made. "What made you choose this whole medieval profession anyway? You're a bear shifter; you don't need blades."

"Kiva." I almost smile. "She'd been an expert fighter for years before we met. I went into blacksmithing for practical purposes since the rest of what's left of civilization isn't as well off as Syn City. She convinced me to go into exclusively making weapons."

Beryl crosses her arms as if defending my mate. "Smartest decision we could've made for the business. Plus, with Kiva showing off the goods at demonstrations, orders came in faster than Stone and she could fill them."

Chase frowns at her. "Why would Kiva have known how to fight with swords as a human?"

I glance at my sister, unsure how much of this is my story to tell and not Kiva's, but Beryl lifts her shoulders in a *might as well* gesture. "My mate's mom died before we were together," I say, "but she taught Kiva all about blades."

"But why?" The mountain lion shifter won't let go of the questions. Such a cat.

"She had Kiva hunting the gods-spawned before she could legally drive."

"She hunted her own kind?" Chase looks aghast.

Beryl glares at him. "Not every gods-spawned creation has the integrity of those in Syn City. Some gods brought back monsters and nightmares-made-real. Plus, Kiva wasn't an immortal's child then."

"Right." The cat shifter backs down, seeming to realize he'd crossed a line that a momma bear shifter wouldn't leave undefended. "She was human."

My sister gives him an uneasy glance. "Sort of," she says. "You know what, I have a meeting with one of the House leaders to sell more weapons." Her voice becomes all hustle and impatience, and she turns a decidedly fiercer glare on me. "Make your choice about whether we're staying and let me know. I can do more research if we need to check out Trick's fortune teller to keep Kiva safe, but only if you're staying to fight for her in her current life and home. Otherwise, I'm not meddling when she's not here to speak for herself or know that you two are mates."

Chase waits until Beryl leaves to chuckle. "Your sister's intense. I'm glad she didn't come to Syn City after a mate. The shifters here wouldn't have stood a chance."

"She seems content making our alpha crazy for now at least." Grabbing a couple of honey beers from the fridge, I offer him one and crack mine open. The frigidness of the can doesn't stand a chance against the sticky heat, and the sweat dampens my palm.

"What'd she mean about Kiva being sort of human before being turned?" Chase asks. "Everyone knows the Furies only turn humans."

I don't see any reason not to tell him. The man's the only person other than Beryl who knows why I'm really here. "Kiva's mom was witchborn, magic-blooded."

"Half-human, half-witch. Unless she had natural powers, I guess the witches and even the immortals would've counted her as a human." He says the last as if that's all they would've seen, which is likely true.

"From what little Kiva would tell me, her mom could've gone to one of the sanctuaries, but she fell in love with a human crazy enough to be a monster hunter. They had two girls."

"Kiva has a sister outside her Fury triad?"

"Had." I don't wait for the next question I'm sure will be coming. "Her family's dead, and I couldn't find her. That's why no one has come for her since she became a Fury."

"She has nobody else?"

"No. Her dad and sister were murdered when Kiva was just a kid. All she ever had was her mom and someone her mom conjured to watch over her while she was away—a poppet or a golem but made of sticks and stones instead of clay or cloth. I honestly don't know much more than that since she refused to talk about her life *before*." I huff a rough imitation of a bitter laugh. "To think now I would give anything to offer her all those memories back. She wanted to kill me for keeping the truth from her."

"Not *kill* you," Chase drawls in his slow Southern accent. "Her House might be the avenging angels of the immortals, but they follow rules. They don't kill unless they're on a mission from the immortals to take vengeance on a crime like rape or murder, and they go full Fury mode, which makes for a piss-your-pants scary look—hot, but terrifying.

"You saw how pissed she was."

"Yeah, but you'll know if she hits full Fury activation. Trust me." He takes a long draw from the beer. "She didn't even pull her hatchet on you."

"The hatchet I made her?"

Chase's eyes go wide. "No shit? You made her weapon to call?"

"Yep. It disappeared the night she died, and I searched everywhere for it—everywhere but with her."

"Huh." He looks impressed.

"You sure they didn't go full Fury? Sadie pulled her whip." The leather handle had appeared in her hand between one blink and the next.

"Nah, that's not personal. She hates all shifters."

"That feels pretty personal." I can't imagine what could've happened to the woman to make her hate our entire species. "Kiva almost pulled her hatchet at the party when Marina first told her fortune."

"Yeah, I can't explain that." He looks as though he's considering options. "She could've been pissed off or scared."

"Scared sounds right. She said something about a sea witch the night she died."

He stares at me, the predator sliding behind his green eyes in a golden gaze as if he's ready to hunt. "Marina smells like magic and ocean to me."

"Me too, but I don't know anything more. Like I said, Kiva didn't talk about her past."

"Your sister offered to do research for you. Maybe you should ask her to dig into that past and any sea witch that might be connected to her family."

I clench a clammy hand around the beer can until the metal crinkles. "I once promised Kiva I wouldn't dredge up her history."

"She won't remember you making that promise."

"But I do."

The gold in his gaze intensifies. "This concerns your mate's safety. Nothing matters more."

"True."

A heavy bell clangs in the distance, and Chase looks up. "Speaking of which, roller derby practice will be over. Thanks for the sword fighting lesson."

"Any time."

"Got to go see my Fury. Best of luck with yours."

His words circle in my brain long after he's gone. *My Fury.* I don't need to choose, regardless of what Beryl thought. Kiva is still Kiva no matter what form she's in now. I would love her in any. I'll always be hers. Mates beyond death, the same as Chase and his sweetheart. If I can convince my Fury to love me, I can break this damn curse and tell her everything I know about our past. But how to persuade her to even speak to me again?

An hour later, I'm no closer to a plan. Back in my hotel room, I shower off the sweat. I'm wrapping a towel around my waist when there's a noise from the bedroom—a tapping. I rush in, half-certain it's a prank because the *tink, tink, tink* seems to come from the window that's a few stories up. What the hell do they put in the honey beer here? I only drank one can.

Crossing the room, I throw open the curtains, ready to scare off whatever little flirt might be tossing rocks this way in hopes of finding Trick Peterson's room. But the words shrivel on my tongue. A panic grenade pulls the hope pin to kick off a fear-driven *tick-tock-boom* in my gut, and my heart sprints in a thundering beat that any supernatural in the pleasure district could hear.

Kiva's outside my window—my third-story window. I wrench the glass open and grab her, hauling her against my chest and checking every inch of her for injuries, taking in the cocky smirk that makes me want to kiss her. Time slows as I memorize the curve of her mouth, the dimple in one cheek, the trio of freckles below her bottom lip. I don't miss the rage and hurt and confusion churning, turning, burning in her gaze, but I would expect nothing other than a powder keg of emotions in the minefield remnants of our mating bond.

The rustle and whoosh of feathers fanning has the rest of what I'm seeing crashing into my suspended reality like a mega-anvil of magical no-way.

She has wings—huge, black wings tipped in silver arrowheads like the one that killed her.

14

KIVA

Stone stares at me like I'm the holy grail, a full-blown miracle, and an incoming ass-kicking all wrapped in one tempting package. I'd paced the walkway outside ready to tell him off, to kiss him, and yes, to run away, but I hadn't imagined this kind of welcome. Hell, I'm still not sure how I found his room. I'd simply reached out with my senses like seeking a bag of salty chips or sour gummies, and *bam* I'd known where he was. *Like the weird fated-mates thing Dottie can do with Chase,* the logical part of my brain yelled before I shut that bitch down.

He's half-naked with damp hair and droplets clinging to his broad shoulders. I focus on the muscles there instead of flicking another glance at the tiny towel slung around his hips. One little tug...Nope, nuh uh, I can't follow that train of thought, or I'll never get to the point of coming over to get some answers out of him. As soon as he stops looking at me as though I'm the eighth wonder of the freakin' world.

A drop of water races along his angular jaw, down the strong column of his throat, and I can't help but wonder if the skin there tastes as good as his kiss did. And there my libido goes again, distracting me.

"Wings—you have *wings*." His deep voice sounds rougher, more awestruck than the dangerous edge of the villainous voice my mind had given him in my replays of our last conversation. Of course, I might've been biased considering he'd been a damned liar, holding out the secrets of a life that'd been mine. And still... while he sounds deliciously wicked, he doesn't sound like an evil mastermind determined to hurt me. No, he sounds half in love with me.

Ridiculous. I need to demand answers and get out of here. Except he traces his fingertips over one of my wings, and a shiver of pleasure ricochets through me. Wings rock—not just because I can fly—but because the sensitive spaces between the feathers? The delicate folds where no one can touch in battle? The softness beneath the shields where he's stroking me now? Nerve endings there can manifest ecstasy with a few well-placed touches. As if he reads me like steel to be sculpted, he zeroes in on those bliss buttons, and I can't fight the sigh that edges into a moan.

His gaze meets mine, seeking permission, but whatever he finds in my expression has him continuing his exploration with a steady, sure hand. "These—" His voice catches as though the rest of the question sticks in his throat. I've had people look at the silver blades embedded in my wings with fear or revulsion or even surprise that I don't slice myself open, but never with such deep sadness.

"They're dagger tips." I don't know what makes me want to reassure him, to soothe away that sorrow. "The same as you make with iron and steel."

"No," he whispers in a gravel and grit voice. "They're silver arrowheads." His eyes widen as if he's surprised by his own words.

"How do you know?" Because now that he has said arrow-heads, I see something I've known so well as the freckles on my face or counted on as thoughtlessly as my feet to take another step in an entirely different light. He's right. They must be arrowheads, although I'd never considered the possibility and no one else had ever suggested it.

He doesn't answer.

So much for openness and second chances. Anger chases away everything but the annoying attraction to him that I can't fight. "Are you certain they're arrowheads?" I don't keep the nasty from my tone.

"Yes." He looks pained, his mouth drawing down at the corners and creases deepening in his brow.

"But you won't tell me how you know." I'm not even asking now, just launching accusations.

He opens his mouth, closes it, opens it again. "I can't."

Frustration fizzles through me, bubbling lava that devours my already thin patience. "Can't?" I'm done with the word. It's so anti-Fury.

"Can't." Except this time, he emphasizes it like I need a decoder ring of bear-shifter talk.

I rewind my memories of the conversations we've had—him being sweet but cautious, protective. "Oh gods, you really *can't* tell me?"

Relief rushes through his gaze, the tense lines around his mouth ease, and his shoulders drop as if he'd been ready for an attack. "Yeah, that's what I've been saying." His tender hold on my arms becomes gentle strokes instead of a grip.

A terrifying thought hits me. "Do you have amnesia too?"

He curves his mouth into a boyish grin that does handstands on my heart. "No."

I rein in the desire to trace my fingers over his smile, to hide my need to touch him behind the excuse of trying to jog my memories. "But you answered me this time."

"Because I could." He says the last word as if it's a clue in a murder mystery game, the mystery of *my* murder.

No way can I stay mad at this man. My rage over betrayal fizzles into guilty. What if I had listened instead of assuming? I stop that incoming rockslide of regret. I'd come here for answers. There might be a way to still score those, no matter whatever block Stone has on talking about my past. "So I need to ask the right questions—ones you can answer for whatever reasons that you can't just tell me?"

He nods.

"We can turn it into a guessing game," I say. "I'm better at rushing in and getting shit done than I am at planning, but I can work a puzzle." Perhaps. "Especially one with my memories at stake. Are there good memories at least?"

He does the open-close-open routine again with his mouth, probably testing what answer he can give. "Some." He doesn't seem able to say more.

Okay, I need to limit my scope so he can give a response. Maybe yes or no works best. We're playing a game with invisible rules. "You'll answer me when you can?"

"Yes."

Here goes nothing. "You didn't kill me." All right, so that's not a question, but more of statement since he yanked me through the hotel window as if he'd rescue me from anything, including myself.

"I didn't." Hurt fills his expression. Grief, maybe? I don't know him well enough to pinpoint the emotion, but there's sadness radiating off him that I can feel like a tangible weight in the air.

"Do you know who did?"

"No."

Disappointing, but at least I'm getting answers. "The same person who killed Rylie?" I swallow the pain that fills me when I remember the teenager's broken body on the ice. While I can't remember who the girl was or what she meant to me, I don't hurt less at the memory. "Did they kill me?"

"I don't know, but probably, given what we found with her body."

More than one or two words this time. I guess at the reason. "You can say more when you're not talking about me directly."

He parts his lips as if to answer, but nothing comes out. The poor guy seems as if he wants to force himself to talk, but there's just no way. His broody bear look is adorable, but this? He struggles with his inability to speak as though it torments him. Finally, he nods.

Hmm. Where did I go wrong with the question? Or did he try to give away too much with his answer? More than simply saying something about me?

"Did I know Marina in my last life?" I ask.

"If you did, you never called her by name."

"Did you know her before..." Before I died. Before I turned Fury.

"No, I'd never seen her until Trick's party in the tent beside you. I didn't like her even before she made that wrong prediction."

"About Trick and me being fated mates?"

He doesn't speak but nods, his jaw tightening.

I go with my gut for the next question because I'm pretty sure Stone and I had been an *us* at some point, even though I have nothing more to go on than the longing looks he throws my way, his bringing me stuff that would be traditional shifter mating gifts, and whatever power pulled me to his window tonight. "Can you talk about us?"

He shakes his head, but his gaze lights with a heat that has my insides twisting into the best kind of tangled knots, and I give in to my need to touch him, resting my hands on his massive chest that has just the right amount of damp, dark hair. He snags my hips and pulls me so close to his near nakedness that my toes and wings curl. His body screams how happy he is to have me near, and I want to rub myself against him.

The man's huge, but his presence, his all-consuming essence, feels bigger, like he's a giant, sexy cuddle bear who'd pummel anyone who tried to touch me. Fantasizing about my were-bear isn't helping with the whole thinking thing.

"If you can't tell me about us, can you show me?" I hate charades unless we're playing it drunk with daggers, but if it'll help with my memories, I'm game. "Give me something to go on." I'm damn near pleading because the answers to my past are here if I can figure out how to unlock them.

He trails his knuckles along my jaw, his hand so big that his thumb brushes my ears when he slides his fingers into my hair to cup the back of my neck. Tugging my hair so that I tip my head back, the pressure of his touch screams possession and passion, yet he stops with his mouth close to mine. Gods, the man twists me up and has me craving the next touch, the next kiss, the next everything.

His expression—so intense and searching—leaves me breathless. He waits one booming heartbeat, then two, so patient that he's either waiting for permission or until I make the first move. As if I hold all the truths instead of a blank slate of a past and no idea what the future might hold.

Then his mouth comes down on mine, and I can't think of anything at all. This isn't a kiss. It's a claiming, and I want nothing more than to revel in the fire there, to burn in his heat and demand more, more, more.

I'd almost imagined that, in the wake of what I'd thought had been betrayal after our earlier kiss, I'd exaggerated how good it'd been. If anything, I'd forgotten how overwhelming this man could be. He holds me as if he'll never let go, as if afraid someone will yank me away. Stone kisses me like his life depends upon the crush of his lips on mine, like he can't get enough of me, like I'm what he's been looking for his whole life long.

For now, I can ignore the nightmares, the confusion, the need to know who I was before.

For now, I can sink into this kiss as though it's the only answer.

For now, there's only us.

What seems like forever and a too-brief moment later, he breaks the kiss and lifts his head. A flash of red in my peripheral vision grabs my attention, narrowing my focus to the thin scarlet line on his shoulder.

"You're bleeding." Not my keenest observation or greatest comeback to the best kiss of my life. I damn near pant the words between the pounding of my heart and my shortness of breath. Who needs air when they could have a lip-lock like that?

"Doesn't matter." He leans in as if going for another kiss, but there's blood on a silver tip of my left wing. *His* blood. "It's only a scratch."

"Shit, I cut you." Shock jolts through me.

"It's okay."

"No, it's not." I tuck my wings, withdrawing them into my body in the next second. "I could've really hurt you."

"You're worth more than a little pain."

I draw back, aware that his towel might be slipping, and while he doesn't seem to give a damn about his near nudity, I need to focus. For almost two years, I've had amazing control of my wings. What is so completely mind-blowing about this man? His taste's on my lips, and yet, I still want more of him. "That kiss?" That amazing, exhilarating, life-altering kiss. "That's who we were?"

He opens his mouth, and he's mute again.

Persephone's pink panties, I'd gone too far. Swallowing a sigh, I struggle not to show my disappointment because he looks sad enough for both of us, as though he'd expected the kiss to fix whatever stole his ability to tell me about my past. "You can't give my memory back by kissing me."

He touches his forehead to mine in the sweetest gesture. "You sure about that?"

Not at all. "Yeah," I lie when all I really want to do is suggest we test his theory, which is exactly why I need to leave before my emotions get too mixed up to sort out. "I, uh, should go." The wobble in my voice, the pause in my words? Not even I buy the line I'm selling.

Except Stone steps back, trailing his fingertips along a lock of my hair. "All right."

It's the smart play, so why don't I feel better about his giving in to what I asked for? His moving away steals the warmth from the room, the air from my lungs. If I don't work out my feelings for Stone, our past, however complicated it might've been, then I'll stay in this limbo of *maybe*, and I don't want to be trapped in this holding pattern forever.

I walk to the window in a daze, latching on to the need to sort everything out in my head when the longing for Stone blares so much louder everywhere else in my body.

"See you soon?" he asks.

"Come to The Rink in a couple of nights. It'll be an exhibition for some of the local shifter communities instead of a true bout, but it should be fun." And I want him to see me skate, want him to see me at my best when maybe he has seen me at my worst.

"I'll be there." There's no hesitation on his part, just a plain, straightforward answer that I wish he could give me the rest of the time. Until then, I'll play this game as long as I can keep my heart out of it because something tells me if I offer that to him, I'll never get it back, and I'm not sure I'd survive that.

My throat goes tight, and I wonder for a second if whatever's keeping him silent might be contagious. But no, he means too much. *We* mean too much when I'm not even sure who I was before the turn to Fury. Pushing off the window, I watch his eyes light with fear for the moment I fall and then something akin to pride when my wings unfurl and I zoom into the air.

At The Rink two nights later, cheers ring in my ears with deafening animal roars and an occasional elephant's trumpeting blasting. No human fans allowed tonight unless they came with a shifter for the exhibition games that make us uber famous in the supernatural community. Roasted peanuts, grilled big game meat, and herbs from the salads on the special menu fill my nose with spicy scents that have my stomach grumbling.

Tonight's skating comes down to money and prestige without the pressure of a championship trophy on the line. We're the feature act with the Fair Furies versus the local Murder Scene of crow shifters. The other team's name pricks at the emotional crap we're all still dealing with here in town considering the serial killer who targeted the Houses so recently, but there will be no killing tonight except on the track.

An opponent rolls up beside me, the wind from unfurling her massive wings slapping me in the face. *Keep your skates on, birdie.* I brought my own feathers, and these bitches have blades—well, arrowheads. I'm still getting used to knowing what those sharp, beloved pieces of me are. She mutters an "I'll ugly up that pretty Fury face" from under a beaky, too-pointed nose. I'll enjoy making her face-plant her snarling snoz on the concrete, or I would if I could get my head in the game.

I'm distracted beyond belief tonight, and I'm not thinking of the know-it-all Huntresses coming between me and a championship victory, the freaking zoo packing the stands, or the shifter team out for blood. No, I'm concentrating on the buzz low in my gut that lets me know my were-bear is somewhere in the crowd.

I toe the second starting line on the track and push forward, rolling my shoulders and then my neck to work out the kinks so I can become a one-woman demolition squad. Glancing upward, I spot the catwalk section where Trick and I talked. The star has a well-publicized party at the House of Muses tonight, but I swear I see a shadow moving near the railing. I look again. Whatever I imagined has disappeared.

Shoving down the temptation to check above or glance toward the stands to confirm what that pull in my gut means, I remember Doc Bomani's advice the other day that I need to decide what future I want and to go for it, no matter the past.

Tonight, win or lose, I'm planning to celebrate with Stone in our own private afterparty.

15

STONE

THE RINK HAS MORE SHIFTERS OF DIFFERENT SPECIES IN ONE PLACE than I've ever seen, apex predators and weakling prey alike. Getting our bears and the neighboring wolves to work together back home took years, yet in Syn City, we all sit on the edge of our seats as if we're one big pack. Well, not everyone. Some have shifted and stomp around the concrete middle circle like it's the damn watering hole in a safari park.

Buzzing on a honey high, Beryl makes her rounds through the crowd, drumming up business when we already have enough orders to keep me busy for months. Chase sprawls next to me in an oversized chair, the perks of scoring seats in the Furies' family VIP booth. I dip a spoon into one of the jarred honeycombs he brought us from a literal Queen Bee who wants me to forge some new fencing for her hives. The sweetness explodes on my tongue, almost as delectable as Kiva's kisses.

"Why's Kiva behind the others?" I ask, tipping my head toward her stance on the track.

"She's a blocker."

"So she's defense?" I know nothing about this sport. Kiva

played center in hockey, and I'm surprised she's not playing offense now.

"Blockers block the opposing team, but they also push their jammer forward to score." Chase gestures with his glass, neatly avoiding a slosh of his booze at the last second. Such a cat trick. "Sadie's playing pivot tonight, so she's up on the first line and will skate on the first whistle. The rest of them wait for the second."

"Why's your girl starting last?"

"Dottie's the jammer. That's also why she has the star on her helmet. She has to lap the other team's blockers to score."

"I still don't understand the rules." My mutter sounds as broody bear as my sister accuses me of being, but I need to learn Kiva's new world.

"It's about fun and watching them get mean, especially during exhibitions." Chase leans back in his chair all lazy feline. "Dottie's skating her first winged event tonight." He sounds super proud.

I can relate to the feeling. Watching Kiva play hockey always had me cheering nonstop when she'd hurtle toward the goal or super worried she'd end up starting and finishing yet another brawl. Tonight, she begins her bout with the same slow skate to setup and by circling her neck and rolling her shoulders until I know she's making awful cracking pops that would make me shudder if I could hear them above the crowd.

A couple of whistle blasts, and they're off. I don't know what I expected after barely paying attention to the one practice I crashed on my first night in Syn City, but the exhibition's a rolling fight of thrown elbows, hard shoulder blocks, and wings taking each other out. A crow shifter smacks Kiva in the face with her wing, and my mate slams into her in a full body blow, knocking the woman into the railing with what looks like a vomit-inducing force. The crow flips over the side, launches into the air, and flies high above the track.

"Penalty box," a ref shouts at the crow. "No sustained flight over three seconds allowed."

Kiva skates backward, aiming two middle fingers at the crow from a low position that the ref won't be able to catch. My woman's gone from aggressive champion forward to brutal all-around badass.

I can't take my gaze from her when she darts along the track, tucking her wings for speed at some points and unfurling them at others for quick stops. It's as though she has grown up with those wings for decades instead of learning to use them over the last couple of years. She flies better than the born bird shifters, kicked out of their human nests as toddlers to discover their animal natures alongside their parents. She moves like she's gliding on ice except she's airborne now and then, executing perfect jumps, spins, and turns. If the Olympics had winged sports, she'd rack up gold medals.

The yells from the players compete with the cheers of the unruly crowd, and I join in, roaring each time she blocks an opponent or shows off a trick move. For once in the world outside my den, I don't need to hide who I am or how much I adore my mate. Even if she refuses to acknowledge the link between us, I can feel her happiness, her excitement, her confidence, and if possible, I love her more. Maybe my love could be enough for both of us in the future, whether or not she remembers our past.

Chase smacks at my arm in a shifter-fast move. "Across the track, mid-level." He looks toward the opposite side of the stadium, and I follow his gaze.

Marina stands there—still and apart—in the center of screaming fans, staring at me. From this distance, I can only imagine the coldness of her eyes, but a shiver runs through me as if the track had iced over and the chill worked its way up the stands to where we sit. She smiles a nasty curl of her lips, glances toward the track where Kiva skates and then up toward the ceiling. I narrow my eyes, trying to get a better view of what might be above. A maze of steel walkways and railings weaves above the skaters.

"The catwalks," Chase says.

His words barely register when the groan of steel overpowers the cheers. The crowd goes silent, supernatural hearing straining as most shifters wait for another telltale sound, to identify where the awful noise came from. A screech of metal and a clang of pipes from above break the quiet. Winged creatures take to the air, parents shield their cubs, and the screams turn from happy cheers to shrieks. A section of the catwalk breaks apart and crashes toward the track.

"Kiva." My yell booms, but the pandemonium around me drowns the sound. I push faster, faster, *faster*.

I can't lose her again. Not this time.

16

KIVA

THE CATWALK—THE HEAVY STEEL SECTION WHERE TRICK AND I HAD swapped stories—rockets toward me like a deadly toy tossed by a giant during a tantrum. My heart pounds as loud as the groaning metal as it peeled apart a second ago, my breath catches in my throat, and icy venom races through my veins.

The crow shifter with the pointy nose seems to forget I sent her to the penalty box earlier tonight, grabbing my arm as though she's a kid and I'm her security blankie. No way am I dying my final death with this bird clinging to me. Glancing toward my triad sisters, I take flight, zooming out of the steel's path and dragging the crow with me.

Dottie and Sadie fly behind me, a V-formation that arrows through the skaters, scattering everyone away from the danger a nanosecond before the metal crashes to the ground with a thunderous boom. Dust and debris explode from the floor, shooting in all directions and blinding me momentarily beyond the faces within my reach.

Terror rips through me, so overpowering that I can't force air into my lungs, a horror of a past repeated that spins through my gut. Except the fear doesn't come from me. No, I'm cold and breathless, but rage has settled my nerves in true Fury style. I look to my sisters, but both show the lethal calm of our House under pressure, the reason our kind thrive in chaos. So who's the source of the panic? Not the crow who comes to her senses and flies to her coach and kin.

"Kiva." The voice roars louder than the ringing in my head. Or does it? The call comes from the very same source as the scared *must-find-her-must-get-to-her-must-not-lose-her* panic litany that shouts from deep within me.

"Stone," I say, although he won't hear me unless...unless he's tied to me the same way as I am to him. It's stupid, crazy, impossible—except I found his room last night in a hotel that houses hundreds, I tracked him to his forge before that, and the first day he came to the track? That's when this *pull* inside me started humming.

Pushing aside the insanity of what I'm asking in this world full of magic, I open my senses to focus on him and only him. Shrieks hurt my ears, grit burns my eyes and stings my nose, and below those overwhelming sensations?

There.

I wing toward the stands, trusting intuition as my GPS. Stone jumps to the track, Chase beside him with his gaze locked behind me where Dottie must be.

"You're alive." Stone wraps me in his arms. "You're okay. Thank the gods." Fear—*his* fear—ebbs from me, relief surging in its wake. I don't fight his hold or whatever tentative bond exists between us.

Somewhere, somehow, I'd gone and gotten my foolish self entangled with a broody bear shifter. What the hell am I supposed to do about that?

He holds me like he won't let go. "I won't survive watching you die again." His raw whisper sends ice slithering along my spine. *He'd been there.* For whatever reason, he can't talk about my first life, but he'd known me before I turned, and my death had nearly killed him, given the heavy heartbreak in those words.

"Come on." I'm not going to push him for answers and end up back somewhere between annoyed and enraged. Not when that sort of fear and loss radiates from him. Not when I can grab hold of today for both of us, regardless of yesterday or tomorrow. I haul him—or he lets me pretend to drag him because a massive bear doesn't go where he doesn't want—to the locker rooms. "Wait here. I'll be out in five."

"She means half an hour." Chase stretches his cougar self out against the opposite wall, looking cat-couldn't-care lazy except for the tenseness in his gaze. I don't give him more shit than a snarl because he's trailing Dottie like yet another serial killer has locked onto his mate as their next target. My triad sister pushes her cousin into the locker rooms in front of us, and I shut the door in the men's faces.

Way more than five minutes later (because showering and changing alongside a team of freaked-out Furies wishing for someone to beat on to relieve the tension takes time), I walk out to find Stone alone except for the security. "Where'd the cat go?" I ask.

"Home with his mate and her human cousin." He tips his head toward the still-loud locker room. "Do you need to stay with your teammates?"

"Nope." I take off, not waiting for him to stalk behind me. Dude's massive. Why doesn't he lumber or plod? No, he moves in more of a sneak attack, just like whatever this magical mood-ring link might be going on between us, but this time, I'm taking the lead.

In a couple of seconds, he's beside me, taking the duffel bag full of clothes, gear, and skates from me. He loops the strap over his shoulder like the thirty pounds of crap I lug around weighs nothing.

"Got more of those crab chips?" I ask.

"Uh...back in my hotel room." He sounds uncertain. I can't tell if he didn't expect me to ask about snacks instead of the disaster we left at the track or if he's remembering that hotter-than-Hades kiss in his room before I cut him with a wingtip. Not that I'll lose control of my wings this time.

"Let's go." I could've died my second death on the track tonight if I hadn't moved Fury fast. No way I'm letting another day slip away without enjoying this life, starting with making some supernatural moves on a shifter with secrets.

We push out of The Rink's lower exit, away from the spooked crowds heading for the ferry or piling into party shuttles to the pleasure district.

"Where's everyone going?" he asks.

"The Nymphs threw an impromptu screening party, a marathon of their favorite soap opera, *Covens to Covet.*"

"Never heard of it, but then electricity's sporadic where we... where I live." He covers his almost slip so fast that I don't have a chance to pounce on the information about my past. "Got a desti-nation in mind?"

"This way." I reach for him, and he twines his fingers with mine as if he's held my hand a thousand times. No matter that he's huge with hands the size of dinner plates that could crush a concrete block, he keeps his touch tender, and my heart goes as gooey as a caramel candy.

"You want to talk about what happened tonight at The Rink?"

I fight a shudder. "You mean my almost being squashed like a mosquito?"

He tugs me closer, and I let him. "Anything like that ever happened at the track before?"

I think of Coach's murder that left Maizie in charge, Connie's kidnapping. "Horrible stuff has gone down there, but with people, not the actual building, and not during an event. Magic runs our city, sure, but tech and solid construction also hold everything together." Or I'd thought as much. "But tonight?

Another second and both teams would've been crushed. We got lucky everyone walked away with no injuries worse than usual."

"A shifter with a broken nose? One with a nasty gash to her leg? You consider those the norm?"

"For roller derby? Yeah. Some bouts end with players hauled out on stretchers. The repair crews will push to get the pit area patched before the charity concert." When he stares at me, I add, "The infield area with the penalty bench and coaches? Where the Muses do the pre-show stuff? That's our pit."

"Oh." He makes the tiny word sound so heavy, as if I'm explaining astrophysics and skipping the first few chapters.

"New to roller derby?" I ask.

"Yeah. Chase ran through the basic rules, mainly on how the Furies don't want to follow them."

"We think of them more as suggestions."

"Ever thought about playing ice hockey?" He grins as if I should get an inside joke there.

"Why?" I ask.

But he doesn't answer.

I've talked to Sadie, our resident kitchen witch, about his sudden muteness when discussing my past, and now seems as good of a time as any to interrogate him. Glancing up at him, I'm not surprised to find him staring back at me with that quiet strength of his. "You're under a secrets-to-keep spell, aren't you? Did you piss off a witch? Or did I?" The latter seems more likely.

He stares, a fierce look in his eyes, not speaking but not disagreeing either. Oh yeah, a spell's at play here. I don't know how to break it, having only fairy tales and the soap opera the Nymphs crush on to use as reference points.

He rubs his thumb against my jaw in the gentlest touch, dragging silver glitter away.

No matter how much I scrub, the damn stuff ends up everywhere. "Part of roller derby," I tell him.

"I like it." Except his gaze seems pinned on my mouth, and

I'm not sure if he's saying he's a fan of body sparkles or if he means something much bigger with his simple pronouncement.

I'm hoping it's the latter but stick with a safer topic. While I'm ready to complicate us, I have no idea how far I want to push into this new uncertain territory. "Comes with the fishnets and protective gear." The black tank top cut for wings, shorts, and sneakers I wear now don't stray much from the Fury's on-the-track uniform. "We tried to get them to allow us to skate exhibitions without helmets, but the Syndicate ruled against us, arguing the whole mortality thing."

"I'm glad they did." He continues lazy strokes with his thumb, swiping as if he might spend hours just looking at me. "When I think of how close I came to losing you tonight with whatever Marina did—"

"Hold up. Why do you think Marina had anything to do with what happened at The Rink?" Suspicion thrums through me, settling beneath my skin in a flush of anger.

"Right before the structure fell, she gave me this awful grin like she knew something was about to happen. She glanced at you and up at the roof. I don't have proof—"

"I thought I saw a flicker of something or someone up there earlier tonight." I wait for full Fury mojo of a *target acquired, revenge rage initiated* to blast across my senses as a sign from the immortals, but...I don't feel anything. That's not entirely true. Plenty of emotions battle to twist my gut—mad, hurt, frustration, confusion. Why does this have to be so difficult? "I could confront her."

"Not without me you don't," he says with a near snarl.

"Nuh uh, I don't need some grizzly security guard."

"I'm a Kodiak, bigger and smarter than your common grizzly."

I poke him in the chest. "I have a magical hatchet that can't miss its target. What do *you* have?"

"Claws, fangs, and a shifted form that's over ten feet tall."

Damn. Okay, so the man has big-guns kind of fight game, but I'm not letting him win this argument. "If vengeance needs to be dealt out, my sisters and I will handle it."

He presses my hand flat over his heart, over the hard muscle and warmth there, covering it with his. "You're her target. She sent giant steel beams crashing down at *you*."

"You don't know that." Although she'd seemed to center her attention on me more than anyone else in town. "What if the building had some structural malfunction? The welding that held the metal together must've been an inch or so thick at the seams, and nothing looked weird a few days ago when I sat up there with Trick, but—"

"Rewind. You went up to the rafters with the pretty boy musician alone?" His earlier *me-big-man-bear* overprotectiveness didn't compare to this level of grouchiness, but the hurt in his eyes doesn't read like suspicion or even jealousy. No, he seems worried about me.

"Yeah?" Not knowing how to take his concern, I stick to the basics without elaborating on the specifics.

"You could've fallen or Marina could've—"

"I have wings, remember?" I tug him closer and almost grin when his tension melts under my touch, his broad shoulders losing some of their tightness and his body curling around mine.

"Promise me that you'll watch your back?" he asks.

"Not warning me off of Trick?"

"Don't have to. You came to my hotel room, and you left The Rink with me."

"Awfully sure of yourself there."

"I'm sure of you."

Aww, when he goes all teddy were-bear on me like that... "Fine, I'll be careful if that'll make you feel better."

"It does. I would be even happier if you said you didn't have practices or events where Marina can get to you anytime soon."

I think about my calendar, ticking through derby stuff like

normal people probably do their birthdays, anniversaries, or whatever. Not that I know any of my "special" days, and it's hard to celebrate when you got turned into a deity daughter because someone murdered you. "I don't have anything planned for the next week except Trick's charity concert. I'm working a shift at the autograph tables signing merchandise for the kids. Judging by the grumpy bear face you're giving me, you don't like my answer."

He quirks that sexy mouth of his, and I can't help but stare at his lips. He's cute when he worries, but if he's right, Marina has decided I'd be better as a squished Fury than a destined mate for Trick. Nothing like having a few thousand pounds of steel hurtle toward me to serve as a wake-up call. I need to live for the moment, to embrace the *now*.

I don't have my memories of whatever might've been my life before turning, but if I shut off the anxiety and my brain long enough to listen to my heart, I would take a chance on Stone. Still, I prefer some certainty.

"You can't tell me how to break the spell that keeps you quiet, can you?" I ask.

"No." His big bear eyes go soft and sorrowful.

"What if for tonight we concentrate on the present instead of the past?" Which he can't talk about. "Or the future?" Because while I would wager we had a past as an *us*, I'm not gambling any commitment. Certainly not to a bear shifter who brought me food because after tonight, I would bet we'd been mates or something close to it. "I'm not agreeing to forever or even a real date, but I'm pretty sure you're interested in more than just kissing me."

"Yeah." His voice rumbles around the agreement like filthy, delicious demands lie beneath the word.

I'd be lying if the unspoken promises there didn't have me moving snug against him. His quick inhale, the heat in his eyes, the hardness of *all* of him make me almost skip straight to smooching. But I can't. "I like you, but I'm not *her*...whoever I was when you knew me before. If we're going to talk about the possibility of more than kissing, I need to know that you want me for who I am now."

He studies me as if comparing me to her, and it makes my stomach twist even if I'm only jealous of whatever connection my past self might've had with him. "All right," he says, "finish laying the ground rules so I know what's expected. Bears don't like surprises. We tend to react badly."

"Violently?" I catch the last syllable on my tongue as if I'm parroting him. Not the smartest idea to mock the man who just told me he goes to ten feet tall, but what can I say? Provoking him has been fun so far.

"Only to those who aren't mates or family." He hitches a grin that I swear to gods has the corner of his eyes crinkling, and I stare, losing whatever smartass response about not coming under those two protected categories that might've been in my head. Yeah, I'm guessing I'd been considered to be on his short list for protection in my first life.

"Your plan of attack?" he asks.

Huh? Oh yeah, we're sticking to the *now*. I drag my thoughts away from might-have-beens and play along. "What makes you think I have one?"

He huffs a laugh. "I saw you skate, watched you terrorize that crow shifter. Don't tell me you didn't have a strategy outlined since you walked out of the locker rooms."

I had, but damn him and his charm, now I can't remember it. Has my amnesia spread to current short-term forgetfulness? Or does Stone steal every thought from my head? Faking a hover-truck load of brashness I don't currently possess, I lift my chin and paste on a *boss-babe-in-charge* look. "We could start over. Pretend we're meeting for the first time?"

"Kinda hard when you showed up at my hotel room to make out with me."

"Oh, cocky." I like that. "Okay, fine. Knowing that you're

getting me and not past-me, what do you suggest for a starting strategy?"

"Whatever you'll let me get away with. But not tonight. First, I need to convince you that I'm interested in you exactly as you are. You deserve that and more."

Great, why did I have to go and run my big Fury mouth? Now that I have my were-bear with his muscles—so many muscles... I don't consider myself a man-ogler, but I might become one for this guy—he wants to woo me? I sigh. "I need something to work off the adrenaline dump of the almost catastrophe at The Rink." Especially since I didn't get to knock that crow on her ass at least a couple more times.

"Understood." He touches the small of my back, and the intimacy of the gesture buzzes through me. "Want to come with me to the pleasure district? I've got just the thing to take that competitive edge off."

17

STONE

THE ONE NIGHT I TAKE MY SHIRT OFF IN FRONT OF THE MASSIVE shop window of my temporary forge, the crowds of female tourists usually swarming the pleasure district have disappeared. Blasting the A/C doesn't do much to stop the heat with how fast Kiva and I move together with perfect timing because we've done this thousands of times before—although I shouldn't think about the past because she said to stay in the here and now.

As if reminding me of the present, she slams her blade into mine, leaning into the blow with enough force to send stinging vibrations through me. Clearing space to spar had been my best idea in a while. Her tight, black workout clothes cling to her curves, and the strappy sports bra strains over her breasts with every labored breath.

"Not the kind of exertion I expected you to suggest," she says.

"I don't hear you complaining about my choice of activities."

"Why would I when fighting's one of my favorite pastimes?" She fills her last words with wicked innuendo.

"Am I supposed to guess the others?" Flirting at the edge of steel hadn't been my intention, but it works.

"Roller derby, of course."

I want to snap back something funny that would make her smile, but she comes at me in a quick flurry of hacks and slashes. My grunt seems to work the same as the best humor. Her combat skills have progressed from expert to legendary. Being a Fury means she moves faster, strikes harder, and recovers quicker. She uses a thrust-and-spin combo that I haven't seen anyone attempt since the last time we fought back at a Warrior's Den Weaponry exhibition, and her simple execution of the complicated maneuver has me hesitating to block.

The clang of steel on steel turns to a *zing* when she steps closer, not releasing her hold. "Almost gotcha that time," she taunts.

"But you didn't." I can't help myself. She's too easy to provoke. Or she once was.

With an adorable snarl, she attacks again, but she uses a dancing lunge comparable to a slap instead of a punch, something designed to show me her irritation as if the little furrow in her brow and annoyed gaze couldn't get through my big bear brain. "Stop holding out on me." She whips the blade through the air like a lethal exclamation point. "You've got shifter speed and strength you're not using."

"I haven't seen those wings yet." Yep, poke, poke with the verbal jabs. My mate's at her finest when riled and snarky.

"You can't handle those babies."

"Try me. Show me what you've got, and I'll show you mine."

"Ooh, dirty talk." She curves her mouth into a smirk that might as well be a direct shot to my heart. "Promise?"

Damn. My brain fizzles at the thought of seeing all of her. Strip sword play should be a thing with my woman. I flex my fingers in a come-at-me dare.

With a loud snap, her wings unfurl—dark and lovely and powerful. Then she's on me. She'd been dangerous as a human; she's a destroyer as a Fury. Fast, cruel, and beautiful, those wings arc and curl with her as though they're lethal extensions. She feigns right, and they arc outward to block as though she has blade-tipped shields running half the length of her body. Gods, I've never seen a more deadly and graceful fighter.

I counter with shifter speed and strength, my bear keeping an easy leash on our worst instincts because toying with our mate means pushing her to limits we haven't seen before while still refraining from damaging that rich, soft skin that glows with happiness.

The mating bond wraps around me, rich golden chains that I yank tighter. Just like that, I fall in love with my mate all over again.

Kiva retreats, staying a couple of feet off the ground with a lazy beat of her wings. "Holy Hades, I needed that."

No surprise there. She always craved a fight or sex after a game. "Feel better?" I could watch her bear-with-the-honey-jar grin and that slow flap of wings for hours.

"Yep, although I'm starving."

"I ordered food to be sent to my room if you're interested."

"Oh, I'm interested. Shower first. Feast with crab chips afterward." Her tone holds challenge, as if I could deny her anything.

"Come on." I won't question what might happen, how she might react, how I could screw this up, how I could blurt out my feelings and lose her. Think on the present, she'd said. So I take in her scent, the sarcastic cuteness of her commentary on the crow shifters, the sway of her hips when she passes me on the stairs up to the room since she says she'll use the door this time and not the window, the knowledge that she's safe and naked and perfect in the next room when the shower spray kicks on and steam creeps from beneath the bathroom door.

She comes out in a towel wrapped around her, and I almost swallow my tongue. Droplets of water cling to her skin the same way I want to touch her, to ghost my fingers along her curves to make sure she's real.

"You're good with me staying over." She says it as a decided fact instead of a question. "Except I didn't bring anything to sleep in, and I mean just *sleep* since you're determined to be old-fashioned with your whole *what you think I deserve*." She raises her hands to throw air-quote fingers with the last, and dear gods and all the baby demons, the towel slips an inch. "Got some clothes I can borrow?" My mind catches up to her words, and my bear wants to roll around in pleasure. She plans to sleep here. Best idea ever.

I've missed her smiles, her smartass comments, and her tough sweetness, but most of all, I miss the way she latched onto me at night, using me as a personal heater for her cold hands and feet, her naked body pressed close to mine. Right, don't think of her naked when the towel's slipping lower on her breasts.

If I'm going to get her to stay without scaring her off, I need to stop staring at her. Pawing through my clothes, I drag out a faded "Axe to Grind" T-shirt with a cartoon anvil.

"Blacksmith humor." She snort-snickers. "Love it."

She should since she gave it to me. "Uh, my sweatpants won't fit you," I tell her. They didn't in her last life and she's the same size.

Snagging the shirt, she shakes her head. "You mean the custom fit jobs you must order to find size *extra-loaded Viking god*? I think your shirt will hang like a dress on me." It will. She retreats to the bathroom, the swish of the towel dropping to the floor and rustle of cotton calls to me, sending the memory of every delicious inch of her body straight through me. There will be no hiding how much I want her.

She walks out with my shirt falling almost to her knees, showing a peek of thigh with each step that's as tantalizing as the shorts she wore earlier. "Your turn to shower."

I crank the water to its coldest, flinching from the shock of it but resolved to give my woman the courtship she deserves before jumping her like a love-starved shifter who has missed his beloved mate for two long years.

A glacier dropping on me wouldn't kill my libido, but the shower chills me enough I won't be so damn obvious. Other than staring at her as if she might disappear in the next instant. No wonder she mandated we stay in the present. Our past tangles me in knots, and the fear of a future for her without me in it shuts down any sexy thoughts. Play it cool. Worship her. Get her to let me adore her every second of the day without me being creepy-stalker bear.

A thud from the bedroom has me hurrying shirtless to check on Kiva.

Stretched on her tiptoes, she rummages inside the massive trunk of weapons, her ass in the air wearing the tiniest red lace panties. She keeps her wings angled as if she's holding them out to balance on a tight wire. "Oh my gods, you have a giant toy box." Leaning further, she comes off her bare feet and holds herself aloft with her wings. The show's sensual if unintentional, and I sit on the bed to watch.

"You're cool if I go through your stuff, right?" she asks.

My mate, the eternal snoop no matter which life. "I wouldn't have left the trunk unlatched if I'd wanted to keep you out of it. Though even a lock might not have worked."

"Nope," she agrees in a chipper tone without a hint of remorse in pawing through my things. "Mmm, chips. Hey, what're these?" She rises, hovering upright, which still staggers me how easily she flies. In one hand, she clutches chips, sour gummies, and honey taffy. The first two had been her favorites. I'm guessing she didn't ask about the food. In her other hand, she waves three knives without an ounce of caution for the sharp edges.

"Juggling knives."

"You made them?"

"Yes." For you.

"Righteous." She makes the word sound like the best compliment ever. "I wonder if I could juggle them."

"Why don't you start with normal clubs sometime before you go tossing blades."

"You've got a thing for safety."

"*Your* safety, yeah."

"Fine." She doesn't pout, protest, or push any real argument, just puts the knives back. "What's for late night snacks?"

I pull the tray from the heated cover, revealing a full dinner of some of her past favorites, and she moves to the bed beside me, grabbing a fork and knife.

"That's what I'm talking about." She digs into the food, not seeming to be bothered in the least by our closeness or that I never got around to putting on a shirt.

My attention lasers on the brush of her bare thigh against my leg, the curve of her ass pushing into my hip, the way her breasts sweep against my arm when she reaches for another bite, the plumpness of her lips as she sucks sauce off her finger.

"So good." She makes a humming noise that undoes what little progress I'd made with the ice-cold shower. "What sexual favors did you have to trade the Nymph who owns the hotel for her to send all this to your room?"

I cough at the first part of her question but recover by the time she's finished. "Some ironwork."

"Ooh, sounds kinky." The delight in her voice? I can't tell if she's teasing or interested in exploring the topic. This is an entirely new side of Kiva.

"Sorry to disappoint you, but I repaired her staircase railings and designed new door handles."

She quirks a brow and finishes chewing. "You're right. That's not nearly as exciting. The weapons you make are way cooler."

With the comment that's so typical Kiva, I feel like I'm in familiar territory again or at least have a rough idea of how to find a way back into my mate's heart. "With the deity daughters here, Beryl has been fielding weapons requests daily, but people still need things fixed around the house." An old argument that my mate had found boring.

"I guess. Hey, you owe me the dagger you promised me in exchange for a kiss. I've paid you double by now."

"Done." I tug the sheath from the nightstand and hand it to her.

"This the same blade?" she asks.

"Yep."

"Why do I feel like there's something significant about it? Something you can't tell me?"

I lift my shoulders, not a don't-know gesture so much as a she's-right-and-I-can't-explain one. No way the curse will let me go into the details of my last proposal, the one she'd accepted. "I could try, but it won't work. Besides, no talking about the past tonight. Your rule, remember?" It's nice not to stammer over every other word while I'm around her. It makes the curse seem less like a boulder strapped to my back to remind me her death was my fault.

If only I'd refused to let her lead the rescue mission to find Rylie.

If only I'd kept her from running out on the ice.

If only.

"So what do you wanna talk about?" She runs the words together between bites.

"You." Such an obvious answer that I can't believe she had to ask.

"Then you're asking for an in-depth guide to roller derby." Setting the sheathed dagger on the only table in the room, she pulls her legs up on the bed to sit cross-legged, edging her knee into my lap. Her exaggerated hand gestures, wide smiles, and stories about tricky moves on the track—they suck me in to the point that I'm learning less about her passion and more about *her*. This new, exciting, amazing version of Kiva who has my love's best qualities and extras.

Despite being warned away from thinking about the future, I can't help but consider how I can explain a move to Syn City to Beryl, to my alpha, because if there's a chance to build a life with Kiva, I'm taking it.

She yawns, stretching her arms wide before wrapping them around me. "Thanks for the dagger. I know your work means a lot to you."

"You mean more." Yeah, I said it.

Holding my gaze for a long moment, she studies me but doesn't let go of me. "Still plan on waiting before we go past kissing?"

"As much as I'm hating myself right now, yeah. You were right earlier. I need you to know I appreciate you exactly as you are right now—smart, funny—"

"Hot," she interjects, not in the least bit humble, and I grin, a laugh rumbling through my chest that doesn't stop when she lays her head there as if listening to it. The action melts me.

"Smokin' hot," I agree. Although tenderness steals through the teasing, making me sound like a man in love rather than in lust, and yeah, that's true. I push the tray away, moving back on the bed, and she follows me, snuggling close with her head on my bare chest again.

"Keep going with how awesome I am." She rubs the space right above my heart.

"Driven, always out to win—"

"True. I must vanquish the Huntresses in this year's championship. What else?"

"You're fearless."

"I don't know about that," she says. "I may run on rage, but the whole serial killer in town a few weeks ago terrified me."

Fear sends a rush of ice through me colder than any shower. "Does Syn City have many murderers?" Please say I've misunderstood and she's using *serial killer* as some kind of code.

"Just the one. A deity son, if you can believe it, and a total twerp on top of being a psycho murderer. We're still mourning the loss of our Coach. I'm working with my therapist on that and the amnesia thing." She lifts her head. "It doesn't bother you that I go to counseling, does it? Because that kind of unenlightened caveman shit might be a dealbreaker."

"I'm glad you see a therapist." After all she's been through, she has another lifetime of issues to deal with. "Do you like the person?"

She puts her cheek back on my skin, snuggling closer as though I've narrowly avoided a battle. "My therapist? Yeah, Dr. Bomani's nice. Says I don't feel safe enough these days to sleep. The nightmare..." She trails off, and I wait, but she doesn't finish whatever she'd been about to say.

I hug her tighter, wishing I could ward off her bad dreams. "When's the last time you slept through the night?"

"Almost two years." Her whisper breaks my heart. "You?"

"Same."

"I probably won't be able to fall asleep tonight."

"Try. If you can't, we'll just talk."

"Okay." She pats my chest as if reassuring herself. "Can you tell me a story? Something that won't trigger whatever silence spell you've got on you? Hearing the way your voice rumbles under my cheek...I don't know...it soothes me."

She'd said the same when we'd been together, but remembering now with her pressed against me? The sadness ebbs away to leave the sweetness. "A story, huh?"

"Yeah, do it right with the once upon a time and everything."

I chuckle and savor the scent of her hair when she tosses her ponytail. "I suppose you require a happy ending?"

"Uh yeah, I'm not camped out at the soap opera marathon. I need closure and happy thoughts in my bedtime fairy tales."

"All right." I run a hand along her spine, edging closer to her ass. "Once upon a time, a handsome bear shifter—"

"Grumpy bear shifter," she mumbles.

"You telling this story?"

"No." She sighs. "The handsome, grumpy bear shifter. Go on."

I do. Spinning a tale of a warrior princess and her loyal shifter servant, I tell her about us without mentioning us. I tell her what she meant to me, how I kept trying to prove myself to her, how they fell in love and promised to love each other forever. Like most fairy tales, I leave out what comes after the vows, but it doesn't matter.

Kiva's breathing evens out somewhere between the seventh proposal's acceptance and the wedding. By "the end," she snores softly. Switching off the light, I kiss her head and close my eyes, thinking I could live with this here and now for as long as she'll let me. The knot that's been my constant for years unravels; the tension from tonight's fear for her at The Rink unwinds. I hold her close as though I can shield her from her nightmare with my body, my love, and sheer bear stubbornness.

Only my mate matters.

I breathe in her scent, enjoy the weight of her soft curves against me, and drift to blissful dreams in the darkness with my wife in my arms.

A pounding on the door jolts me from sleep, and I spring to full alert, pushing Kiva off me and blocking her from whatever threat might be outside. Whoever would be stupid enough to surprise a bear shifter deserves the scare I plan to give them.

18

KIVA

T<small>HE MORNING SUN SHINES BRIGHT THROUGH</small> S<small>TONE'S HOTEL</small> window, streaming in rays with tiny specks of dust floating like glitter from last night's derby fashion. I woke a moment before him, watching him sleep—how peaceful he looked, how untroubled and at odds with his normal serious self—before someone banged on the door. In an instant, Stone went from dreaming about honey or whatever had put that boyish smile on his face to jumping upright and shoving me behind him.

Now, I can't see anything around the muscled wall of his broad shoulders.

"Stop it," a female voice comes from the hall. "What did I tell you about startling any of our kind?"

"Beryl," Stone mutters, rubbing a hand over his face. "If my sister's out there, guess I can't punch whatever idiot woke us."

Staring at his grumpy gruffness, I fight a smirk and drag the sheet over my bare legs. "Wow, you meant it when you said you don't like surprises."

He grunts and stalks across the room, glancing over his shoulder as if checking me from my messy ponytail to covered toes before opening the door.

"Thank goodness you're awake." Beryl pushes through the cracked door and rushes inside, Trick Peterson behind her. Her perfectly styled hair and makeup seem at odds with her yellow pajamas decorated with honeycombs, flying bees, and dotted-heart flight lines. "Oh." Her gaze locks on me, her rose-painted mouth rounding. "Um, we're interrupting."

"Yes, you are." Stone stares at Trick as though wondering what the man's doing with his sister or in his hotel room.

"It's good to see you, Kiva." Beryl doesn't seem bothered by her cranky brother. Or by me being in his bed wearing only his shirt.

I almost explain that the situation's not what it looks like, but I don't get the chance.

"I heard about what happened at the Rink," Trick blurts out. "I'm so glad you're safe." He hurries to sit on the foot of the bed, staring at me as if reassuring himself that I'm uninjured. What's with men examining me this morning?

Stone growls, yanking him up by his collar as if the music superstar was a naughty kitten.

"Wait." I hold up a hand, taking in Trick's bloodshot eyes, wrinkled clothes, and the dirty jacket he carries. The man's shirts and jeans usually appear pressed, starched, and ready for concert spotlights. Not this morning. He looks like he hasn't fallen asleep in days, a feeling that I completely understand after having gotten my first good night's sleep in years. "Put him down and let him explain."

Stone glances at me and drops Trick. "Stay off the bed. Start at the beginning."

"All right." The singer drawls the last word, straightening his shirt. "No murdering me, bear. I came looking for you, *and* I put in a good word for you with Kiva."

The questioning stare that Stone gives me seems to require an answer. "He did," I tell him.

Beryl butts in. "I found him downstairs in the lobby asking for the blacksmith."

"In your pajamas?" I ask her. "I mean they're fabulous, but—"

"Coffee," Stone says. "She can't function without caffeine in the morning."

"It isn't my fault they only stock the rooms with enough for two cups." His sister sounds annoyed. "The rest of us can't have whatever food or drink we want brought up to us. *Anyway*, I found Trick asking for the blacksmith, so can you let him say whatever he came here to tell you?"

My were-bear stares at the singer like he caused this mess. "Why'd you ask for me?"

"I figured you'd be my best shot at getting the message to Kiva and that you'd do whatever it takes to protect her."

"Protect me?" I sit up, fully alert, no need for java. "I'm a Fury. I can take care of myself."

Beryl puts a hand on Stone's shoulder, ignoring me. "Sit down." She looks to Trick. "Start at the beginning."

Stone joins me on the bed, his heavy arm settling around my shoulders. Normally, I would snap at such a possessive move, but he doesn't seem to be staking a claim. Worry radiates off him. I seriously need to talk to Dottie about the mate-mood-ring thing that goes off with maybe fifty percent accuracy. Until then, I'll try to fake patience with the room full of people who seem to know more about me and my past than I do. "Come on, Trick. Talk." Yeah, screw patience. Waiting sucks.

He runs his hand through his blond hair, messing it with a movement even more awkward and clunky than his norm. No wonder the man refuses to dance as part of his act. He lands in the chair with a heavy thud, tossing his jacket on the table next to my bargained-for-a-kiss dagger. "It's Marina. She doesn't make sense since we got to town. After I heard about what happened with the catwalk falling on the track, I went out looking for her because she never showed up at the House of Muses. *None* of this makes sense."

I don't know if he's trying to convince us or himself, but I want to yell at him to get to the part about where I supposedly need protection.

"Marina was invited to their party with you last night?" Beryl asks, prompting him to continue a whole lot nicer than I would've.

"Yeah." Trick sighs. "She insists on attending functions with me these days, doesn't like me going off on my own for very long. Saving my reputation, she tells me. After the episode in New Orleans—"

Stone interrupts him. "Whoa, that's a magic sanctuary run by the voodoo priestesses. What kind of connections do you have that allow you to play there?"

I smack my were-bear in the arm. "In case you guys haven't noticed, Syn City? Built on magic. Everyone in this room? Supernatural. Except Trick unless you haven't...you know what, doesn't matter and it's rude to ask. Get to why you think I need protection."

"Details *do* matter," Beryl says in a spa voice so soothing I wonder if she practices it. "I know you rush into stuff, but Stone preps every battle strategy for our den's alpha. He needs all the information, and trust me, you'd rather I ask than let him shake it out of our singer so close to a charity concert."

Trick jerks his head up. "Huh?"

She waves her hand at him. "Nothing. What do you remember about this New Orleans episode that made Marina an overbearing psycho?"

With that very pointed and loaded question, I think Stone's sister and I might become friends after all.

"I don't..." Trick spreads his fingers over his knees, the knuckles going white. "I don't remember what happened. I don't even remember being in New Orleans."

"Amnesia?" I ask.

Beryl shushes me. So much for future friendship.

Trick shakes his head. "Not amnesia. Pieces of my short-term memory sometime come through fuzzy. The stress of fame and the attack in New Orleans, according to the doctor Marina hired. Whatever the stalker fan did, I blocked it, but Marina's my manager and since then, she travels with me to supervise security, location, the event, everything."

"Sounds like she's your handler instead of your manager," Stone says.

Trick lifts a shoulder, and the gesture comes off so awkward that it looks painful. "Life got weird as a celebrity. She represents what's left of home for me—everything stable and familiar. Or she did."

"What changed?" Beryl asks.

Finally, we might get somewhere with this conversation.

He meets my gaze. "She started acting weird when we showed up here, reminding me about how I've been looking so long for the fated mate she foretold that I would meet, for the person destined to share forever with me. I'll admit, the idea of someone I'm meant for, who's meant for me? It hooked me from the start. Who wouldn't want to meet the exact right partner?"

Stone tightens his hold on me and interrupts him. "Sounds like career suicide for a man who makes his living writing heartache."

Looking away, Trick mumbles, "Doesn't mean I want to live that way. I see how you protect Kiva. I want to do that for someone. Hell, I wanted to do that for her."

A sound suspiciously like a growl rumbles through Stone, and I smack him in the gut. "Stop it. *You're* not helping, and *you*," I snap at Trick, "speed up to the part that made you come here this morning. We've got enough backstory and details." I inject a super-sized dose of scary-ass Fury into my tone, daring anyone to challenge me.

"All right." Trick lifts his hands in surrender. "I heard about what happened at the track. After asking a lot of questions, I figured that the part of the catwalk where Marina saw us talking —or somewhere close to there—coming crashing down toward you. No way that could've been a coincidence."

Stone cuts me a look so damned heavy with annoyance that I swear I can feel it in that internal tug-of-war we have going. "You failed to mention that Marina saw the two of you talking."

I hold up a finger. "We can discuss your mushy-wushy feelings later, *after* I freakin' finally hear some solid evidence of why Trick thinks I need protection. Which may never happen if you keep interrupting. Now, shut up or I'll show your big bear self some real surprises."

Trick eyes us as if deciding which one of us would be more dangerous if pissed off. I make sure everyone in the room can see I'm the biggest threat—no weapon to call necessary.

"Uh, so..." The singer clears his throat, clearing his momentary lapse into a squeaky voice climbing toward soprano. "I looked for Marina, but she didn't show for the party."

"No, she didn't," I say before anyone else can interrupt or he can pontificate on bullshit minutiae. "She came to The Rink, and we already know that part, but you found her where?" I twirl my hand in a *continue* motion.

"At the swamp's edge talking to the water," he says.

Now it's my turn to butt in. "Okaaay." I realize after I've opened my big mouth that I don't know what to make of his answer. "Do you mean she spoke to the water metaphorically like she talked through her problems beside the water?"

"No. I mean she talked *to* the water." He rushes on as if anticipating another interruption. "Even creepier? The water answered."

Dread tiptoes up my spine, an insidious and ghastly presence that steals my breath and makes my skin go clammy.

Beryl gasps and stares at her brother with wide eyes. "The sea witch," she whispers as though that means something big, something monumental, something I'm totally missing.

"What?" I demand. "What do you know that I don't?"

Stone's jaw goes harder than the anvil in his workshop, and he shuts down whatever connection we have so that I can't read his emotions. I glance at Beryl, who looks as though she wants to spill every thought she's ever had but can't. *Ugh*, these two and whatever spell has been put on my past.

When I glare at Trick, he pushes back in his chair. "I can only tell you what I saw."

Doubt threads through me as hard as a Gorgon's block in a derby bout. "How long after you left the House of Muses do you think the water talked back to Marina?" I ask. "And were any Mad Maes at this party? It wouldn't be the first time the maenads slipped a hallucinogenic into the booze."

He snorts. "I wasn't high, and I didn't say the water talked back. I said it *answered* her. You wanted me to tell you everything, so let me finish. Marina said that it was almost time, that her children had nearly come into their own. I didn't have a clue what she meant because she doesn't have kids, hasn't ever mentioned family. I would've felt sorry for her except she said she needed to push you to a breaking point to siphon enough pain from you to bring them to life." He stares at Stone. "She called Kiva by name."

"Holy Hades, what'd I ever do to Marina?" Because none of this makes sense. The woman claimed she wanted to be friends when we met. Sure, she has said some weird shit around me, but if what Trick says is true, she's magic-born and has prettied up her hatred of me with the pretense of helpfulness. "What else did you hear?"

"I don't think you did anything to her," Trick says with such sincerity that his conviction surprises me. "Or at least I can't imagine you hurting anyone."

Little does he know. "I'm a Fury. Dealing out hurt tends to be a specialty of ours when it comes to dishing out vengeance." I want to curse because I've stalled us yet again to getting the full story. Or as full as he might know it to be.

Trick quirks a brow and cocks his head as though he doesn't buy my explanation. "You said you hadn't met Marina before I threw the welcome party for the Houses. True?"

I nod, not wanting to delay whatever he's about to say but not wanting to hear it either.

He blows out a long breath like he's having second thoughts about sharing. "Look, this will sound nuts, but here's how it went down. Marina gave a damn near villain's monologue to the water about her master plan to siphon pain from you to bring back her children, and I confronted her."

"Nooo." Beryl puts her hand to her throat, and if she had pearls beneath those PJ's, I'd bet she would be clutching them. "What were you thinking engaging with a mad sea witch? She could've hurt you." The way she emphasizes the last and gawks at him makes me feel a little sorry for Trick being treated like eye candy by the mobs of women in town. "Are you okay?"

"I didn't know what she was—I still don't—and I'm fine." He doesn't sound fine. "I accused her of coming after Kiva, asked what she'd done at The Rink and if she'd had any part in the accident. She has magic, but I've no idea how much. Other than invoking standard pre-bought spells, she does some fortune telling and predicts future stuff for my career. But last night, she didn't deny anything I alleged. No, she said we both *need* Kiva's pain."

"Why?" I ask, knowing there's no legit reason he can give. Sinking into Stone's side to borrow comfort from him, I wonder what I could've ever done to someone in my past life that might've been so bad to make them want me to suffer. Had I been terrible enough that a Fury could've been sent to punish me for my sins? Was that how I'd died? Was this the secret that Stone and Beryl kept? Had I died for a crime I committed? My nightmare of blood, so much blood comes to mind. "What did I do to make her hate me?"

"I don't believe *you* did anything. Marina told me your mother slaughtered her whole family, that your mom's creation magic hinges on your pain." Trick's voice goes flat. "That with enough heartache, Marina could bring her children back and start a new family to replace the one your mom stole from her. I seriously thought she'd lost her mind, but then she called to her children." Fear edges the sorrow in his gaze. "The water? It came alive. Spikes of waves in shapes that could've passed for four, maybe five adult humans appeared on the surface." He pauses, searching our faces. "You don't believe me."

"Oh, I believe you." Stone's voice comes out hard, cold, and certain. I wouldn't want him using that tone on me. He doesn't elaborate, probably because whatever gods-damned spell hides my past from me won't let him. "Tell us exactly what you saw."

Trick looks defeated, as though he'd rather no one had believed him. "I mean I'd heard to stay away from the swamp. The Muses love to talk about gators and sea hags lurking beneath the surface waiting for some drunk dumbass to wander into the water. These beings? They didn't come out of the water; they *were* the water. Up they emerged, bits of leaves and sticks and every-thing else in them, swirling and churning like monsters moving toward land." He shudders. "I'm glad they're stuck out in the swamp, for now at least. Marina seemed to suggest they wouldn't be trapped there once they got enough of a charge from Kiva."

"Through my pain?" I'm stuck on the concept. How'd this happen? How did Marina find me? For month after long month, I waited for someone to come for me. Now, I have visitors, and I'd like one less.

Beryl pipes up, still centering on Trick as if he holds the secret to the world's happiness in his pretty-boy looks. "What does Marina's obsession have to do with you? Why would *you* ever want to cause Kiva pain?"

He slides his long legs out in front of him, his boots scuffing softly against the floor. "Yeah, I told her she was out of her mind if she thought I would help her hurt Kiva. Marina said that she found me, made me who I am, and could put me back to what I was. That I'm *her* creature now, whatever that's supposed to mean." He meets my gaze. "She told me I could never be your happily ever after, said that's not happening for you, ever. You need to watch yourself. I don't think she's out to end you. No." His voice goes from its mellow crooner smooth to quiet, jagged shards. "For you, she's planning something worse than death."

19

STONE

Minutes after kicking my sister and Trick out of my hotel room, Kiva quick-changes into a tank top and shorts. She heads for the door, bag slung over her shoulder.

My pulse pounds deafeningly loud in my ears, and my heart rabbits as if it could outpace her wings in flight. Worse, my bear rises under my skin, ready to burst forth and protect our mate whether she likes it or not. Getting between her and the door, I try my best to keep a calm, reasonable tone. "You can't leave." The boom in my voice shocks even me, echoing off the walls and coming close to a roar.

She gives me a look that says she'll go through me, but at least she doesn't summon her hatchet. Not yet anyway. "I understand this morning has been a lot and that you don't like surprises," she says, doing a much better job than I did at composure. "Regardless of your *big-caveman-protect-little-woman* feelings, I need to talk to Sadie and figure out how to break the spell on you. While I enjoyed pretending last night that history and future don't matter, my past holds answers about whatever Marina's current issue with me might be."

"But if Marina can attack you at The Rink, she can come at you anywhere. You're not safe out there."

"Agreed." Kiva taps a short fingernail with chipped black paint against my bare chest. Not a claw, but effective at snagging my attention. "Until I get my memories back, nowhere is safe—including here."

"*I'm* here. I won't let her hurt you." I won't let anyone hurt my mate ever again.

"Maybe that's how things work for shifters and their sweeties where you come from, but I take care of myself." She moves to sidestep me.

My size alone means I fill the doorway, so I simply shift my weight to block her. "I don't want to scare you—"

"You don't. Now move."

"I can't let you go out there alone."

"And how are you planning to make me stay?" She doesn't sound mad. No, that's mischief in her voice with a thread of desire.

All right, I'll play along. "Chain you to the bedpost?"

"No bedpost." She glances around the room, exaggerating the movement so that her hips sway and her ponytail swings. "And I don't see any chains."

"I'm a blacksmith. I'll improvise."

"Kinky."

I take a moment to think with my brain instead of my cock. Lust thickens her voice, and if I didn't know her as well as I know myself, I might think the innuendo came from nowhere with the threats and danger. But it doesn't. Beneath the swagger and flirtation, she's afraid. Not of me, but fear radiates off her all the same.

"You looking for an escape, love?" I step closer, crowding her. "Not from me or this room, but from your problems?"

The tiniest flare of purpose lights her gaze, as though daring me to cross whatever imaginary line stands between us. "If I said yes?"

"I could be that for you." Hell, yeah, sign me up as her distraction any day. "But it'd have to be your choice. No regrets later." Not that my impulsive mate ever bothered with guilt or shame except when it came to her past with her mother and whatever horrors they'd faced in hunting down the gods' spawned. Even then, she hadn't drowned in sorrows or problems. No, she'd simply blocked them from the conversation, from her present as if she could cut away the pieces of herself she didn't want to face. Now, her natural inclination to forget the past has been amplified to the millionth power. "Tell me what you want." My voice goes grizzly gruff.

She catches her bottom lip in her teeth, and a world of want and need collide in her gaze, but she shuts down the passion in a blink, the same as curling her twitching fingers into fists as though her restraint hangs by a tangled thread of past, present, and ugly possibilities for the future. "You can't tell me how to break whatever secrets-to-keep spell stands between me and my past." Her voice goes determined. "But can you show me?"

Technically, no. The immortal Fury who thought it'd be fun to toy with us by shoving this curse down my throat and stealing her memory? That eternal bitch wouldn't have left a loophole for something so simple as charades. How might I express true love to the extent of our mating bond, fulfilled so completely that we're two halves of the same whole? I have no idea. Except my bear roars from within me that a kiss would show her, and my body agrees with all-systems-go screaming intensity. My pulse spirals into the stratosphere, and heat surges through me.

Snagging the back of her neck, I haul her close and kiss her. Not a hesitating, careful kiss. No, this is a savage mark of claiming —one that would tell her she's *mine* and I'm *hers*. It's a bruising clash of lips, tongues, and teeth that's territorial and downright obsessive. Kissing her as if I can burn away the two years of separation, the torment of her death, the uncertainty of ever finding her again? I'm almost positive that hot, open-mouthed branding doesn't count as the sweet, tender courtship I promised last night. But she said show her how to break the spell, and I won't waste a chance to pour my immeasurable heartache and hope into the carnal connection between us.

"Wait." Kiva's one word shuts me down, splitting open the moment as raw and painful as a gunshot shattering the tenuous bond between us.

Dragging in one ragged breath after another, I hang my head, waiting for her judgment, for her to rush past me regardless of the dangers, just as she did the night I lost her. I slam closed every link associated with the mating bond, shoving my emotions down, down, down where she won't be touched by my despair and longing.

A *whoosh* fills the room as Kiva unfurls her wings—those beautiful, dangerous, haunting wings with silver blades that multiply her murder weapon by a hundredfold. Could she intend to use them to slice what's left of me to ribbons? Would I put up a fight if she did? No. Without her, I have no reason to live.

She wraps them close to me, so close I can feel the cold slide of metal against my skin. I don't pull away, don't flinch when the bite of a blade stings against my bicep. A pinch, the same as if she dug her fingernails into me. The sensation pulls me into the past when she left red marks on my back, my ass, running her nails along my neck and up into my scalp while out of her mind with orgasms and ecstasy.

We hadn't been a perfect couple with my need for slow deliberation and her fast impulsiveness, but we'd been pretty damn close, and sex had never been a problem for us. Regardless of any issues we'd had when she rejected my proposals or as we worked through the day-to-day petty problems of married life, the chemistry between us had been inferno levels of hot from the start.

Pulling my gaze to hers, I watch the hunger in her eyes, imagine the heat there burning for an entirely different reason than anger. I lick my lips to catch the lingering taste of her on my tongue. If she's going to kill me slowly, I might as well savor the sensations as long as I can.

She spreads those deadly wings and kicks off. How many have watched her do the same in the last couple of years before she brings the full vengeance and judgment of her kind with lethal coldness? Except she stops short of the super tall ceiling —a gods-send for me during this trip so I could stand and stretch without smacking my head every other minute—and wraps her legs around my ribs, bringing her heavy-lidded gaze level to mine and her mouth within strike distance for another kiss.

"Better." She curls those gorgeous full lips into a half smirk. "Now where were we?"

I don't need more of an invitation. Cupping her ass with one hand and her breast with another, I haul her close and kiss her as if it's the secret to unlocking the other half of my soul—because it just might be. I want to lose myself in her, to find myself there in the surrender whether she remembers *us* because I could imagine a future with this version of my mate, regardless of the past, if she'll simply let me claim her today and all of her tomorrows.

She sinks her teeth into my bottom lip, not hard enough to break the skin. "Now that I have your attention," she says, her mouth red and swollen from my kisses.

I touch my tongue to the tender spot she bit, torn between listening to whatever she has to say and pushing her to see if she'll nip me again. "Glad you don't have fangs."

"You wish," she drawls in a voice so sexy that I go for another kiss, and she lets me as though she hadn't pulled away in the first place. "Before we go further than kissing—"

"We don't have to." I don't want to rush her. Hell, I promised last night that I wouldn't. "I—"

"Stop talking." She puts a finger to my lips, and I suck the tip into my mouth just to mess with her because damnit, she's fun to provoke. Winding a wing between us, she points it at me. "Don't make me hurt you."

I release her finger with a pop. "Now who's talking kinky?"

"Be serious for a second. A kiss isn't going to break the spell. I mean, we've kissed before."

Wishing I could tell her that the right kind of kiss is exactly what would break the spell, I try and fail. Of course, that's not allowed under the curse, but I had to give it a shot. "You never know. It works in stories."

"Cleaned-up fairy tales. Not the real f'd-up versions." She glares at me as if she can see secrets beneath my skin. Who knows? Maybe she can.

"You said we could try to live for now. I can honestly say I know nothing about Marina. Never met the woman and never heard of her."

"But maybe I have," she says. "Or *past* me had."

"Or maybe you haven't, and what she told Trick is part of her head games."

"Answer two things for me before we go further."

"If I can."

"Fine." She whips her wings back, a snap that's somehow as frustrated as the little sigh she gives. "First, did I kill anyone in my past life? Because my nightmare seems to suggest I was a horrible person."

Settling for a non-answer will let me get around the moral dilemma she seems to be having. "Lots of people need killing. The world's not a nice place, not a safe one. But *you* could never be a horrible person." There, I used her words, as distasteful as they might be, in connection with her. "Next question?"

"Not that it matters, and I'm not asking about *this* life but for the last one, and no judgments or anything." Her ramble goes full nervous-nonstop mode. "I'm pretty sure you'd know, but maybe not, and I would like to be prepared if there's pain or whatever—I mean outside of derby or Fury stuff. Or what if

I'm awful at it, and that's not okay. Except the kissing came easy—"

"Love, do you want to ask your question, or should I settle us in to sit while you talk it out?" Either way, I'm good because she'll be here and safe.

"Do you know if I'm a virgin?"

Shock has me almost dropping her, and she lets out a squeak, tightening her thighs around me and stretching her wings. Grabbing her ass, I clutch her closer. A flush worse than any sunburn steals over my face. I cough, and it comes out somewhere between a snort and a chuckle.

"Why's that funny?" Her frustrated expression takes adorable cranky to another level, and I laugh.

Once I start, I can't stop. The full, deep chuckle rolls through me until tears come to my eyes. Oh, the many ways we tore up the sheets, the walls, the trees, the workshop, and everywhere else because we couldn't keep our hands off each other as newlyweds, and now she wants me to answer this? I can't. Some egotistical part of me takes satisfaction in the fact she hasn't fooled around anymore than I have since I lost her. But then the thought of losing her sobers me.

"Oh." Her annoyance slides into a crumpled expression of disappointment. "I'm bad at sex, aren't I?" She loosens her hold on me as though she'll slide to the floor, but I don't let go.

"No." My throat closes around the rest. Damn this curse. I don't need words to answer her. Not about either of her lives, not on this. Cutting off conversation with a kiss, I walk toward the bed, tasting her sweetness and not stopping until my shins bump the mattress. While I offered her escape, I'm the one drowning in her sexy whimpers and soft skin.

She tucks her wings, a move I'm learning to recognize comes before she vanishes them.

"Don't," I say, spinning to sink into a sit on the bed with her straddling me. "Leave them out."

A throaty laugh comes from her, one I want to hear again and again. "I'll bring them back." The wings disappear so fast that the movement sends a rush of cool air against my hot skin. "But they'd be a bitch to work around to make stripping sexy even with the customized clothes." She peels the thin black tank with those extra slits for the wings up, up, so slowly up to reveal a sliver of stomach and a red lace bra that barely covers her gorgeous breasts.

The flow of falling fabric brushes against me, and I curl my fingers into fists to keep from touching her. "You're perfect." My mate's built solid with generous curves that fill my hands, and I can't wait to stroke, to taste, to bury myself inside her. But I won't rush this, so I force myself to hold still and watch because she's putting on a show, and I don't want to miss a second.

She traces a hand from her throat to her chest, drawing a tempting path over the swell of each breast. "You like?"

"Love." My mouth goes dry, and my brain short-circuits.

"Want to touch?"

"Yeah." My voice has gone to a painful scratch of hoarse whispers that have nothing to do with the curse.

Continuing that lazy pull of her fingers from lush curve to shadowed dip and the shiny satin below the lace, she crooks her mouth into a knowing smirk. "How badly do you wish you could have your hands on me?"

"Depends. How much do you want to keep that bra in one piece?"

"I don't see any blades around," she taunts, bringing her lips so close to mine that I can feel the warmth of her breath. "The weapons trunk's closed, so I guess you're out of luck."

That's it. I can't take another second. The beast inside me screams *don't scare our mate*, but he'll understand the chase, the need to prove ourselves to her. I uncurl my fists and breathe through the partial shift, the advantage of those with alpha blood

—even those of us who don't want the title. Flashing sharp claws, I give her a grin as evil as hers. "Problem solved."

"Well, damn. You put those away this time, okay?"

This time. Which means she plans on a next time. I fully intended to touch her with nothing but the gentlest caress, but the way she phrased the question, she's throwing down a challenge. "Or?" I ask, needing to know the rest of the unspoken dare. "Because those little straps holding your bra up look like they're working overtime."

"Or I don't bring out my wings."

The threat works. I flex my hands, and the claws disappear. "Done."

She hums an approval that shoots straight to my cock. "I guess you deserve a reward." She's driving me insane, and from the teasing look in her eyes, she knows it. A quick reach of her hands, and the bra falls away to reveal dark peaks, heavy curves, and luscious skin that I've seen a thousand times before and a million times not enough.

"Tell me I can touch." I don't beg, but it's a near miss.

Unfurling her wings, she winds her arms around my neck, and I swear I'll give her anything just to sit here in my lap with her tits pressing into me and her sweet body grinding on my erection for the rest of time if that's what she wants. Blue balls be damned.

Nipping my earlobe, she whispers, "I think we've proven *show* works better than *tell* for us, so why don't you show me what you'll do if I say yes."

"I thought you'd never ask." I yank her to me. "Tap out if I go too far."

20

KIVA

WHAT HAVE I UNLEASHED IN MY WERE-BEAR?

Stone stares at me like he's a great big predator, which—*duh*—he is, but I didn't imagine he'd look at me as though I might be the weak, little prey. I'm not petite. Hell, I'm the opposite of short, waifish, and pixie-like. Stacked, muscled, and tough with the wings to match and a weapon to call, I'm a scary badass, but he doesn't seem at all afraid. No, he looks turned-on and outrageously sexy.

My heart kicks into a thumping drive I know he can hear, and everything in me tightens in a hot rush better than any Mad Maes drug trip. He kisses me as though he can devour me, licking into my mouth in a tangling of tongues punctuated by quick nips of teeth.

The man's huge, and it makes me wonder how big he might be all over, but before I can reach down to those loose sweatpants in size giant to find out, he's stealing my thoughts with teasing that overwhelms my senses. I struggle to concentrate on one thing, just one simple sweep of his fingers or suck of his mouth, but he touches me as though he knows every play in my body's handbook and executes them in complicated combos as a joint assault on my sanity.

Why does everything sound louder in the quiet? My harsh breathing, his groan into my mouth, the rustle of my wings, the slide of my knees on the crisp cotton sheets when he pushes me off his erection right as the friction had become so sensitive. I fight a whimper, not wanting to admit I've become the prey in this scenario, but I craved that pressure. The emptiness, the hollowness of missing something I've never even known washes over me like the swamp swelling to drag me down.

"Up." He wrangles me into a standing position with his hold on my hips despite the fact my legs shake so badly I can't remain on my feet.

Thank the gods for wings. Two harsh beats, and I float a few inches off the floor. Slowing my breathing, I need to take a moment, to take control of the situation, to take over this game because that's what it is, right? A power struggle, no different from roller derby's head trips with only one opponent to check and conquer, except a loud part of my brain laughs that this is *nothing* like that.

He flicks his thumb over the button on my shorts, loosening them with a pop in what seems to be a practiced, deliberate movement. Oh, so it's a strip he's after? After teasing him with the peel of my shirt and bra, he's ready for more? I'm down for that. Naked time for both of us sounds great. I grab for the zipper, but he swats my hand away.

"No, let me," he says.

I want to argue, yet there's a heat in his eyes that tells me he's not unaffected by this. He might be tormenting me for earlier, but he tortures himself at the same time. *Fine.* I can outlast whatever mind game he's playing. Except his slow, oh-so-slow drag of my zipper pushes my patience to its limits. How could a couple of inches take this freakin' long?

He eases the shorts over and off my hips as though he has the whole day to undress me. His gaze locks on my panties, and I want to hit him with a yeah-I-win grin. Yeah, that's how real women take back the power—with sexy, showstopping undies that no one can resist staring at because I'm worth it.

My curve-a-licious booty can't be limited to teeny thongs. This ass comes from years of skating long, hard strokes around the track, lets me drop into a one-legged squat to bypass blockers while flying a middle finger, and should have its own derby nickname given how much hip checking I do. That's why I treat myself to lacy red naughtiness that hugs every round, swirls up to my stomach, and plunges in a deep *V* in the front as if pointing to the best bits like a "you wish you could peek" arrow.

I hook my thumbs in the waist, dipping the lace even lower. "I'm sorry." I'm not at all sorry. "Did something interrupt your whole game plan there?"

"Nope." His voice bottoms into a dirty roughness that makes me want to brush against him to see if the filthiness rubs off. "Why would I rush unwrapping you?"

"Like candy?" Because while the man devours honey taffy with a happiness to rival my love of sour gummies, I don't fully get his reference to wrap.

"The sweetest kind." His gaze pins to the whirls of lace between my thighs, and I shiver, goose bumps having nothing to do with cold spreading along my arms.

Time to speed this along before he rakes in so many points that I lose track of the score. Ignoring my nerves, the uncertainty zipping around in my brain on how this will play out, I say, "My turn to unwrap you."

On a mission, I trail a hand down to cup his hard cock beneath the soft fabric of his sweatpants, stretching my fingers to run along his length, and gods, what a length. He shifts his hips beneath my touch, sucking in a quick breath when I squeeze. Surprise, intrigue, and wicked curiosity flare through me. I don't know how we'll fit, but I'm ready to figure it out.

The asshole pulls my hand away from my prize. "Still my turn."

"Says who?" I try to sound pissed, but the question comes out more petulant *give me what I want.*

"Says me." He moves so fast I don't see it coming, don't block, don't counter. No, he lets go of my wrist and pushes his hand between my thighs to stroke the lace above my sex, and my heart flips faster than any of the aerial acrobatics I do pre-show at The Rink, tumbling over and over, a fluttering pulse than matches the throb beneath his touch. Oh gods, can he hear my pounding heartbeat? Can he feel how much I want him?

My skin heats, the flush burning away the earlier shivers. He's a shifter. He can scent my arousal. There's no hiding from him, and it's not embarrassing. No, it's hotter than the flames in the deepest pits of the Underworld. I push my wings to lift me higher, not risking a stumble that might cost me a second of him touching me, and yeah, I'll confess, rocking against his hand to find the friction he deprived me of earlier.

"More," I demand.

"I plan on it." He nudges my panties aside and works me with two blunt fingers. "Soaked for me?"

I give a half-assed yes that comes out breathy and needy. If this is losing at whatever power play we have going between us, I don't want to win. "Feels so good." I sound drunk on him.

He pushes a finger inside me. "I can do better."

"I don't know if I can take better." I'm coming apart at some inner seams that I didn't realize existed, and he's the only thread stitching me to the here and now.

"You can," he says in that devastating voice of sinful promises.

Cool air hits my skin when he strips my panties off, and I open my mouth to protest, except the man hauls me up so that my legs wrap around his shoulders.

My wings snap out in shock. "Uh, I d-don't," I stammer.

He buries his face between my thighs, and whatever I meant

to say comes out in a long moan. Screwing me with his tongue, his fingers, his uplifted gaze, the man takes whatever lingering control I had and shatters it. His intense devotion, his fierce reverence, Stone worships me like I'm one of the immortal goddesses. My wings beat in a frantic rhythm to match my heart.

My body clenches as though I'm a knot, twisted and tangled around my bear shifter from the burn in my lower belly to the hardening of my nipples that ache for me to pinch. Every part of me feels and wants and *needs* him. Pride has no place in the infinitesimal space between us, and I ride him until I shake and shiver and splinter into a thousand pieces. In my climax, I almost forget to keep myself in flight, a rookie mistake I haven't made since becoming full Fury. But Stone doesn't stop, supporting my weight and driving me higher and higher in my orgasm until I'm spent, every emotion wrung from me.

I go limp as he pulls me onto the bed, gathering me to him as if he knows I need a second, a minute, an hour to come back to myself, to some semblance of normal if there can ever be a *normal* again. He props against the headboard, sitting where he did when Trick was here. Then, Stone held me in solidarity, in comfort. This is nothing like that.

Now, he lounges like he's sated on his favorite vice with me sprawled in his lap, idly rubbing the back of my neck in slow circles with one hand. The other, oh gods, the other—he licks his fingers clean as if savoring the taste of *me*. The sight almost makes me come again. He grins like he knows exactly what he does to me.

Two can play at torment. Moving down his body, I stroke my hand along his erection, earning a groan from him.

His eyes half-close, and the hunger there steals my breath. "I'm good, love," he says. "We don't have to—"

"My turn." I curl a wing until the blades brush against his cheek, a threat without bite, but he doesn't know that. "Get naked, bear."

Miracle of miracles, the man follows instructions, moving so fast he almost gets twisted in his pants. I would laugh, but catching sight of his erection, I swallow. Hard. No pun intended. I had briefly planned seduction, domination, conquering. My boldness stumbles, a deafening *clack-clack* rattling in my chest like the roughest hits in a derby bout. But there's no going back now. Not unless I want to admit I have no idea what the hell I'm doing.

Faking a cool calm that I definitely don't feel, I wait until Stone props against the headboard again, the same position, but this time, he's deliciously naked and all mine for the taking. But what to take first? I should've asked for those chains he teased about to tie his giant bear self to the bed. Too late this time, but maybe in the future. Shaking off my spinning thoughts, I crawl up his big body, taking pleasure in the way he stares at me—as though I can grant him the greatest passion with the least effort or destroy him with a look.

My mouth waters at the temptation of returning the favor of what he did to me with his mouth without the acrobatics. Only I'm not sure how when he's so big. No way can I take all of him. I'll approach this the same way I do a new weapon, experiment with the safety on until I get the hang of the handling. Licking, touching, stroking, sucking—I try different techniques, delighting in every groan and growl.

Here, surrounded by him, I can savor the scents of him, wallow in being wrapped in the sensations. Taking him until he bumps the back of my throat still leaves a lot of Stone to manage, so I curl my fingers around him, twisting my fingers slowly one way, then the other. Each time, I pause, listening for the quick inhales, watching for the tensing of muscles. Oh yeah, he *loves* what I'm doing.

Settling in, I reach down my body to touch myself, planning to stay here as long as it takes to unlock both our pleasure. I'm lost in the slide and slip and slickness of us.

"Enough." Stone yanks me up his body to straddle his lap.

"What?" I wriggle against his erection. "Didn't like that?" He's huge beneath me, and I know the obvious truth. Still, teasing Stone is so much fun.

He rumbles a full shifter growl that rolls through me, getting beneath my skin as if I can feel the desperation of the sound. Except he has shut down whatever emotional mating bond we share. *Fine.* I can push him into losing his precious control.

"Something you want?" I ask in a *who-me* voice while rubbing his cock through my folds again and again. Enough to taunt, to tantalize, to torture, because what's the fun of making this easy for him? Only I didn't count on how much the same teasing would drive me to crave *more*.

"Same thing you want." He wraps an arm around my waist, careful to avoid my wings.

He's right. Of course, he is. For once, I don't want to argue, don't care if I win or not in our power play. I just *need*.

"You're in charge, love." His deep voice sounds no less sexy in an almost whisper between kisses. Sweet, tender ones. Hot, sloppy, open-mouthed ones. Kisses on my lips, my breasts. It isn't enough. I still feel empty.

A soft whimper escapes me.

"It's your turn," he says as if answering a question that I didn't ask aloud. "Take what you need."

Lowering onto him, I drown in sensation—the ache, the pleasure, the pain, the stretch, the feel that he splits me in two and I don't ever want to be whole again, not without him. Another inch, and I gasp.

I can do this.

I can't do this.

I can't *undo* this.

He will own me as no one ever has. He'll be the face I search for at Family Festivals. He'll be the one I wish had come for me all those nights I've wandered alone in my nightmare. He'll be my new *everything*.

I study his face, the flicker of expression from desire to destroyed to determined. What would I do to become *his every-thing*? Can I risk what it might cost? Will I survive not marking him as mine?

The possessiveness, the territorialism spirals through me as I move, taking him deep within me and releasing him only to sink down once more. I climb to the shaking, spasming heights closer and closer to orgasm, but it's just out of reach.

"Almost," I mutter. *Almost, almost, almost.* My inner chant taunts me. Yet, I can't get there, and hot tears prick my eyes.

"Let me." Stone makes the solution sound so simple, so *this* plus *that* equals incredible uncertainty made certain. He grips my hips, his hands—so strong, so big—make me feel powerful and fragile, commanding and vulnerable at the same time.

"Yes." I'm not sure what I'm agreeing to, but I'll give anything to crest out of this limbo, this stuck place between yearning and satiated.

He lifts and lowers me, driving up into me, setting the pace from the bottom while I stretch my wings, taking up space, allowing myself to fill the room the way he fills me. I can't think, can't move, can't do anything but meet his dark gaze. I'm lost in the scents, the sounds, the sum of us in what feels like a rush to ecstasy that might tear me apart and put me back together. Those contradictory climaxes hover so close, just over the next wave of pleasure. But I can't get there. Not without knowing how he feels, but he has locked himself away.

Pressing my hand over Stone's heart, I spread my fingers. "Put it back." My order comes out breathy. "The emotions, the mood ring, the whatever lets me feel what's inside you."

He hesitates, still inside me, under me, all around me. "You don't know what you're asking for."

I lean closer to him, moaning when the angle takes him

deeper, presses against my clit. I'm close. *So close.* My wings push me forward, and the ache intensifies. "Don't tell me what I can and can't ask for. Those emotions. This bond. You offered it to me. It's mine. So give it back."

"All right. But remember, I warned you." He doesn't look away from me, and an avalanche of emotion crashes into me, making the world spin sideways. Colors explode in my vision. Warm amber, the color of his favorite honey taffy, radiates from him, wrapping around and suffocating me.

I gasp for air, and Stone tightens his grip on me.

What have I done?

21

STONE

I SHOULD'VE KEPT SOME OF THE SHIELDS IN PLACE, BUT NO, LIKE A big dummy, I let passion steal my common sense. Kiva demanded that I stop blocking the mating bond from my end, the call to her that lets her feel what I feel, that tempts her to say yes and accept me as her forever fated mate. I'd only wanted to keep my feelings from complicating her own, and now, I've unleashed the full force of my love on her and almost killed her.

"Kiva, love, you okay?"

She gasps for air as if she can't catch a breath, and the way she swayed a second ago? I thought she'd topple over. Even her wings had gone still.

"I'm not sure." Her whisper sounds hoarse, distant, confused.

My blood pressure skyrockets, nudging my breath faster and faster. What have I done?

"I didn't expect that." She sounds more like herself this time, but I'm scared to know what she's talking about.

I pull her close, wanting to lock the emotions up tighter this time but not wanting to start a fight either. My mate doesn't like being told she might've been wrong, and she certainly can't stand for me to go back on a promise. I'd been protecting her, but I'd also denied her the basic connection of mates.

She studies me, and I fight the need to hide from her gaze that looks as if she can pull me apart and inspect each sliver left of me. "Don't stop." Her voice takes on a dreamy quality, and I stroke her face, hoping to catch a hint of what she's thinking.

"Stop the feelings or the—" I cut off before the curse. Fucking sounds too coarse, too vulgar for what we were doing.

"Neither." Taking the choice from me, she rides my cock, slowly at first and then picking up the pace to a frantic beat that only she can hear.

I want to slow her, to check in with her, to take care of her, but her desire devours me, pulling me along in her wake. The slap of skin, the erotic sounds she makes—they urge my painful need toward martyrdom. For her, I'll do anything, give anything, become anything.

She comes with a scream loud enough to wake the entire hallway, and I pound up into her, wanting to give her more before I can't, before I lose myself in her all over again.

Cupping my jaw with a touch so gentle that I marvel at her tenderness, she smiles the softest curving of her lips. "Your pleasure? That's mine too," she says. "Let go."

I do. As if my body responds to her command, I orgasm, crashing so high only to plummet back to reality too tired, too drained to move. Gods, two long years without her. I'd kept the memories of our lovemaking locked away in a place tightly guarded enough that no one could ever reach it, but nothing compared to the reality of Kiva.

She grins, a sleepy, smug curl of her lips with a satisfied gaze. With her hands cradling my face, she kisses me, a soft brush of her mouth once, twice, and then once more as if she has decided something and needs to test the thought. Jolting away, she sits upright, her wings snapping to full width. Her wide eyes and tense body have me half-expecting her hatchet to appear from whatever magical pocket where it resides.

"What?" I check between her wings, searching for the threat. The door's still closed and locked. My shifter senses don't hit on any unusual scents except sex, no out-of-ordinary sounds except Kiva's racing heartbeat.

"Stone?" She says my name as if she's seeing me for the first time, as if her world didn't just come undone as mine did.

My stomach sinks, my vision narrows to her, and time seems to slow. "Yeah?"

"I remember."

With those two words, she makes me hope harder than I ever have before, but I need to be sure. "You remember which part?"

Her eyes shine with unshed tears. "Everything."

Happiness floods me. *She remembers.* Which means true love's kiss. She's *my* Kiva again. I kiss her, touching her face, her hair while hugging her so tight that the blades of her wings slice my skin, and I don't care about the stinging pain. Not when I have my mate back.

"Gods, I missed you. I love you." I can't say the words fast enough. "I'm so sorry I failed you. I couldn't believe that I lost you. I would've searched forever for you." I don't stop talking, making promises that I should've made back then, telling her the truths I'd left unspoken between us because I'd thought I would have decades to say them.

"What took you so long?" A hiccup of a laugh or a sob breaks her voice. I'm not sure which it might've been, and I don't wait to find out. I won't hesitate to tell her whatever she wants to know, not again, never again.

"The immortal took your memory, wouldn't tell me what she'd done or where you'd gone. We searched everywhere we could to find you. How could we have guessed the House of Furies skater they called Killa on the derby team might be you? I worried she'd taken you to another dimension, to a place where I couldn't follow. I never stopped looking for you, not for a day—"

She silences me again with her mouth, the kiss raw and full of the fantasies I'd had since she'd died. I wait for the mating bond to connect, to finish, to fill me with colors and light and completeness. But it doesn't. The void there remains. Perhaps it'll take time. Maybe the second life means a different link.

She draws away. A single tear spills, trailing down her cheek. *No, no, no.* I don't want to see her sad or scared or uncertain. Catching her tear with my thumb, the heat scalds my skin. My breath catches, my chest burns hotter than a stoked forge, and I want to fight whatever's coming. Only there's no one else here but Kiva.

"I can't," she says. "*We* can't."

"What? No." Despair chases away the joy that'd been here between us only a second ago. "Don't say that." My muscles tense, needing to shift, to rage, to roar. But I can't. Because Kiva isn't the enemy.

She pushes off me, pushes me out of her, pushes an invisible wall between the two of us more substantial than her wings as she turns away from me. With hurried, shaking movements, she yanks on her tank top and shorts, not bothering with the lace bra and panties on the floor.

I catch her wrist. "Wait."

"I can't go back to our life, not again."

Of course, she can't. She's a Fury. I haven't asked her to. I *won't* ask her to. "I know."

"Do you?" She doesn't sound angry. No, she sounds sad. As if she found the best and the worst in her memories, in our kiss, in discovering our past together.

"Talk to me."

She licks her lips as though her mouth has gone dry, as though all the air has been sucked out of the room for her too. "Your life has always been your pack, your den, your home. You worked your ass off to become the second in rank, to be every-thing your alpha needed. Your place will always be there, and my place is here now."

"I thought you were happy." Except I remember those days of sorrow haunting her gaze, of her staring out at the mountains as though wishing she could be somewhere else. Beryl's pitying words about Kiva treating me as the center of her world in her past life, about how my mate might not be content to simply to be the *little wife* anymore—they stab at me like verbal daggers. "I thought *we* were happy."

"I was, but I've lived my whole life in someone else's shadow —my mothers, yours. Now I serve an immortal. I can't go back to what we had."

"We had a marriage, a true mating bond. Who wouldn't want that?" I've mourned the loss of it for two long years, and now that I've found her, I won't let her go. My grip on her wrist tightens, my bear seizing on our mate. She's *ours*. We can't lose her again. We'll do anything.

She jerks out of my hold. "I have to go. I need time to think."

"About what? About us?"

"Don't." She holds out a hand, the warning clear that she doesn't want me coming any closer, doesn't want *me*.

"You can't just take off." I stare, disbelieving as she stalks toward the door. "Don't you love me?" I don't bother hiding my hurt. "We're mates, fated to be together for our entire lives."

She stops but doesn't look back. "I died. Remember? Because now I do. My life—that life? It ended. We aren't mates, not anymore." She walks out as if she hasn't destroyed me.

My head spins, my world tipped off its axis. In the last five minutes, I got everything I'd ever wanted back and then lost it all over again. How could I convince her that I hadn't stopped loving her, that I would give her anything she wanted to say yes one last time. *That was it.* I hadn't asked her. I'd simply let her panic and run away as she always did. This was Kiva, how she operated. It had nothing to do with this life or her past live. It was *her* in all her lives. I'd been drowning in my own problems to the point I hadn't remembered her issues.

Jumping off the bed, I run for the door. I need to tell her to take her time. We've been apart for two years. A few more minutes, days, weeks? We can overcome that. Except she's gone. In the hall, I find nothing more than an open window with sheer drapes that float outward as if she flew out only seconds before. The rush of incoming footsteps has me hoping she's coming back.

Except Beryl rounds the corner. "Shit, bro." She covers her eyes, spinning away. "Cover your junk."

I don't need to look down. The cool air against my naked skin reminds me of my nudity. Not that I'm all that embarrassed. "Like you haven't seen it before after we hunt with the den."

"Did you shift into a Kodiak here?" She lowers her voice, hissing at me in a judgmental stage whisper. Like me becoming a bear in a hotel might be the worst possible scenario.

Going into the room, I grab a sheet and wait for Beryl to follow me inside. "Kiva remembered," I tell her.

"Oh my gods, that's amazing." The happy exclamation in my sister's voice topped off by the glow in her face? It mirrors one of my many emotions in response to Kiva's cursed amnesia being cured. "How?" Beryl wrinkles her nose in an audible sniff. "Don't answer that. I figured it out myself from that scent," she mutters. "But where is she?"

"Gone." My voice grates on the word.

"She ran away? How very Kiva." She shakes her head, holding up a finger so fast that her honeybee charm glinting golden in the light looks as though it has come to life. "What'd she say?"

"That we couldn't be together since her life's here and she thinks mine is back with the den and our alpha. Said she needed some space."

"I'll handle our alpha." She touches the bracelet, rubbing her thumb over the charm while she says it, and I suddenly wonder who gave her that jewelry. Had the alpha? I'd been too far gone in grief to ask when she'd started wearing it. Not that she gives me time to ask now. "Any idea where Kiva would've gone?"

"The House of Furies," I guess, not knowing anywhere else she might stalk off to. "I'll get dressed and go check on her. With Marina after her, she's not safe out there."

"No, *I'll* go ask about her. You don't want her turning you down twice in one day, do you? Besides, as long as she makes it back to the Furies, she'll be safe with her sisters."

"I could go with you. I know where their House is."

"You mean their secret lair that they forbid anyone to enter? I don't think showing up on her doorstep would be our smartest play here. Let me work my connections and see if she'll meet up with me. Hundreds of kids just came off the ferry for bus tours and stuff related to the charity concert. I'll start there and invent a legit business reason to see her."

"About the business..." I don't finish the sentence because I'm not sure how. My sister, Kiva, and I built this business from nothing, and I don't want to abandon it, but I can't leave my mate either.

"We can make it work." Beryl sounds so certain. "Once you're released from your obligations with the alpha, we'll transfer production here. The Syndicate offered to rent us a plot away from the pleasure district's main businesses to establish a training academy if we're interested. We could find some people to run it here with you."

"But you can't stay?"

"Someone has to keep our alpha and our parents in line."

I knew better, but life across the country from my sister makes me sad. She's been no more than a mile away for our entire lives. But her voice doesn't invite an argument, and I've already had one woman take off on me today. "You sure you don't want my help tracking down Kiva?"

Beryl gives a little snort. "*Help* is not what you would be when it comes to your mate wanting space from you."

"I can't sit here in the room waiting. I'll go out of my mind."

"Then go check out the land east of the casino to see if we could turn it into a training academy and secure the forge. The last thing we need would be some punk kids getting hurt because they wanted to play war with your creations."

The horror of the last has me moving to get dressed. "Let me know if you need anything."

"I'll find your bride. Just be prepared to grovel or make her a new, shiny weapon to get another chance."

"Whatever it takes." I'm ready to give anything for my wife to say yes again, but first, I'll need Kiva to stop running long enough to give me another chance.

22

KIVA

Since I woke in Syn City as a Fury, I thought curing my amnesia would solve all my troubles. I hadn't counted on my memories bringing new problems.

Flinging another throwing knife into the practice dummy with a reassuring thwack, I want to scream my frustration. Marina might as well come for me. At least I'll have a legit target to destroy whether or not she's the sea witch my mother tracked to the ends of civilization to avenge the murders of my dad and big sister. I take aim again, but the door to the training room crashes open.

"I'm here," Dottie calls, huge wings worthy of the biggest butterfly ever fluttering behind her. Looking at her, anyone would assume she has spent years zipping through the skies instead of crashing into trees, people, furniture, and anything else in her path only weeks ago. "Reporting for sister duty."

"Thank the gods." Sadie jumps off the weapons bench and stalks toward the door like it's the only way out of a raging inferno. "I can't handle the shifter-mating bullshit. You deal with her. Yell if you need backup for anything other than shifter drama, preferably something violent." She spreads her wings and jumps off the landing, not wasting time with stairs.

I point the next knife's handle toward her, giving Dottie an out. "I'm not great company right now." Triad sisters can be awesome in a fight but having them butt into every personal matter? Not as cool.

"Quit trying to get me to leave." She tucks away her enormous wings in a blink. "Sadie told me about Marina coming after you. No way we're leaving you alone."

"Let the witch come." I toss two more knives, almost severing the practice dummy's head. "She wants pain? I'll give her plenty. Besides, you should be shacking up with your mountain lion."

"Nice try. You're stuck with me." She shuts the door without anyone following her in, surprising me.

"Where's your mini-me?" I ask, hoping Connie the teenaged terror hasn't come to witness my meltdown while also wishing she might be here to take the pressure off me. A training session with her might take my mind off Stone.

"Helping coordinate the invasion of the screaming teenaged girls and roaming packs of kids who arrive today. She volunteered to staff one of the registration booths at The Rink."

"We should go check on her." I wrench the blades out of the dummy, having to wiggle one that has managed to stick in the rubber base. Damn, guess I'm even madder than I thought. "I could use a skate. Or a fight. Maybe some Huntresses will want to scrap. Punching one of those know-it-all's might make me feel better."

"The last time you were at The Rink, the ceiling came down on you, so nope, we're going to stay here and talk."

"Ugh, I don't want to talk. Even my shrink hasn't made me yet."

"That's because Dr. Bomani's out of town to lend trauma support. The shifter community fifty miles north of here had another murder."

I freeze, my heart stuttering over a beat. I hadn't known. The way she says *another*. "The same murderer as suspected in the other shifter killings?" The mutilated corpses, the savagery has me cold in an instant. "Like whoever killed Rylie? The shifter kid from Stone's den. She was only fifteen years old, just a heart-broken teen who'd gone through her first crush." Having my memories back means I have the good, the bad, and the truly awful. "She was Connie's age and killed for sport. Tell me her murderer isn't close." Or better yet, that they are so I can destroy them.

Dottie pales under that eternal sun-kissed tan of hers. "Chase thinks so. He stayed with Connie as extra protection. She's not a shifter, but he can't shake the feeling that whatever's happening with those murders might be coming here. He said the wolves are ready to send a marshal to Syn City."

"They won't be allowed here. No law enforcement is—human or supernatural." None but the Furies could bring down vengeance for murder in our territory.

"True, but shifters have their own rules, which I'm assuming you know now that you have your memories back."

"I see what you did there, turning the convo back to my problems." I would be impressed except she corners me in a way Sadie didn't bother. "Yeah, looks like you and I both have a shifter mate. Well, I *had* one." Putting Stone and I in the past and not the future physically hurts.

"That why you're hiding in the training room and scaring everyone away with your terrifying blade skills?"

"We're Furies. I'd hoped for a decent fight to take the edge off."

"That's not *why* we fight."

Great, now she makes me feel two inches tall. I know the immortals gave us a higher purpose for our rage, but I'm just so freaking sad. Everything hurts, and I need it to stop if only for a few seconds. "I know."

"But it could be an excuse for training." She picks up a dueling rod, designed to mimic the weight and length of a sword without the slashes and gouges. The things can leave nasty bruises. "You game?"

I catch the rod she tosses at me and give her a cocky salute with it. "I'll go easy on you."

"Awesome. I score a hit, and you answer a question."

"And if I score a hit? What do I win?"

"You still have to answer." She sinks into a lunge, stretching out the words in her slow Southern drawl. "But you can choose which question gets tackled first."

"This doesn't sound at all fair."

"Life isn't." With a Fury-fast move, she smacks my arm hard with her wooden dowel.

I resist the urge to rub away the sting. "Hey, we hadn't started yet."

"I had. Keep up." She doesn't withdraw, simply stays on guard with the skills I taught her. "First question, if you have your memories back, why are you here and not getting busy with your bear boyfriend?"

"Husband." The truth slips out before I think through the consequences of admitting it. I've barely accepted our forgotten marriage myself. "Or at least we were married in my last life. I don't know if it still counts or not since shifters have weird laws about mated pairs. Plus, Stone gave me a wedding because the silly tradition seemed important to humans."

Dottie's eyes widen as if surprised I had been married or perhaps about a shifter marriage. "Okay, still doesn't answer the question about why you spent the last hour skewering Bob the fight dummy and not enjoying a happy reunion with your man. Don't tell me you didn't spend last night in his bed. Judging by your swollen lips and the whisker burn all over your neck, either you had some fantastic sex, or you had an unfortunate run-in with some branches on your flight home."

"It's complicated." I take a swing and hit the stick in her hand with a loud crack.

"Shifter stuff doesn't have to be. The human side messes things up."

Not stopping my attack, I work to control my breathing so I don't sound like a wheezing walrus. "He worked his whole life to become second to his alpha. Getting the promotion? It was the happiest I've ever seen him. Everything else sort of fell in line around his role in the den."

"All right, I get his work's important to him, but nothing outranks a mating bond."

Except it did. Our year of marriage? He spent most of those days either in his workshop or defending the den. I'd understood it—hell, I'd encouraged it—because my whole life had been a crusade to stop the bigger monsters before they found someone's home. "I can't ask him to give up his role in the den, his work, his business, his family."

"That's not your decision, and you thinking it might be is utter bull crap." Ah, the sweetness of Dottie not wanting to curse but not knowing she sounded more profane with her cute creativeness.

I giggle at the ridiculousness of a grown woman saying *crap* like it's a three-syllable, five-dollar curse word. The wench takes advantage of my distraction and jabs me in the ribs. "Ow. That'll leave a shiner for days."

"Next question." She doesn't sound the least bit sorry. "What's the real reason you're mucking up this mating bond? You're fated. I fought it like an idiot and have kicked myself for wasting time. You *know* how good a mated pair can be so what are you afraid of?"

I don't want to answer. Voicing my fear makes it even more real. I advance on her, but she uses my own moves that I drilled her to master against me, blocking my hurried assault. My arms shake from holding her off, but she narrows her eyes. I rush through the confession. "He wants who I used to be, not who I am now. Even if he says he won't resent me for changing, he will. Someday, we'll wake up and he'll want *her* back." I break the hold, dropping the weapon and backing away so I don't have to hear her throw my dread back at me.

"Did you ask him?" She says it like the reality's so simple instead of being wrapped up in death, amnesia, and messy love.

"No." I huff the answer with a sneer because I can't admit to her that, through the mating link, I stepped inside Stone's truth as surely as living it myself—his steadfast love, his strength, his struggles. I hadn't expected a single kiss after I'd stopped lying to myself about loving him to both complicate and uncomplicate us on so many levels.

Dottie stares at me, lowering her weapon. "I never thought I'd say this, but you're a fool, Kiva. You know more about skating, fighting, and being a good sister than anyone I've ever known. But if you believe you're not worth your mate's love in your last life *and* this one, then you're not the baddie I believed you to be."

Anger sizzles through me, boiling in my chest, bubbling in my gut, and flaming over my skin. How dare she judge me for something she doesn't understand? Defensiveness slips on like an easy, worn set of armor, and I sift through memories as though I'm shaking the dirt away from hidden pieces of bitter gold to defend my actions. Except I don't find any shiny nuggets beneath the soot. No, I'm left with hurt and hatred so deep I wonder how I haven't drowned in self-pity.

"I took off." My voice comes out small. "Running away is sort of my M.O."

"Maybe it could've been once, but now you're a kick-butt Fury."

"True, yet I learned early in life that fleeing today leaves you alive to fight tomorrow."

"How early?" She sounds suspicious, and I know my answer won't help her feel better.

"I started weapons training at four." Which explains why every killing machine, blade, or pointy edge in this training room seemed so familiar. Muscle memory indeed.

"Dear gods." Dottie looks like she wants to track down my teacher and tear them apart. Too late. My mother died before I met Stone. "Why ever would you need to learn how to kill so young?"

"Because my family hunted the gods-spawned." I pull the pin on that verbal grenade and count the seconds until *tick, tick, ka-boom.*

"Your family killed our kind?" Her tone says she doesn't want to believe the accusation.

"Wasn't my kind then, seeing as how I—like every other Fury —had a first life as a human. Well, half-human, half-magic slinger for me. But we tracked the monsters, the scary kill-or-be-killed kind. I didn't know Nymphs or Muses existed. My bedtime stories revolved around chupacabras, wendigos, and spider-shaped bloodsuckers who ate babies. I can't remember what my mom called those last ones."

"Charming childhood." Dottie sounds like she might be sick.

"It wasn't all bad. After a sea witch murdered my dad and my older sister, I didn't go out on missions until I turned twelve. My mom left me behind while she hunted."

"A sea witch...Marina?"

"I don't know. My mom left on a mission when I was sixteen and never came home. Tracking down the sea witch who'd killed my father and sister became her obsession, but she never gave me a description. She said the witch's children walked out of the water and drowned our family while they stood on land."

Shock rolls through Dottie's gaze, and her voice comes out scratchy. She clears her throat, tries again. "Who took care of you when you were a kid? Don't tell me you stayed by yourself."

I touch the spelled cuff my mom gave me, the one with my name engraved inside, the one warded with protection from sea witches. "She gave me a doll, a poppet, she called it. I named him Peter. Whenever I felt sad or lonely or hurt, he came to life. Sort of a golem but made of wood instead of earth. Peter took care of me until I could take care of myself."

"Which was at what age?"

"Nine or ten maybe. I sent him with my mom on her last mission. Stupid teenaged me thought she might want a reminder of who waited at home for her."

Dottie stares at me as if I grew up on an alien war planet. "With that childhood trauma, Dr. Bomani will keep you in her office talking for a solid week."

I groan. "I already have enough issues to unpack with my present-day problems. No need to add past baggage to the mix." Except Marina had probably walked straight out of my family history. "After I stop the current threat, we can discuss mating bonds, maybe-still-valid marriages, and mommy issues."

"Plus, the fact your murderer's still out there." Dottie slides the last bit in like it's not a major trauma trigger on its own, but she's right, and she would know better than anyone as the immortals granted her full Fury rage with black eyes, flaming weapons to call—the whole terrifying total package—to avenge her death.

To kill *her* crazy psycho murderer. Not mine. "I'm betting whoever shot the arrow that killed me is the same one tearing apart shifters."

"How do you know an arrow killed you?"

"Stone told me. I didn't see the weapon, just his face while he watched me die." A memory that torments me, and I can't imagine how it must torture him.

Dottie's gaze goes sad. "Chase still blames himself for my death no matter that he couldn't have stopped it. We're working through stuff with Dr. Bomani, but..." She glances away.

"Yeah, I hear you. I need to schedule a session after I figure out how to deal with Marina. At least she'll be too busy with Trick's charity concert for a few days to fool with whatever sadistic plan she has for me."

"You don't know that." She hurries to talk before I can interrupt with a what-the-hell-else can I do comment. "But with the swarms of kids in town, it'll be harder for her to do anything as long as you stay put at the House of Furies. This might be the only kid-free zone in Syn City. With the exception of Connie."

"Your cousin's an honorary member of our House." I want her to talk about Connie, the concert, anything but my problems. "Kid invasion, huh?"

"They're everywhere. From little ones missing their front teeth to mouthy teenagers. Trick's entourage has them out touring the city in big groups on the hover carts, or The Rink would be overrun for registration, swag distribution, and photo ops."

"With Trick?"

She frowns. "I didn't see him when I dropped Connie off, but I could've missed him in the crowds. The Muses and Nymphs had lines waiting for pics, and the Gorgons had hologram games set up. It seemed sort of a frantic chaos, less organized than our—"

Sadie slams open the door, wings outstretched. "Dot, come on, we need to get to Connie. Two hover carts full of kids and a chaperone took off hours ago and never came back. Maizie says we're—"

I gasp and double over, my breath sawing out in rough chops that catch in my hot chest. A pain stabs through me as though a phantom sword guts me, radiating hurt, fear, worry, danger in staggering emotional blows one after another. I can't think, can't move, can't feel past the sensations overloading my body. A flare of red, green, and violent purple pop at the edge of my vision followed by waves of gold that fizzle and blink out.

What the—

Awareness slams into me, flooding my system with adrenaline and sending my heart rate into a panicked pace that has me freezing cold and fiery hot at the same time. "Stone. He's in danger."

23

STONE

I DIDN'T FIGHT MARINA OR THE MEN SHE BROUGHT WITH HER WHEN she tracked me to the location that I planned to turn into a training academy for the new branch of Warrior's Den Weaponry. Not when she showed me Kiva's dagger and Beryl's honeybee bracelet. How could I if it meant I jeopardize the lives of my mate or my sister? What would I give to save them? Anything.

Swallowing my hot anger and the sour bile on my tongue, I'd followed her to this storage facility. Biding my time, I allowed the entourage members I'd assumed to be Trick Peterson's body-guards to surround me.

As if they could stop me should things go sideways.

As if I would allow these assholes to harm my wife or my sister.

Walking through the air-conditioned hallway that smells of bitter chemicals and mold, I count the closed doors that we pass and the roll-up gates with padlocks in different sizes and colors. When Marina stops outside a room and unlocks it, I sense only one heartbeat. The stink of camphor and ammonia cover any other scents.

"Inside," she says.

Fine, given it must be Beryl or Kiva in there.

Only I find neither.

Stepping through the door, I almost stumble at the sight of Trick slumped against the wall, the singer's face beaten and bloodied. What the hell? I'd expected the worst, but I hadn't guessed I might find her star client with shiners on both cheeks and a cut on his forehead.

I'm done playing her twisted guessing games. "What's going on?"

"I'll be back soon to talk about your mate and your sister." Marina curves her mouth into a smile, a shark's smile—all coldness, no warmth. "Lock them in."

A guard slams the door, clicking deadbolts into place.

"Trick?" My shifter vision adjusts to the dim light, and I hurry to the singer's side. "What happened?

"I'm sorry I stole the dagger from your room."

Relief surges through me, and my chest unwinds from the tight knot of shallow breathing that it's been since I saw the dagger in Marina's hand. She doesn't have Kiva. "What about my sister's bracelet?" A thief I can deal with much easier than losing either woman. "Did you take it too?"

"Beryl lost a bracelet? Did she have it on this morning?" He seems to lose focus, and I fight the urge to snap my fingers at him.

"A gold one with a honeybee charm. Did you steal it?"

"No." He sounds sincere. "I wanted a weapon to protect myself, to defend Kiva if necessary. Sneaking things comes easy to me, and that blade drew me like I was meant to hold it if only once. I would've given it back, but once Marina found out that I'd warned you..." He hangs his head, and blood drips from a gash next to his ear. "Why'd you ask about Beryl's bracelet?"

"Marina says she's holding both my sister and Kiva."

"What? No." He pushes as though he'll stand but falls.

Or he would've fallen if I'd let him. "We have to get out of here, find the women, and take you to a doctor."

He laughs a sad, brittle sound that's all hard lines and jagged edges, so unlike the crooner that it has my bear rising within me. "No need for a doctor," he says. "I'm not even real."

Something's very off about Trick, but I don't have time to figure out his riddles. "I'm gonna need you to make sense."

"Marina told me the truth. I'm not Kiva's mate. She told me the lie to convince me to get close to her so she could do the same."

My gut sinks. Whatever Marina's plan might be, it can't be good. "Why? Did Marina give you a reason?"

"I'm Pinocchio without the long nose or any hope of becoming real. Marina called me a Pygmalion from the myths like the Furies, but I don't know that story. She says Kiva's mom created me, that I'm tied to Kiva by her mother's magic, spelled to come to life only with her pain."

"That's impossible." Except memories of Kiva telling me about her mom conjuring a poppet to watch over her flash through my mind as bold and blaring as the massive signs on the side of The Rink. What exactly had my mate said about the spelled doll? She didn't mention much. Only that his name was... "Peter."

"A trick, Marina told me." He shakes his head. "I'm nothing more than a trick that she named Peter's son."

Trick Peterson. Oh my gods. He's the manifestation of Kiva's emotional pain. Her worries, fears, and loneliness as a child fueled the magic that fed him. Reclaiming her memories had sent my mate running this morning, so what would discovering none of his life had been real do to Trick? "What can I...how can I..." Damn, feelings are hard. I can't get a full question out.

Trick sinks lower against the wall. "The past I thought I knew? It's nothing more than lies. I didn't come into existence until two years ago."

"When Kiva died and came back as a Fury."

Hurt fills his gaze, so tangible and cutting that it carries weight the same as a piece of metal in my forge's fire. "I feed off her pain the same as Marina's monstrous creations. My existence means she suffers. How can I live with that?"

"Hey, you make your own decisions. You came to us, warned us, tried to protect Kiva."

"Because I was made to take care of her. Which made it easy to believe she had to be my fated mate, my reason for being." His voice cracks on the last, and he looks away, smearing the blood on his face with a jerky swipe.

No wonder the man moves differently. My bear sensed something *not right* with him from the beginning, but I couldn't have guessed the awful truth. To believe—to feel down to your bones, to the core of your essence—that someone's the other half of your very soul, and then to have it ripped away along with your reality. I can't breathe past the tightness of the tragic rage and bottomless grief he must be going through.

He glances my way, his eyes shiny. "I won't let Marina torture Kiva. It goes against everything I stand for." Coughing a sorrow-soaked chuckle, he shakes his head. "Literally."

All right. As much as I want to help him, we have bigger dangers to face right now. Marina's the enemy. She's the threat to Kiva, to Beryl, to us. Eliminate her, and we can deal with the emotional fallout later. First, we need to get out of here.

The lock unclicks. Great, I'll take out the guards and go from there. I strip off my shirt, preparing to shift.

The door swings open, and flashlight beams cranked to sunlight-brilliant-levels blind me. I blink past the circles and spots floating in my vision.

"Don't bother changing forms," Marina snaps. "We have high-powered rifles trained on both you and Trick."

"You won't shoot your meal ticket." I taste the lie on my tongue.

"Won't I? We both know he's expendable, but he's your bride's only link to her mother, her family, her blood kin. Without him, she has nothing of them left. How convenient of her mom to carry him on her hunt for me. I enjoyed taking his poppet off her corpse."

"You killed Kiva's mother." I didn't meet the woman, but that doesn't stop me from wanting to lash out at the witch who hurt my mate.

"The witch-born with creation blood who should've known the value of life? She slaughtered my family." The barbed accusation doesn't hold misery or mourning, only wrath.

"You murdered hers." I don't know that for a fact, but I say it anyway.

"I did." She drawls the confession as if savoring the taste. "The girl I drowned—Kiva's older sister?" She doesn't wait for an answer, seeming lost in a memory. "Her hurt made for such a satisfying snack, but her father's anguish at watching his child drown on dry land without being able to save her? Delicious."

"You're an abomination." The word doesn't cover the horror of what Marina truly is—one of the creatures in the dark that stories had taught us to fear long ago when fire was still new. "A monster."

With a *naughty child* tsk-tsk, she stares at me without remorse or guilt. "Who's calling whom a monster? Ask the humans and they'll name you and your kind as nightmarish enough to be hunted and eradicated. We're not so different."

"We're nothing alike. You can't kill my mate. I'll end you if she doesn't first."

She gives a cruel, twisted mockery of a laugh. "Kill her? Oh no. I need her alive. Good thing you bargained for her second life. I would've been so disappointed if I'd lost her out on that frozen lake while I was trapped beneath the surface."

"You were there?" I remember the smell of the salt air seeming so out-of-place over a freshwater lake. Other memories haunt me—reaching for Kiva when she heard the eerie call across the ice that she swore was Rylie, but I'd known it to be something else, something dangerous. The way Kiva had pulled from my grasp. Trying to chase her with the *pop-crack-pop* of the ice splintering beneath my feet. The scarlet of Kiva's blood against the stark white of ice and snow. The arrowhead clinking against the ice. "You watched Kiva die."

"And listened to you beg that an immortal spare your mate. Kiva's suffering in her second life has helped birth my children. You see, Trick's magic puzzled me until I realized it didn't feed off the mother's blood, no, it was cast in Kiva's. I tied the spell to raising my own new family to replace the one stolen from me, and it worked. The more she hurts, the closer to completion my babies will grow." Stepping aside, she nods to the hallway where a slick, oil-skinned being stands.

No, not oil.

Water.

The creature appears formed of water and muck made solid with no facial features, nothing more than a shape of the head where a face should be. The hollowness sends chills through me. I can't let this woman hurt Kiva, can't let more of these terrors become flesh.

"We leave in five minutes. The bear sow will be joining us." *Beryl.* "You can have your little knife back, Trick. It did the..." She pauses to give a nasty grin. "*Trick* of getting the bear here. As for you..." Glaring at me, she waves two fingers at a shooter behind her.

I move. Not fast enough. A bullet hits me in the chest, a *thwopping* hard punch to the solar plexus that knocks the air from my lungs and stings my skin as though I've been stabbed with a hot poker from my forge. The next slams into my stomach, ripping at my skin in a searing slash. Staggering into the wall next to Trick, I struggle to bring my bear to the surface, to allow the shift to heal me faster so I can save my wife and sister.

But nothing happens. My body goes so heavy, not with the weight of the bear settling over my shoulders, but as though my head's made of iron. The room spins, Marina's image goes hazier than the faceless water freak with her, and my vision tunnels. Kiva's face flashes through my mind, her wings outstretched, love in her eyes, and I wish on the dream.

Darkness drags me into oblivion.

24

KIVA

I CAN'T FLY FAST ENOUGH, NO MATTER HOW I SWOOP AND SWERVE around trees I know as well as my own curves by now. The whole place smells wrong. Our swamp doesn't hold the same brimstone sulfur and decaying rot stench of most marshes. It's more citrus, cypress, and sweetness thanks to the immortal magic, but tonight? I could swear ocean winds sweep salt-soaked air into my lungs that burn as I push harder.

Stone's pain vanished minutes ago—long, agonizing minutes that ticked by like years while I waited for Maizie to give the signal for the Furies to move out. She sent me and my sisters first, promising backup would be close behind. I don't know if our leader wanted me to show the House the way, if she telepathed with the immortals, or if she simply couldn't stand another moment of my frantic need to get to my mate. I might've run away from him, but the mating bond stands between us.

Not being able to feel his emotions, to sense his pain? Fear rips at me, driving me past caring, except Dottie and Sadie flank my sides, and I can't risk my sisters. The immortals haven't sent me into a Fury rage, and I hold on to that as my one hope that they believe I have nothing to avenge. Not yet anyway.

He has to be okay. While I'm not sure it's *me* who he wants and not my past, I'm not letting anyone else make that decision. He's my were-bear, whether I'm ready to gamble with his eventual rejection or not. No damn sea witch gets to take him from me.

"Slow down," Sadie urges.

"Can't." I don't.

"We need a plan," she argues.

"I *have* a plan," I tell her. "Save Stone. Hope the immortal Furies let me kill a sea witch. See? Two plans. Even better."

Sadie flies in front of me, holding out her hands as if that'll stop me. "You don't—"

Dottie yanks her out of the way before I barrel over either of them. "She can't stop," she tells Sadie. "It's mating instinct to keep each other alive." The last she says in such a serious voice that I almost give in to the need to sob for what I may have lost for being a fool.

Swallowing past the knot of emotion choking me, I glance toward the cloudless sky. A full moon lights the water, silver playing across the dark surface as if it's a shiny, round marble ready to spin us all off. Another night, another moon, another dance of light across shimmering ice haunts me. Stone lost me then. I won't lose him now.

I swoop toward the round banks that are lined with trees, a bowl of swamp carved into the edge of the city far from the pleasure district. The curve reminds me of the ice that stretched endlessly at the lake, and I want to scream at the similarities. Not this time. I'm not a scared half-human trying to save someone already gone. There will be no deaths tonight.

Dark shapes float on the water, a large raft with multiple figures huddled together on it at the far side. Two smaller crafts drift closer to the shore, though not close enough to allow an easy swim through snakes, sea hags, and gators. While gator shifters might not attack people, their animal counterparts do.

Spheres of water hide more than a fuzzy outline of anyone on the three shapes as though the element itself has decided to play along with a grand reveal.

"Someone has a Muse-level sense of showmanship," Sadie mutters.

I don't bother to answer, landing hard at the water's edge. The impact jars me with a jolt that shakes my whole body, but I'm numb to the pain that should rip through me. Does the failure to feel pain come from me running away or from something that has happened to Stone? I can't tell.

Several members of the House of Nymphs come out of the trees, hurrying toward me and my sisters.

"Thank the gods you're here," one says.

I don't answer her, don't even look her way. Where's Stone? Our bond tells me he should be here, but I don't see him.

"What's wrong?" Dottie asks. "Has someone from your House been hurt?" Her voice cracks on the last. *Killed*, she means. The Nymphs suffered from this city's last killer the same as we Furies did.

"No." The musical voice cuts short as if she too remembers their grief. "But the saltwater, it's killing the waterlilies, ferns, and carnivorous plants that can't withstand the change. Some of the animals below as well. We're doing what we can to keep them alive."

I sweep a glance around the curved shore, noting other slender figures with hands raised toward the air and glowing, magic orbs shining on the green, blue, and purple shimmering hair that's a signature for so many Nymphs. But other taller, broader forms push into the water, only to be shoved back again by the waves. *Gorgons.*

"What are the Gorgons doing here?" I ask. They like few things in life, respect even fewer.

"Children." The Nymph looks away so fast I don't catch her

face, but she's one of the older ones who have retired from roller derby. "They say children are trapped on the water, that they can feel their sadness."

Shivers roll through me cold enough that I could be standing at the edge of another shore by a lake of ice. Fear clutches my heart, wrapping it in a fist. "Kids?" They must be the children and teenagers here for the charity concert, those from the two missing hover carts.

Maizie touches down beside me. "We haven't received any commands from the immortals."

"But we're sort of the police here, right?" Dottie spins the question into a decided fact, a call for action.

"Hardly." The leader of the Huntresses, Devlyn, announces her presence in the same superior-to-everyone way those bitches handle everything in life. I want to fly at her, to put her in the ground, but I glance at the bow in her hand, the quiver of arrows strapped to her back, thinking of the silver tips on my wings.

I glare at her. "Any of the Huntress's arrowheads made of silver?"

She looks at me as though I needed permission to speak to her and glances toward Maizie. "They're not arrowheads," Devlyn says finally. "They're called points, and we don't waste resources such as precious metals, unlike some of you." She glares at us as if we've offended her by existing.

"Yeah, yeah, y'all do no wrong." Pushing aside my need to know about *my* killer, I concentrate on the here and now. "Marina?" I yell.

Maizie curses and spins on me. "Don't attack. Don't provoke. Don't engage until the immortals give us a sign. If that happens, then you and your sisters can take point, but only if."

"Understood." *Whatever.* I can't concentrate on the petty rivalries between Houses. Stone's here. I know it. So why can't I see him? I stare at the spheres, wishing the water would part long enough to allow a glimpse beneath them. "Marina! You put on a show, and we're all here. Now, come out." *So I can kick your ass.*

"Kiva." A voice much like Rylie's, the bear cub who I looked after the way I wished someone had looked after me, whose ghost I see in Connie's teenaged drama moments—her voice skitters across the water to make my stomach churn and my heart race.

I won't let Marina win. Not this time. Not as she did when she called me out on the ice to find Rylie's body and my death. "Come out, sea witch. Stop with the tricks."

The swamp shifts and parts in the center of those shapes, the water giving away to a stool, a chair? What is that?

"Holy Hades," Dottie says. "She's sitting on a throne."

Yep, Marina parks her ass on a giant royal throne fashioned out of water instead of metal. "Cut the crap," I call out. "No one wants to see your sad, little show."

"Then why have your great Houses turned out if not to watch?" She waves a hand at the Nymphs, Gorgons, and Huntresses. "Besides, I have something you won't want to miss."

One of the water spheres surrounding the throne disappears, plunging back into the surface. High-pitched yells pierce the night as kids and teenagers crowd together on the raft that's far too small and narrow for the group. In the middle, a woman attempts to pull them tighter, to keep them afloat without anyone falling.

Nymphs send the colored orbs out over the water to shine over the kids, one after another in an eerie chain of glowing colors.

I squint, staring hard at the woman in the center. *Beryl.* How did Marina get to Stone's sister? The woman can swim, but not in a swamp riddled with venomous snakes, and if she shifts into her bear form, then that raft will sink in a split-second.

"The sea witch kidnapped children," Sadie says, and the snap of her weapon to call cracks beside me. She summoned her whip.

"It's a crime that calls for Fury vengeance." She announces it as though we don't need permission from the immortals.

"Wait," Maizie says.

"For what?" Dottie asks.

"The immortal mothers say not yet." Our leader doesn't sound happy about being the go-between in this situation.

Sadie grumbles something that sounds like a curse on our immortal mothers. "Wait like they waited to watch us being murdered? Those are *children*."

The raft dips wildly, and a teenaged girl goes over the side with a shriek cut off on a gurgle. I can't breathe until her head breaks the surface.

Styx, the undead House rumored to shepherd souls to the Underworld, appear at the edge of the water. Their cloaks and faceless masks reveal nothing, but they could only be here for one reason. Death is coming.

As if making the same awful realization, a group of Gorgons again rush into the water.

"Uh uh uh," Marina says, pushing a wall of waves toward them. The rolling surface knocks another two kids off the raft and makes it impossible for the others to drag them back to safety without risking more going into the swamp.

The first girl to go into the water screams. "Something slithered against my leg." A head emerges near her, not an alligator. No, it's worse. With long, stringy, dark hair and a greyish face, a sea hag swims closer. The girl thrashes, grabbing the raft and almost tipping it over as she tries and fails again and again to pull herself up.

"Quiet." Devlyn bellows the word so loud that I'm not surprised when the sea hag twists to look at us, and by twist, I mean the hag cranks her neck a full 180 degrees until her chin sits over the spot where her shoulder blades meet. The spirits of women drowned by the humans for suspicion of witchcraft, the hags supposedly have lost their sight and react only to sound. They drag their living victims down into the deep with them. I hadn't seen them in action before tonight, and I hope I never see them again.

Gorgons fight a losing battle with the waves to reach the downed children.

"Screw it," Sadie says. "I'm grabbing that kid." She pushes into the air just as a Huntress's arrow goes whizzing past, barely missing her. "What the hell?"

The sea hag disappears beneath the surface, and Devlyn nocks another arrow.

"No." Maizie puts the full force of Fury coach into her tone. "You can't kill a sea hag, and you could've hit the kids."

"I don't miss." Devlyn's boast comes out as conceited as the rest of her Huntress vibe. "I'll kill this Marina, and we'll be done."

Maizie shakes her head hard enough that a dread swings loose of her high bun. "You don't have jurisdiction to bring a sanctioned death. Only a Fury under the immortal wrath can do that. You shoot, and you're a murderer, not a gods-endorsed vengeance dealer."

The Huntress curls her lip into a sneer. "We don't bow to your power trip." She shoots, and the arrow blazes across the swamp, zipping *through* Marina to thunk into the raft holding Beryl and the kids. Shrieks and splashes follow as another teenager tumbles over the side.

"Stop making things worse." I don't hide my rage at Devlyn. Whatever political power games she plays, I'm not here for them, and neither are those kids.

"Marina wouldn't be here except to find you." If a Huntress could hiss, she would be spitting at me. "If we give you to her, she'll release the hostages."

"And if she doesn't?" I'm done with her messed-up logic and hatred of anyone not a Huntress. "You going to shoot your little arrows through her again? Piss her off some more? Step back and let us show you how to get shit done."

My sisters move next to me, using their wings to block out the rest of the world. "Game faces on," Dottie says. "We need to pray for some divine rage."

I step into the water. "This is between you and me, Marina. Let the kids go. You don't need them."

"I don't." Marina sounds positively giddy, and the wrongness turns my stomach. "But they make sure everyone else stays out of our negotiation. You see, I called you here because you have a choice to make."

"There's no choice." No matter what my mother may or may not have done to her. "I'm not holding still so you can kill me."

"Kill you?" She laughs, and I want to punch her in her fluid face. "Why does everyone assume that? Oh no, I need you to live a long, tortured second life."

"To bring back your weird water babies? No thanks. I'm too focused on my career right now for kids, especially monstrous ones. Maybe you should adopt a sea hag instead. They seem to need a lot of love, and you could fulfill your crazy mommy dearest fantasies that way." Yeah, I need to stop cracking lame jokes, but I'm trying—and failing—to assess her weaknesses.

Marina had been plenty real to the touch when she'd taken my hand, but that arrow went through her as if shot into a waterfall. Even if I have the immortals' blessing, how do I hatchet someone without a solid form?

"You'll help." Marina seems so sure that her certainty slides cold along my spine as if she trickled ice there. Raising a hand, she gestures to the waves, and a small army of human forms come out of the water—translucent but gaining solid form. Four of the most clearly defined figures step out of the swamp and onto the shore.

"They have no faces." Sadie sounds as horrified as I feel.

"She made monsters," Dottie whispers. "You can't help her create more of those."

"But the kids," I remind them. "And Beryl. We have to save them."

"Your choices," Marina booms as if she's a Muse announcer calling out plays in a roller derby bout. She sweeps a hand toward the smaller rafts that I'd almost forgotten with the way the water spheres camouflage them in darkness. The shields drop.

My heart plummets to my knees, my pulse pounds so hard it's louder than the kids' screams, and I go dizzy.

Stone. He's knocked out and strapped down with chains and what looks to be an iron gate, the load so heavy that his raft dips until he's partially submerged. My mate has had nightmares of water his whole life. While it's a blessing he's unconscious, how the hell will he get free of those bindings if he can't fight, can't move, can't think through strategy the way his quick mind works best?

I act on impulse, the need to reach my mate overpowering any thought as I kick into the air and fly toward him. Marina works magic so that the water rushes over him, and I freeze, yanking my gaze to her. "What do you want?" I ask.

"Wait for your other choice." She makes the request sound as if she scolds a naughty toddler.

The other sphere slides away. Gasps and cries come from the shore. Marina has chained Trick to a massive iron ball that has to be heavy the way his raft sinks as low as Stone's when the singer doesn't have my mate's mass. An orb controlled by the Nymphs floats his direction and shines pulsing green light across the ghastly blood and bruises coating his face. He sits up, not unconscious the way my were-bear is, but slumping from his hunched shoulders to his bowed head. What has she done to him to steal the cocky swagger and smooth charm, leaving a broken shell behind?

"You choose who lives," Marina says. "And who dies. Choose the supernatural children if you're feeling especially altruistic. Or perhaps your mate from your first life. Or the only living tie to your mother, your family, your blood kin. I believe you called him Peter."

Peter? The poppet who became a boy when I needed a playmate, a man when I needed a grown up to take care of me? The one person who kept me company, read me stories, and made sure I wasn't afraid when I was all alone as a child? My sister's doll who had been spelled just for me after she died. So special for so many reasons as a simple toy, but the sole person I could count on in childhood? Trick Peterson is Peter. No wonder he felt so familiar. How did I not see it before?

He stares at me with a sad hollowness, as though he has disappointed me. "I'm sorry." His low voice carries over the water. "I didn't know. Not until she told me. I immediately felt drawn to you, connected to you, but I didn't guess why."

"You couldn't have." My throat scratches, and I drag the words up past rawness.

The yells of the kids and the calls from the shore fade into a roaring background, and I don't know if Marina has worked a spell or if panic has taken over.

"Choose," she tells me. "Quickly, before both their times run out. Oh, the delicious pain that would incite in you? It would fuel my children for years. Think of the havoc we could cause. They'll devastate everything in their path. The mass destruction they can create will make drowning your entire family seem like nothing in comparison."

"You killed my family?" My question comes out too high-pitched, too fast, too scared. I'm suddenly the little girl who lost her sister, her dad, and then her mom.

"Just like your mother butchered mine. You'll watch me take away everything you love. Your mother tied her creation magic to your blood, to him." She jerks her head in Trick's direction. "Now, I'll have a new family, an unstoppable one."

Beryl yells at me to save her brother while the waves push her and the kids farther from shore, from the drifting teenagers.

Stone doesn't move, his wrists and ankles chained to the gate in an X-cross that can't be escaped. Trick holds my gaze as though trying to convince himself that I won't let him die.

How can I choose a life? How can I live with myself if I'm responsible for any of their deaths?

25

KIVA

My heart breaks again and again with the impossible choice Marina gives me. Gorgons and Nymphs push against the water, fighting to gain an inch when they would need a quarter of a mile. The Styx remain still and silent, a solemn sign of what's to come.

Hopelessness drowns me as if Marina has decided to murder me the way she did my sister, my father, my mother. She must've taken Peter from my mother's backpack and somehow created Trick Peterson from the spells. My mom's magic had been so powerful, and yet she'd walked away from her own kind for my dad, for her children. So how can I leave Trick? But I can't give up Stone, and no way can I let those children go into the swamp.

Sadie's voice calls me to the present. "Distract the sea witch and grab one of your men. We'll get the kids. Stop thinking, and act on impulse. It's what you're best at."

But this isn't a derby bout where the only stakes might be losing a championship. My actions mean life or death.

I fly at Marina, but she appears and disappears as easily as water splashing from one puddle to the next, as quickly as an alpha's shift. Her laughter seems to come from everywhere, stalking me from every side. "Not so easy to take me out," she says. "Even your mother couldn't do it. Here I am, being kind enough to let you pick, and you throw a tantrum. Who knew tormenting you as a Fury would be *so* much fun? Choose." She slips out of reach and repeats the word over and over in an agonizing cat-and-mouse chase where I'm the prey and an army of predators wait to pounce.

"No." Trick looks up, his defiant gaze locking on mine. "I don't remember our past, Kiva, but I've loved you from the moment I met you. Not the way you want, not the way you could return, but enough to sacrifice for your happiness." He scoots the heavy iron toward the edge of the raft, tipping it wildly.

"Trick, no." I zoom toward him, but a chuckle from Marina has me spinning. She drags Stone another inch lower.

Trick shakes his head, blood-stained blond locks falling in his face. "It's okay, Kiki." My mother's nickname for me. My heart skids into a frantic beat. He *knows* that name. Some part of him remembers. He pushes the iron another inch and raises a hand as if saying good-bye. "I was never real anyway." Overwhelming sorrow punches me, suffocating me in the heavy tragedy of his words. He felt real to me. The possibility of losing him feels so very real. Over the side he goes with a splash, the metal dragging him toward the murky bottom of the black water.

"No." I scream and rush toward him, my hatchet coming to my hand when I call. "No, no, no."

But Marina blasts me with a wave that has me flapping wet feathers, slinging dripping hair out of my face, and blinking the muck out of my eyes. The sting of salt burns my nostrils, my eyes, the back of my throat, and the cold water makes my shaking worse. Terror goes though me, the same as when I found Rylie's broken body on the ice and knew I could do nothing to change her fate, felt the arrow's sting and watched Stone's horror. Rage and fear and grief collide within me.

"How wonderful." Marina's singsong cheer over my agony makes me want to tear her to pieces. If only I could catch her.

I'm frozen, and I don't dare let her look away from my misery, or she might see the Gorgons creeping through the water to the children. Trying again, I get slammed with another wall of water. My heart's quick *boom-boom* drags into a sluggish *thud-thump-thud* that can't keep a steady rhythm, a broken metronome where my fight moves come in a shuffling quick-quick-slow tempo. My wings go heavy with grief, and my stomach feels as if an icy knife stabs at my middle. Misery ripples through me the same as the water's waves above the spot where Trick went down.

He has been under so long there's no way he could've survived. He sacrificed himself for me. Even if I could bring him back to life with my mother's spells, which I have no idea how to do, he won't remember *this* life. He'll be like me, trapped by amnesia with no hope for a cure, no reality to anchor him, and no guarantee the magic would last. I've lost my last connection to my family so quickly after discovering it—the hurt and helplessness magnify until they are all I can feel.

"Such rich pain will sustain my children for years, but can you give me more?" Marina lowers her voice as if sharing a secret between friends. "I think you can."

Like a horror hologram playing in slow motion, she lifts a hand, and Stone's raft flips to stand vertically in the water, his heavy body strapped to the gate, his head hanging forward.

"Please." I'm not sure who I beg, but I put everything I have into that one simple word. An echo of Stone's deep voice imploring the same over my body runs through my mind. A ghost of a memory? I'm not sure. Just like I don't know how she keeps that damn raft upright or manages to make his slide into the water excruciatingly slow. But I'm certain of three things.

I can't lose him.

I can't watch him die.

I'll give my second life to save him.

Tucking my wings and banishing my hatchet, I take a deep breath and plunge toward the swamp's surface. I have one chance to get this right. If I can't free Stone, if I can't hold enough air, if I become tangled in those chains, we could both die. I push every emotion I can through the mating bond—love, terror, dread, the shock of the water as I hit it, pulling my wings in before they can catch in the waves and drag me down. The grit of salt and tangle of vines cling to me, stinging and scratching my skin as I dive further into the dark water.

Our swamp doesn't have the sky blue of hologram oceans or the cloud-mirror lakes of my childhood. The locals call it tannic water because decaying plants and rot color it the shade of sweet tea. Tonight, no matter the moon's light, I'm struggling to see anything beyond my arms sweeping in strong strokes. But Stone's down there. I can sense his fear, his confusion, his concern. He's awake and fighting to get free in the nightmare that has haunted him for decades. Yet the worst of his troubles? His worry for me.

The tug through our bond shatters my heart. Lungs bursting, eyes blurry, and head spinning, I center on him like the North Star that I'll pin my hopes and wishes on. An orb from the Nymphs crashes through the water, tracking me and lighting us in an icy silver glow. The stark similarity to my death does nothing to deter me from my course. Down, down, down I go to the bottom until I can see him, wide-eyed and yanking at the chains that won't give. Love rolls through the bond—honey-gold so thick I can taste it if I concentrate on the emotions instead of the horrible possibilities slithering against my bare legs. Fear for me pours from Stone, sickly green.

Pressing my mouth to his, with a kiss fused so tightly that not a single drop of water can slip between us, I seal a promise of life, of a bond that can't be vanquished. Pulling back, I summon my hatchet and go after the chains that hold him, starting with those binding his arms. *Clang, clang.* The water drags my swings, slowing each.

Air bubbles slip from his mouth, and Stone closes his eyes.

I'm running out of time. Seconds pass, stretching into infinite loops unto themselves.

Faster. I push into a manic pace, hacking at the iron as if it's the vines around the House of Furies that refuse to give way. The shackles finally release his wrists, and he opens his eyes, unwinding the chains from around his arms while I bend to free his legs.

Stone's shocked gaze flies to somewhere behind me. Not stopping to consider whether the threat's Marina, sea hags, gators, or whatever other monster lurks beneath the swamp, I swing my hatchet, my weapon to call that can't miss its target, and the blade goes through Marina. She curves her mouth upward as if in delight at watching our struggle.

I weigh my options, and screw it, go with impulse because Sadie was right. I'm my best when I don't overthink. Slashing at the chains around Stone, I ignore the witch bitch. Marina doesn't want me dead; she wants my suffering. One, two, three swings, and I have his right foot undone. Marina's children drop into the water to surround us like a ghostly army, and I keep going.

She pulls my arm, and I curve the hatchet in an upstroke that should gut her but does nothing. How can she have been so solid before and liquid now? Home turf advantage? With each of her quick yanks at my clothes or tugs on my hair that already splays around me in waves like a demented mermaid in a hack-and-slash movie, I shrug her off and keep going. I'm so close to getting Stone free. Nothing else matters.

How long has he been without oxygen? A minute? An eternity? The last chain breaks loose, and I banish my hatchet to jerk the tangled loops from the gate.

Marina grabs my arm, my bracelet—the cuff my mother made me—and goes solid. I can feel her fingers on my skin, the clamp of her hold and its pressure. I reach for my weapon to call, but Stone slips a dagger from his waistband, *my* dagger. The one he returned to me in this life. The one I left in the hotel room when I ran away. The one he gave me when he proposed and I said yes.

He plunges the blade into Marina, and she recoils, trying to move away. Except I press her hand against my cuff, keeping her in this form. A pain rips through me as if I'd been the one stabbed, a tearing away of part of me. I glance at Stone whose closed eyes don't blink open, whose mouth goes slack and a lone air bubble drifts upward.

No. I can't have lost him.

I won't.

Vengeance pours through me, filling me with divine rage. The wrath I need. The immortals answering my plea at last. My eyes go full Fury with heightened senses that let me see anything and everything I need to take revenge for my mate. I won't miss. I can't. This is my purpose in my second life, my last chance with Stone, and I have the immortal mothers guiding me.

My hatchet comes into my palm as I curl my fingers around the handle and swing at Marina. The magic of the called weapon means it arcs true in one beheading strike, but I've needed this justice for decades. Years of grief and torment and rage explode in the sweep of the blade through her solid flesh. No way she survives that blow, not without her head.

Her monstrous children disintegrate, flying apart to rejoin the water that made them. But I don't stop to check or investigate or celebrate a victory. Not when I may have lost everything.

Sending away my hatchet, another gift from Stone and another reminder that will forever tie our lives together in intricate knots that can't be undone, I haul him upward, sucking in air past a burning throat into a too-tight chest as soon as I break the surface.

"Help." I choke, cough, and yell again.

"We're coming," voices call from above. Dottie and Sadie drop from the sky, seizing Stone and dragging him through the water to the shore. Other Furies surround them, taking his arms and legs to fly faster toward land.

I open my mouth to ask them to wait but shut it again. If they can save him, if they—

"We've got you," Maizie says. She and her triad sisters pull me out of the swamp.

Nymphs kneel around Stone, who lies on his back in the mud, and I collapse beside them. One has her hand on his chest, another his throat, a third on his temples.

"They're coaxing the water from his lungs and sending air to his blood," Sadie explains, translating whatever dead language they're using. "You'll need to give him the breath of life, a kiss to call him back."

A kiss? The bargain. Our trade. The favor he wanted. The key to unlock my past. Our shared breath beneath the water. How could everything come down to a kiss?

"Whatever it takes," I tell her.

Stone coughs, water coming from his mouth as the Nymphs turn his head to the side and continue chanting.

"Now," Sadie says.

I lock my lips over his and push breath through him. *Come on. I reach for the mating bond as easily as taking his hand, as practiced as a hug. Come back so we can be us.*

Thoughts flicker through my mind, and they aren't mine. No, they're his. Images of me as a Fury with my wings outstretched, on the track skating at The Rink, laughing at something one of my sisters said, raiding his trunk of weapons in his hotel room. Beneath each, a thread of love pulses as strong and sure as a heartbeat. Stone's heart.

He opens his eyes and stares into mine. "This mean I get another chance?"

"*We*, we have a last chance. The only one we'll need." For me, a second life as a Fury. Whatever this might be for Stone with Nymphs working air and water magic to save him.

Beryl and the kids head in our direction. We made it out alive, all of us except for Trick. I'll mourn him and the loss of connection to my family later, but for now, I settle against my were-bear's chest, listening to the steady *thump-thump* and enjoying the rise and fall of his breath. Whatever comes next, we'll do it together.

"Give me a minute to catch a few good breaths." Stone's voice comes out in a hoarse grumble. "And I'll be ready to roll."

"Did you make a roller derby joke?" I snicker, laughing despite the sorrow. Grief can pause for a moment. The chatter around us ebbs and flows the same as the waves from an ocean, replacing the salty wrongness of the swamp with cypress, citrus, and disinfectant from the first aid kits. Rescues and reassurances surround us, filling the shore.

"Are there many derby puns?" he asks, holding me close enough that the squish of wet clothes and shivers of shock can't touch his humor.

"A whole handbook. Mostly about skates, jammers, and rolling. Take any variation of a *your momma* joke or a rolling cliché, and go from there." My grin wobbles at the edges, sadness stealing in.

He brushes his thumb against my cheek to the corner of my mouth, chasing away tears and grit. "Let me see what funny I can come up with to keep that smile in place. For whom does the Fury roll?"

"She rolls for you." I kiss him with the tender harshness of truth—the good, the bad, and the work that will come—of a love that doesn't stop. Not even for death.

26

STONE

WEEKS AGO, I CAME TO SYN CITY TO FIND KIVA AND TAKE HER home. Now, this swamp with its magic, technology, and my beautiful warrior mate? It's *our* home.

My gorgeous wife walks into the construction site that will become my permanent forge with a swagger that speeds my pulse and beautiful wings that steal my breath. Those silver tips that once reminded me only of her death? They glint with the sharp edges and stubbornness that brought Kiva back as a Fury, as a wife who would fight death for her life, for mine, for *us*. Not that the time between that showdown with Marina and now has been easy.

Beryl went west, back to our alpha and the den, two brown bear shifter females hoping for mates making the trip with her. She didn't blame me or Kiva for what happened with Marina, but my sister didn't seem the same after facing down sea hags and gators. She says she sees them lurking beneath the water in her sleep.

While the kids got home and Trick was called a hero who gave his life for them in the human news, Beryl couldn't wait to return to the mountains and trails we grew up wandering in both forms. I offered to accompany her, but my home will be with Kiva. Mates fated until death and beyond.

"Your sister's on the comm," my mate calls out, tucking into my side. "Got you on speaker, Beryl. We miss you. Everything all right?"

"Better than that." Static interrupts my sister's voice. The tech and magic powerhouse of Syn City can't fix Sierra Nevada connections. "Our alpha released Stone from his position, from living with the den. He says he can't come between a man and his fated Fury."

"Thank you." Being forgiven by my alpha gives me one less problem to worry about.

"What'd it cost you?" Kiva asks. "Nothing comes for free, not even among shifters."

"A kiss." Beryl sounds annoyed that she couldn't wiggle her way out of a bargain.

Our alpha could've asked our business for money, me to send extra resources, or countless other things we couldn't afford to offer in restitution. But he has his heart set on my sister no matter how many times she tells him maybe. Kiva pushes her cold nose from flight against my neck, and I understand why the man comes back each time with the hope it'll someday turn to yes.

I glance at the foundations of the new forge, at the setup for the training school in the clearing beyond. "Sounds like you got the good end of the bargain."

Beryl laughs. "I don't know. He promised to replace my lost bumblebee charm. That gold won't be cheap."

"Sorry we didn't find your bracelet." I'm not asking if our alpha gave her the first one, which probably sits at the bottom of the swamp along with the poppet known as Peter. We hadn't found either. Watching my mate go through Trick Peterson's things looking for any connection to the childhood friend she'd known had been painful. She hadn't cried, which made her silence worse. "We'll keep looking. It might turn up and then you'll have an extra bumblebee."

"You two doing okay?" Beryl asks.

I look at Kiva, let her answer.

"We're good," she says, and there's conviction in her voice no matter the uncertainty she gives to words when we're alone. We *are* good, but we will be better. A good marriage can mean hard work, especially with the struggles and changes we've faced.

A rustling noise comes through the comms as though Beryl stands outside in the wind. Makes sense since the den only has one working line. "What about Trick?" she asks.

"No signs," Kiva says. The grief in her eyes shines like dark lights on the water, deep enough to hold the loss of her friend, her family. "Sadie says even if we could find a way to bring him back, he might be Peter or Trick or someone entirely different. She thinks it's best we mourn and move on."

"I'll keep you in my prayers," Beryl says. "Y'all. You'd think I'd use the proper pronoun now that I spent weeks with y'all. I'll remember it when I'm back in Syn City next spring."

"You'll come back for a visit?" I don't hide my hope.

"Someone has to check on the business and to make sure you're not driving Kiva too crazy." My sister needles me a bit more before saying good-bye.

Kiva grins as she switches off the comm. "Beryl sounds happy. I bet she'll lead your alpha on a good chase. The man deserves it with the crap he's given her and your family for years."

I don't bother defending my alpha. That's a battle I won't win with my mate. Instead, I pull her close, then think better of it. "I'm sweaty from work. I'd planned to stop by the cottage to shower so I wouldn't get you dirty."

"What if I like you messing me up?" She kicks one corner of her mouth into a smile so deep that it teases a flash of dimple.

"You might not want to smell like grimy man-bear for our appointment with the doc later." We've been seeing Dr. Bomani to get a head start of working through potential problems before they pop up in our second chance at marriage. A mate who saves me from iron chains and a watery grave? She's worth any amount of therapy she wants me to attend. The doc's nice—sort of reminds me of a cat in some of her mannerisms—but I'm no wolf who'll judge an animal by their skin even when you can't see it.

Kiva tightens her hold around my waist, toying with a hammer looped in my toolbelt. "Well, if you're going to your cottage—"

"*Our* cottage." The cottage next to her triad sister Dottie and her were-cougar Chase. The Furies had set us up in the rental, saying we needed privacy as mates and spouses, and the situation has been so much nicer than anything I could ever give Kiva.

A mischievous sparkle in her gaze warms my heart. "If we head home, we could shower together."

"Deal." I move to shut down work for the day and pack up supplies before the word's out of my mouth. Getting my mate naked and needy in a shower with working plumbing and hot water? Definitely a perk of moving to Syn City. Unhooking her sheathed dagger from my belt, I hand it to her. "Thanks for the loan. We've had orders pouring in for designs close to it." Since a sea hag swam to the edge of the shore that night to hand the dagger to Sadie as if she'd known the Fury. Perhaps in another life.

"Both my triad sisters want to talk to you about new weapons." Kiva pulls the blade, runs her fingers along the etchings she now remembers as symbols of our courtship and mating.

"Sadie willing to wield something forged by a shifter?" The woman hasn't grown any fonder of me, but Chase had the right of it when he said she didn't like any shifter. Still felt plenty personal.

"She'll come around."

"Not sure she will." I don't want to tell her the next, but we promised not to keep secrets from each other. No matter if it costs me fun time in the shower. Or the homemade honey candy Kiva promised me tonight. "With the shifter murders hitting so close to Syn City, one of the wolves in their marshal service will be arriving next week."

"The Syndicate won't allow jurisdiction."

"The rumors spreading among the shifter staff at The Rink say the Syndicate has already agreed." I take a deep breath, readying myself for the explosion I've known would be coming since Chase told me an hour ago. "Specifically, the marshal will be re-opening the investigation in a shifter-related homicide that happened outside of Nashville a few years ago. A human family who worked as healers in the community, who practiced spell-craft. Said he wants to speak with the victim who turned Fury."

Kiva's gaze goes suspicious. "Sadie's family?"

"Sounds like it."

Letting out a low whistle, she shakes her head. "I pity that poor wolf. Sadie will make him wish for a fight that's limited to fangs and claws." She helps me finish packing away my tools. "Think we could talk to the marshal about Rylie's murder? About mine?"

"Don't see why not." That wound has been torn open and stitched back together as much as time, healing, and immortal mercy will allow. "It'll be your call what you want to share."

"I thought shifters answered to the marshals?"

"I answer to my mate. Everyone else can get in line."

She laughs and cuddles close, tipping her face up to mine and nipping my lip. "Careful, or I'll fly up there and kiss the smile off your big bear self."

"As if that's a threat."

"Race ya to the cottage," she says.

"What do you get if you win?" I ask. With my mate, games always come with a gamble.

"I get to snuggle my cold toes in your Kodiak fur tonight."

Sounds like a win for us both. "And if I win?"

She pushes off the ground, flies until she can whisper in my ear. "I'll snuggle you naked."

I reach for her, and she rises into the air with a shrieking giggle, those glorious wings outstretched.

"Chase me, my were-bear," she calls and darts away.

I will, and I'll catch her every time. In this crazy Fury life full of magic and beyond.

Thank you for reading! Did you enjoy? Please add your review because nothing helps an author more and encourages readers to take a chance on a book than a review.

And don't miss the next book of the Syn City Shifters, THE FAST AND THE FURIES, available now. Turn the page for a sneak peek!

Also be sure to sign up for the City Owl Press newsletter to receive notice of all book releases!

SNEAK PEEK OF THE FAST AND THE FURIES

My office, my life—hell, my whole world—revolve around the one case I couldn't solve. Sure, I hide the murder board behind evidence from an open investigation so no one can see my failure. But I can visualize every pinned photo and paper scrap tacked to it. The entire office thinks I'm the carefree and cocky wolf marshal who's gunning for promotion. No one else searches for the murderer who killed the Tucker family and my brother because *everyone* thinks he did it.

I know better.

Lowell wouldn't have hurt his mate, Hazel Tucker. He certainly wouldn't have slaughtered her entire family. There's also the impossibility of how he couldn't have ripped himself apart. The wolf marshals deemed it outside their jurisdiction since Lowell was one dead shifter outnumbered by five murdered humans. The human police didn't care. My little brother—the only person who loved me despite my secrets—was just another dead monster to embody the horrors our community represents for them.

"Bankston," my captain snaps. "Daydream about your latest romantic conquest on someone else's time."

Painting a wolfy grin on my face because it's the cliché that's expected, I lean back in my creaking chair far enough that a human would tip over, lace my hands behind my head, and hit her with a super-smolder shifter stare. "You jealous, Zaleski?"

She rolls her eyes so hard that I'm surprised she doesn't strain something. "Don't flatter yourself. There's been another murder, and it's got your boy's M.O. all over it."

Shit. The coffee I pounded earlier sours in my gut. I straighten and go deadly serious in an instant. I'm working the high-profile serial killer case that's left a trail of dead shifters across the country. I can't tell if it's a career-making opportunity or a curse. "The vic in this one?"

"A couple of deer shifters." She raises a hand to keep me from popping off questions. The captain knows me too well. "I realize the vics aren't predators so they don't fit your profile, but it's your guy."

Every major pack and possible power player in the shifter world has been hit—starting with my brother's murder—but none of the victims came from prey species. "How do you know it's the same killer?"

Her face goes green around the edges. "The vics were torn apart."

The same as Lowell and his fiancé's family had been. I fight the urge to glance toward the covered board. "What else can you tell me?" I don't bother with notes as I'll review every report, every photo, every witness interview I can get.

"It went down less than twenty miles from where that bobcat shifter murder happened two weeks ago," she says. "Predator then too. Not a pack leader as your profiling mentioned, but that vic was a well-respected elderly female. The dead deer shifters were the daughters of the herd's buck. Both fall under your category of vics whose loss would be considered a devastating blow to the community."

A devastating blow to the community. Lowell's death left one of the biggest wolf packs without leadership when the resulting shock ended his father's rule.

His father.

Not mine.

Not that anyone outside our family knows *that* dirty secret. It would ruin us all. Without the alpha, factions sprang up, internal wars erupted, and the entire city suffered for it. "So either this is a copycat murder," I say, "or our perp's narrowing the killing field geographically."

The captain shakes her head. "Your boy's slipping. Mistakes will make it easier for you to finally catch the bastard. The local authorities don't have the resources for this so I'm sending you to represent HQ."

I start gathering what I'll need for the trip—reports, recorder, spare batteries and phone signal boosters since electricity and connections are spotty everywhere outside the big cities where humans, shifters, and magic slingers cohabit peacefully. Allegedly. No one likes to talk about prejudice when infrastructure like power, water, and sewer rank so much higher. "Where?" I ask.

"Syn City."

No. Dropping into my seat, I try to keep my expression neutral, pulling out the poker face I've used to clean the meager pockets of patrol and lockup officers at five-card stud. But it doesn't work on her, and I don't want to explain why I have absolutely zero desire to visit the entertainment mecca of the supernatural world. "Their syndicate doesn't allow shifter law enforcement." Or any law enforcement outside some crazy winged avengers who are mortal daughters of Furies—as in Greek mythological legends come to life. "No way will they let me stay there." *Gods, I hope I'm right.*

"Both murder scenes are in the backwoods of nowhere. You can't conduct a complex investigation while staying in some local yokel's barnyard. I called in favors and got you a diplomatic pass since Syn City closed their borders to all outsiders given their recent incident."

"Great." I can't very well blame my heinously bad luck at being allowed into a town I don't want to visit on some kids who almost died and a country music superstar's mysterious disappearance. The news blasted: *Country Music's Golden Boy Vanishes, Musician Hero Sacrifices Himself to Save Children,* and *Syn City No Longer Trusted to Keep Visitors Safe.* No one could've missed those headlines exploding in every media source the week before Syn City shuttered.

"Look at the bright side, no tourists means fewer people to get in your way."

My problem isn't the gawking sightseers there to watch roller derby and concerts. No, it's one of the stars—the younger sister of Lowell's fiancé and my once fated mate who I could never make mine. Sadie Tucker.

"Our Atlanta office can't house me?" I'm man enough to keep the whine out of my voice. Mostly.

"Atlanta isn't close enough. Besides, I hear Syn City has all the tech you could dream of. The magic there supposedly amplifies it."

Yeah, the deity cities always have the best toys. I scan my office, searching for any last-ditch plea to get out of this jam. "We can't trust Syn City's syndicate not to have their own agenda. Any hotel there will have zilch for privacy, and we can't risk the confidentiality of the victims—"

"Zip it, Bankston. You're going. That's final." She glances at the closed office door, and suspicion finally sparks that should've been spinning since she shut it on her way in. "I need you out of headquarters for a couple of weeks until the heat on your use of force investigation dies down."

Anger surges through me, bringing my wolf so close to the surface that I bet my eyes gleam golden. "That guy was about to kill a kid. I took him out so he wouldn't shoot the boy."

"A boy who was a shifter. You killed a human. The interspecies authorities aren't happy."

I want to tear apart the desk, to chuck it at the stupid council who dares question an emergency situation from the safety of their secure chambers. "I'll bet the boy and his family weren't happy about him being kidnapped and kept as some sicko's pet either."

She jabs a finger at me. "I'm not saying you're wrong. Just that you need out of the spotlight. Since you won't take a two-week vacation and no one else can work this case, go to Syn City and find the damn killer that's been terrorizing our kind for years. Solve it, and all this will go away. You'll be promoted and then *you* can deal with the politics."

"Politics are their own nightmare."

"Can be." Captain Zaleski, the woman who can outtalk anyone in our station, goes silent—so quiet that the ringing of phones, squeak of shoes, and slamming of doors boom loud in my shifter hearing. "Look, go to Syn City. The affiliate agency pass will get you access to whatever resources they can provide. Solve the case, come back, and enjoy your promotion. Just don't shoot anyone while you're there and, for the love of gods, don't screw any of their deity daughter darlings. Or the interspecies council and this use of force investigation will be the least of your problems. Got it?"

I nod because there's no other acceptable answer, and she leaves, closing the door behind her.

Syn City. I'm so screwed.

Following her to the door, I twist the lock as soon as she's gone—the lock that I never used until now to keep the rest of the station out.

I can't have anyone else seeing this.

Papers rattle and wheels scrape as I turn the murder board to reveal evidence collected from the Tucker home—a big farmhouse just outside of town, the white clapboards framing the blue door and welcoming porch. I climbed those front steps often enough to know exactly which creaked.

The memory of stepping around the squeaks when I was the first to find the murder scene? It makes me nauseous. A young marshal, I'd rushed inside with my gun drawn in hopes of finding Lowell's killer. Or anyone alive.

Hope. It's such a silly, fragile thing.

On the murder board, a sketch of the house's floorplan covers half the space with drawings of where each victim went down. I trace my fingers over the green lines and circles meant to depict a garden. I can almost push past the station's stink of ink, stale coffee, and shifter sweat to imagine the clean scents of herbs, flowers, and freshly tilled soil.

The garden had been Sadie's favorite place. A green witch, she'd constantly had dirt under her nails and grass stains on her clothes.

I found Lowell's body first, next to trampled rows of her beloved mint, rosemary, and lemon balm. My brother had been naked with scraps of his clothes scattered through the wreckage of vegetables and ripped-up herbs. Which meant he died as a shifter and transformed after death. Running my fingers along the sketch, I force myself to remember each awful detail with as much objectivity as possible.

With the brutality of the attack, I almost didn't recognize Hazel, his fiancé. She went down halfway between my brother and the porch while running for the safety of the house. I figure Lowell had been protecting her as he always did.

When I'd climbed the steps, avoiding the creaky boards, I'd prayed to whatever gods might listen that Hazel's parents and her two sisters had survived. I found everyone but Sadie dead in the kitchen. Two larger X's and a small one in red marker on the sketch seem so inadequate to memorialize a family that'd been vibrant and cheerful. The Tuckers were humans who practiced healing arts and kitchen witchcraft that'd gained them the respect of humans, shifters, and magic slingers alike. When the magic-blooded retreated to their sanctuaries during the Witching Wars, people like the Tuckers were the only ones left who could heal hurts that needed spellwork and white magic rituals.

When I'd followed a blood trail to the attic, I had fully anticipated that I would find Sadie's body next to the altar where the
family kept their grimoire. Hell, I have no idea how she made it
up the stairs with the amount of blood she'd lost other than sheer
stubbornness. But she'd been gone.

The tides of grief drowned out the jealousy, regret, bitterness,
and shame that had darkened every time I'd ignored her instead
of risking real *feelings* for her. Resentment came so much easier
than exploring why the Fates matched me with the awkward but
beautiful girl who was too shy and innocent to have a liar like me
as a destined mate. I'd done everything I could to drive her away
rather than chance dragging her into my mess.

Switching from the floorplan sketch to the photo of Sadie
posted on the board, I study her gorgeous perfection that had
been completely out of reach when I lived one exposed secret
away from losing everything. My hungry gaze devours the curve
of her jawline that I longed to stroke, the dip above full lips made
for kissing, her wide-set green eyes that seemed to see through
me to the not-a-wolf beast no one can ever know about, and the
straight blonde hair that my fingers itched to find out whether it
was as silky as it looked. The love I could never deserve but who I
mourned as the impossible who I could at least watch over and
protect from a distance.

I failed her in even that.

Before her murder. Before she made a deal with whatever
immortal Fury brought her back to life. Before she went from
Nashville's most sympathetic murder victim to her family's
suspected killer, depending on what source the reporters cited.

Now, Sadie's a roller derby megastar in Syn City who inspires
kid's costumes and is the face of a cosmetics brand. While Sadie's
new hometown celebrates the kind of superficial star power she
has, popularity won't help me track a serial killer.

I shove the board back into its hiding space, only pausing
long enough to rip off the evidentiary envelope full of crime

scene photos. Our unfulfilled mating bond couldn't have survived Sadie's death, and my past's too complicated to let it muck up the present murder investigations.

Except, if I'm right and whoever tore apart Lowell has killed again and again, then Sadie's the only witness who lived—sort of. Which makes her the key to solving my case, getting her out of my head permanently, and letting everyone know that my brother was innocent.

She's timid enough that getting her help won't be a problem, and if she decides to make this even more difficult than the memories I'll already be dealing with, I have the ultimate bribe to force cooperation. Even if it means letting go of the last link I have to the woman who haunts my dreams.

Don't stop now. Keep reading with your copy of THE FAST AND THE FURIES available now.

And sign up for the latest news, giveaways, and more from Luna Joya: lunajoya.com/newsletter/

Don't miss more of *Syn City Shifters* series with book three, THE FAST AND THE FURIES, available now, and be sure to sign-up to receive all the news and updates at lunajoya.com/newsletter/

Nolan Bankston isn't just a cocky gunslinger with a badge and secrets tangled up in my family's worst tragedy. He's a wolf shifter and my fated mate. No way this will end well.

Three years ago, a rogue wolf shifter slaughtered me and my family. I swore a blood oath to serve an immortal Fury straight out of mythology in exchange for a second chance at life and brutal vengeance against anyone involved in my family's murder.

Nolan, a wolf shifter who thinks he's the gods' gifts to women, needs my help. Only he's more than a marshal—he was the best friend of the dead wolf who murdered my family. Except he has proof the real killer is still alive and here in Syn City.

I'm a mortal Fury, a divine dealer of execution for crimes that must be avenged. Even if the signs point to the killer being my fated mate.

Please sign up for the City Owl Press newsletter for chances to win special subscriber-only contests and giveaways as well as receiving information on upcoming releases and special excerpts.

All reviews are **welcome** and **appreciated**. Please consider leaving one on your favorite social media and book buying sites.

For books in the world of romance and speculative fiction that embody Innovation, Creativity, and Affordability, check out City Owl Press at www.cityowlpress.com.

ACKNOWLEDGMENTS

For those readers who told me the books had cost you a night's sleep, or you wanted to be adopted into these magical families, or you couldn't wait for the next book—this is for you. Thanks so much to every reader who spends time in my story world.

Thanks to Lisa Green for being such a supportive editor and to the entire Mystic Owl and City Owl teams. To the Paranormal Romance Rock Stars on Facebook, I couldn't ask for a better squad. To the members of Luna's Lovelies, I adore y'all.

A heartfelt thanks Lily who loves my broken heroes and Summer for being my romance fangirl bestie. To Becca Nation and Susan, y'all rock. To Laura the Literary Vixen and Echo, what would I do without you?

A big kiss to my husband. You and Tiny Editor are my world. Love to my parents for encouraging imagination and wonder.

To the BookTok community, Bookstagrammers, reviewers, bloggers, artists, and readers who have spread the word about my stories, thank you for everything. You keep me inspired.

ABOUT THE AUTHOR

A survivor of traumatic brain injury with steel body parts, Luna lives in SoCal with her combat veteran husband and their two-pound terror of a rescue pup, #TinyEditor. She loves Disney, tacos, and dragon shifters.

Luna Joya writes steamy romances that are "wickedly delightful" (*Publishers Weekly*).

The "delightfully devious" Luna writes "action-packed paranormal romantic thrillers, singing with magical power and humming with sensuality that will leave readers breathless." (*InD'Tale Magazine*).

Want to be the first to get a look at covers, sneak peeks, and more? Sign up for my newsletter at lunajoya.com/newsletter/

Want to hear about all my pre-orders? Follow me on BookBub at www.bookbub.com/authors/luna-joya

Facebook Group:
www.facebook.com/groups/lunaslovelies

ABOUT THE PUBLISHER

City Owl Press is a cutting edge indie publishing company, bringing the world of romance and speculative fiction to discerning readers.

Escape Your World. Get Lost in Ours!

www.cityowlpress.com

facebook.com/YourCityOwlPress

x.com/cityowlpress

instagram.com/cityowlbooks

pinterest.com/cityowlpress